MW00461451

TALK HOCKEY TO ME

KELLY JAMIESON

Enjoy!
Kelly
Jamieson

This book is a work of fiction. The names, characters, places, and incidents are products of the writer's imagination or have been used fictitiously and are not to be construed as real. Any resemblance to persons, living or dead, actual events, locale or organizations is entirely coincidental.

Talk Hockey to Me © 2021 by Kelly Jamieson

All Rights Are Reserved. No part of this book may be used or reproduced in any manner whatsoever without written permission, except in the case of brief quotations embodied in critical articles and reviews

HUNTER

We got our asses spanked.

Tampa Bay just eliminated us from the first round of the playoffs.

We played six games of a seven-game series. We needed to win last night to hang on, but we had nothing left. The tank was empty. The juice was drained. Now our season is over.

The team is gathered in the Red Roadhouse, a popular Hoboken eatery. We reserved a bunch of tables at the back, where there's a long black leather banquette. Worn wooden tables are pushed together with wood chairs pulled up on the other side. Considering our season just ended, we're a noisy, jocular group. What else are you going to do? Sit at home and cry?

We're deep into the Don Julio and beers, along with numerous orders of crab dip and calamari, steaks the size of a dartboard on order. We've debriefed about the season and the game, bitched about the reffing, and possibly put a bounty on the head of Tampa Bay's asshole Dman, Dave "The Rat" Buzinski, for next season. He injured two of our players and never got a single penalty either time.

Yeah, yeah, we know we're responsible for how things went. Coach drills it into us that bad reffing doesn't lose games, poor play loses games. Still, sometimes it feels good to vent in a safe place with buddies.

At one point, Alfie pulls out a bottle, shakes a pill into his mouth and swallows it with a big gulp of water.

"What's that for?" Disco Dan asks. "Your ED?"

Alfie rolls his eyes. "It's an antihistamine, asshole."

"Sure." Dan smirks. "Didn't know you had that problem, my dude."

"Too much riding the bike," Hakim says. "It can cause nerve damage in the uh, nutsack region."

"Fuck off." Alfie frowns.

"Seriously." Hakim nods. "Do you have any loss of sensation there?"

"No! I told you, it's an antihistamine."

"Crusher might have problems," I put in. "He's on the bike all the time."

Hearing his name, Crusher peers down the table. "What? What problems?"

"Erectile dysfunction," Hakim calls to him cheerfully. "From too much bike riding."

"Jesus." Crusher shakes his head. "I don't have any erectile problems. My last girlfriend called me Redwood."

We all guffaw, including him.

"No more spin classes for me," Dan says with a laugh.

"Viagra," I say. "Strong enough for a man but made for a woman."

They all roar with laughter again.

"Nah, he's telling the truth," Dilly says. "Look at his hair. Bald men are more virile."

Crusher's hairline is receding and is often the target of our jokes. This year he shaved it all off. "With a body like this, who needs hair," he boasts.

I'm laughing, but still I swallow a sigh. I'm going to miss these assholes.

Once the season ends, everyone packs up and leaves. Almost

everyone, anyway. Lots of guys head home to spend time with their families or travel. I haven't made my plans yet. And next season, the team could look totally different.

Absently, I pull out my phone to check it and see a missed call and a voice mail. From Vern.

My heart jolts in my chest. Jesus. Is this good news? Or bad?

I quickly check the voice mail. But it's not Vern, it's Effie, his assistant, asking me to call her at Vern's number. What the hell?

She answers. "Hi, Hunter."

"Hi. What's going on?"

"Hi." She pauses to clear her throat. "I, um, have some bad news. Vern had a heart attack this afternoon."

I blink and sit up straight. "What? Holy shit."

"Yeah, holy shit is right. He's okay," she says quickly. "Well, sort of. He's alive. He's having surgery as we speak."

"Jesus." I don't know what to say.

"I'm just letting his clients know. We'll keep you posted about his condition, but…he's likely going to be out of commission for a while. Assuming he makes it." Her voices catches.

"He'll make it." He has to. I rub my chest. "What can I do?" Vern lives in Toronto, so it's not like I can zip up to the hospital to see him.

"I don't think there's anything. Gail's at the hospital with him, and his kids are both flying home. As for business things…we'll figure that out."

"Okay. But if there's anything, let me know. I can fly up there."

"Stay put for now. He's probably not going to be in much shape for visitors for a while."

"Right." I exhale a long breath. "The important thing is making sure he's okay."

"Yes." Her voice quivers. "That's right. I'll let you go. And I'll be in touch."

"Okay, good. Keep me posted how he's doing."

"I will."

We end the call and I drop my phone to the table. Then I rest my elbows on the table and sink my head into my hands.

"What's up?" Hakim asks.

I blow out a long breath, lift my head and tell the guys what just happened.

They're all concerned of course, but I'm the only one here who has Vern as an agent.

"Oh man! How old is he?" Dan asks.

"I think he's about sixty."

"Has he had heart problems?"

"Not that I know of." I make a face. "I guess he wouldn't tell me. The guy likes his food. And drink. He's heavy, but he's a big guy." I feel disoriented, with a weight in my gut.

"This is bad timing," Hakim says slowly.

"Shitty timing." I grimace. As of June thirtieth, I'll be an unrestricted free agent. That's ten weeks away. Not that I'm counting. Okay, I am. "I feel guilty even thinking that. It's not about me. The dude's having heart surgery right now."

"It *is* about you," Hakim says. "I mean, yeah, we hope for the best, but it's pretty natural for you to be concerned about what's going to happen. It's your career."

I nod.

I like it here in New Jersey. I've been here three seasons, although my first year I mostly played for the farm team. Last year and the year before, the team signed me to one-year contracts. But this year…I think I've proved myself. This year I deserve more than that. This year I want stability. I want long-term. I want big money. The kind of money I deserve. It's taken me too fucking long to get here.

The only problem? Two little words: salary cap.

I wasn't too worried about it, because Vern is a shark—tough, determined, a predator. But now…holy crap.

I'm concerned for my contract, but I'm also scared for Vern. There aren't many people I care about in my life, but he's one of them. He's been my agent since college, unofficially while I was in school and

4

then formally once I graduated. He helped me get my NHL start after I single-handedly trashed my chances.

This is why I don't care about many people. This is what happens.

"I need to get wasted." I lift my hand to get the waitress's attention. "More Don Julio!"

2

KATE

I get the call at nearly midnight. I fumble around for my cell phone, plugged in and sitting on the nightstand. I'm a deep sleeper and it takes me a while to become conscious, so I don't even know what I'm doing as I answer the call and mumble something.

"Kate. It's Kevin. Beaven." One of my clients.

I don't even have my eyes open. "Kevin. What…?"

"I need your help."

"What help?" I fall back into my pillows, fighting the sleep that's trying to overtake me again.

"I'm in jail."

My eyes fly open. "What?"

"I got in a little trouble tonight. I need help. I need to be bailed out."

I'm still confused. "What kind of trouble? What the hell did you do?"

"I'll tell you about it when you get here."

"Oh my fucking God." I fight through the bedclothes to sit up. "Where are you?"

He tells me which precinct he's at and the address. I click on the lamp and enter it into my phone.

"Okay. I got it. I'll be there as soon as I can."

"Thank you! I really appreciate this."

I end the call and close my eyes again, my shoulders slumping. I can't believe this.

Well, this is my life now. I'm a sports agent. This is what I wanted. I throw back the covers and quickly find some clothes—a pair of jeans draped over the chair in the corner, a T-shirt from a drawer, socks. I shove my feet into short, low-heeled boots, grab my phone, purse, and a jacket, and leave my Greenwich Village apartment. Out on the sidewalk, I pause with my phone to figure out where the hell I'm going.

Despite the late hour, the neighborhood is busy. The Amber Crown Jazz Club on the first floor of my building is still open, music drifting through the door as it opens and closes, and the pizza restaurant across the street is also busy.

It'll be quickest to get a cab, but I'm going to have to hike down to Houston to find one. Or I can call an Uber if I can't find a taxi. I set out, my mind clearing from the sleep fog but now jumbled with thoughts.

Luckily, I hail a cab quickly and give the driver directions to the precinct. "Don't judge me," I mutter. I know I don't have to say it. New York taxi drivers have seen everything.

It takes about ten minutes to get to the precinct.

I walk in and look around. Lovely. I always enjoy new experiences.

They tell me Kevin's still being booked but should be done soon and then will appear in front of the judge in night court.

I can't fucking believe this.

I sit in an uncomfortable chair and check out the room with uneasy glances. This is quite a collection of characters...a dude in a hoodie with his head covered slumped forward as if he's sleeping; a woman in a tight sequined dress and dangerous looking platform shoes; a short man in a suit and a bow tie talking in low tones on his phone in the corner. I sigh.

I pull my phone out, to do what I don't know. Google is always my friend. Apparently, booking Kevin involves taking pictures of him, fingerprinting him, and doing paperwork.

After an excruciatingly boring hour which I mostly spend scrolling through Twitter and Instagram searching for any mention of Kevin's arrest, I agree to be responsible for Kevin's one-thousand-dollar bail and he's free to go.

He looks a little rough but appears to have sobered up. I'm assuming he was drunk.

We get out of the police station and walk half a block away in the dark. "What happened?" I ask tersely.

"We were out celebrating."

The New York Bears made it to the second round of the Stanley Cup playoffs last night. Kevin plays defense on the team. Celebrating is understandable. I nod. "And...?"

He drops his head forward. "I grabbed the waitress's ass."

"Jesus Christ." I pull in a long breath through my nose.

"I know, I know. We were flirting...or, *I* was." He grimaces. "I got carried away. Little too much Jack Daniels."

"Is that all you had?" I hold his gaze fiercely.

"Yeah." He holds his hands up. "That's it. They kicked me out of the restaurant, but...then I went back. I swear it was just to apologize, but the girl freaked out and called the cops."

I want to cry. I rub the spot between my eyebrows. "Who knows about this?"

"Just the guys who were there. And the police."

I shake my head. "Okay, I'll figure out what to say. You say no comment, if anyone contacts you. I didn't see anything on social media yet."

"I was with Wendy and Cookie and Jammer. They know not to say anything."

"I hope to hell they do. Okay, let's get you home."

"I'll call an Uber."

"Good."

I wait until he's in the car and on his way, then call my own car, since we live in opposite directions. Around three-thirty in the morning, I fall back into bed.

Of course, I can't sleep now.

As a relatively new sports agent, I don't have many clients.

Yet.

I will. I'm determined. I know this is what I was meant to do. Only, I never knew I'd be bailing clients out of jail, officiating at a wedding, or talking a big hockey player through a meltdown after finding out his girlfriend was cheating on him.

I shouldn't worry so much about my guys. But caring about them is part of what makes me a good agent, I believe. That, and I'm an excellent negotiator. Also, I love the sport of hockey.

I've been a sports agent for just over a year, including my time at Pinnacle Sports Management and now on my own after that ended up in a fustercluck. As a little girl, I loved hockey and always wanted to be at the arena with my dad when I wasn't playing. I was also fascinated by the business and legal aspects of the league. I spent hours reading the Collective Bargaining Agreement and talking to my dad about it, which made me a huge nerd. I didn't care. Growing up, my dad was the assistant GM of the Chicago Aces, and I got to know a lot of people in the business, obviously the management of the Chicago team, but also players, agents, managers of other teams, and even the commissioner of the NHL. These connections have come in handy.

My love of hockey and my law degree brought me here, although this wasn't originally what I planned to do with my life. But I love it. I love taking care of my clients, taking care of things so they don't stress about them and can do what they're paid to do—play hockey. And with a couple of female clients, I hope I'm increasing visibility for women in the hockey world, as agents and players.

It's nights like this, though, that make me wonder if my old boss was right. *Am* I too mothering? Ugh. I put a lot of hours into my clients because I care about them, but that can lead to burnout and cynicism. Will my unique brand of agenting pay off?

My alarm goes off at seven because I have a Zoom meeting at

eight. I just have to swipe on some lipstick and make sure I'm wearing a nice top. Working from home is great that way. Some day I'll have a fancy office on Lexington Avenue, but right now, I don't need it. I can meet with local clients at coffee shops or the arena, and my other clients are spread out over the country, so I usually travel to their cities to meet.

Before my meeting, I call Kevin and arrange to meet again later to put together a statement for the media.

When Kevin slides into the booth across from me in the coffee shop, I have my lecture prepared. Just call me "mom." Ha.

"Okay," I begin. "First of all, tell me why what you did was wrong."

He chews on his bottom lip. "Um. It was…wrong."

"It was assault."

"It wasn't *that* bad. I didn't hurt her. And nobody's gonna know about this."

My eyes widen. "That doesn't matter! The woman knows about it!"

He grimaces. His naïveté about this is concerning.

"It *was* that bad," I continue. "You did hurt that woman—she didn't want to be groped. You need to own what you did and apologize. Sincerely."

He nods.

"This could be an important moment, if we handle it right. But… it's not only about PR." I lean forward. "I want to make sure you understand what happened."

"Of course I understand."

I'm not convinced. "It's not okay to touch women without their consent. Ever. The 'boys will be boys' thing is a myth. You're not a boy. You're a man. What you did wasn't blatant assault, but it crossed an acceptable boundary."

"I wasn't thinking at all," he mutters, looking down at his hands. "I was hammered."

"You know what I mean."

"Yeah."

"You were flirting. Even if she was friendly to you, that's not an invitation."

He nods.

"Look, Kevin." I lean forward. "I know you're a good guy. But I want to make sure you're aware of your male privilege, so this never happens again. As a professional athlete, you're held to a higher standard. We all know the guys in the league who've gotten in trouble for worse than this, right?"

"Yeah." His mouth sets.

"I don't want that to be you. Okay?"

He meets my eyes and I see the genuine remorse there. "Yeah."

I expect my clients to have high professional standards, as I do for myself. It's tempting to make this just go away; it's my nature to look after things. But then Kevin won't learn anything. "Okay. So. We're going to apologize. You express remorse for what you did. You take responsibility and acknowledge how it was hurtful to the waitress."

"I can't just say I was drunk, huh?"

"No." I swallow a sigh. "That's not an excuse. Is there any way you can make amends?"

His head jerks back. "What? I don't know."

"You could send her a hand-written card apologizing. And we can say you were wrong, and you hope she can forgive you. You can vow to respect women and physical boundaries in the future."

"Yeah." He nods.

After that, I head home and write up the statement which I get Kevin to review, then I send it out. Hopefully this blows over but if it doesn't, Kevin will learn some even harder lessons.

In the agency I first worked at, I heard about one agent who peed into a bottle and gave it to his client for a urine test so it would be drug free. I'm not that kind of agent. If that's what I have to do to attract clients, I'll...well, it just can't be. I may be slow in growing my client list, but I'm not going to resort to things like that to do it.

I'm sitting in my home office a few days later when my cell phone rings. I don't recognize the number. "Kate Bridges."

There's a brief silence, and I open my mouth to repeat myself, but a low, husky male voice says, "Kate."

"Yes." I roll my eyes with impatience.

"Hi." Another pause. Then, "It's Hunter."

A tingle starts at my chest and spreads all over my skin...up into my face, down to fingers and toes.

Hunter.

I blink several times rapidly, and my heart knocks against my breastbone.

"Hunter?" I croak.

"Hunter Morrissette."

I only know one Hunter. He didn't need to tell me his last name. Images swirl through my mind, images of Hunter...deep-set hazel eyes, brown hair with coppery glints, square jaw...his lean, muscled body and thick thighs...his big smile as he laughed with me. When I first met him, that smile had been non-existent, but gradually it had become more frequent and he'd become more at ease. More fun. Then images from those days in Cancun after the Frozen Four championship our last year in college flood into my head...sun, surf, lots of tequila...also lots of bare skin and horny hormones.

I give my head a sharp shake. "Wow. Hunter. What a surprise."

We haven't talked in nearly four years.

"I know." I picture him shoving his hand into the thick curls that used to aggravate him. "Uh, how have you been?"

My eyebrows lift. "I've been great, thanks. And you?"

"Eh. Doing okay. I guess you heard we're out of the playoffs."

"I did hear that, yes." My tone is dry. I didn't "hear it"; it's my job to know what's going on in the NHL. "I'm sorry."

"Thanks. It was disappointing." He pauses. "Did you also hear about Vern?"

I frown. "Vern?" Then it clicks. "Vern Tayhan?" Hunter's agent. "Oh my God, yes. How is he doing?"

"He's doing okay. He had to have major surgery. There were some complications…it's been a rough ride for him."

I hear the strain in his voice.

"I'm so sorry."

"Yeah. Me too. It sucks."

Why is he calling to tell me this? Ohhhh…I jerk back, my eyes wide.

"I need a new agent," Hunter says, confirming my hunch. "I'm a UFA at the end of June."

I nod. I haven't talked to Hunter for years, but I've followed his career.

It's my job.

He's followed mine, too. At least, superficially. He apparently knows I'm working as an agent now.

"Yeah," I say slowly.

My mind is racing, and it should be thinking of numbers— Hunter's stats, dollars, cap space, and my potential commission. But instead I'm thinking about Cancun and Hunter's mouth and soft laughter beneath moonlight and rustling palm trees…

Oh God. Heat washes down through me and I wave a hand in front of my burning face.

"I held off for as long as I could," Hunter continues. "We kept hoping he'd make a quick recovery and be back to work but looks like he's not going to be able to work for a long time. I'm hoping you can take me on as a client."

Me?

I might as well be on the floor comatose for how well I'm dealing with this unexpected call. One thing I've learned in this business, though, is not to show any weakness or lack of confidence, no matter what I'm feeling inside. On the outside, I am as cool as the ice my clients skate on. Usually, I *am* confident. Right now, I'm a shamble of uncertainty, self-doubt, and, frankly, disbelief. My hockey-ice cool is melting rapidly.

Me?

"I'm not getting a good vibe," Hunter says dryly. "You don't seem to be jumping at the chance."

"Jesus." I blow out a breath. "I'm surprised, Hunter."

"Yeah, I get it. How about I take you out for lunch tomorrow and we can talk about it?"

My lips twitch. Usually, *I'm* the one wining and dining prospective clients.

Then my stomach clutches. Lunch with Hunter? God.

I press a hand to my forehead. Both are sweaty.

"Okay," I say, attempting a casual tone. "We can do that."

"Great. What's convenient for you? I'm in New Jersey."

I swallow. "How about we meet somewhere in Soho?"

"Sure."

I give him the name of a casual place just off Seventh Avenue. "I don't think we'll need a reservation."

"Is one o'clock okay?" he asks.

"Perfect."

"Great. Thanks, Kate. I really appreciate it."

I tilt my head back and make a face. I still don't know what to say. "Well. See you tomorrow."

I end the call and stare across the room. Holy shit. What just happened?

I jump out of my chair and walk around the room. My apartment is slightly bigger than a postcard. My office is in the living room. The kitchen is also basically in the living room. I have a small island from IKEA that acts to separate that space and give a bit more storage and counter space, but this one room is definitely multi-purpose. I feel lucky to have an actual bedroom.

I pause at one of the windows that looks down onto the street. Trees outside soften the view of the brick buildings opposite me. Right now, I'm not really seeing them. I'm...flummoxed.

I press my hands to my still-hot cheeks.

Hunter Morrissette.

I turn and shuffle over to my couch. I sink down onto it and lean back.

Get your shit together, girl.

I can't help remembering that last night in Cancun, the last time I saw Hunter. The time I let my guard down and acknowledged to myself the feelings I had for him. Feelings he didn't share.

Okay. This is actually great! Hunter's not a mega star player, but he's become known over the last year or two as someone dependable, hard working, a character guy to have on your team. This season... okay, I haven't memorized his stats, but I think he played well. He needs a new contract.

And I need clients.

Perfect.

Suuuuuure. Perfect.

Can I do this without things getting all weird? He would probably be better off with someone else. Why *isn't* he with someone else? There are lots of great agents out there. Why did he call me?

Just when I'm questioning my abilities to keep my feelings separate from business, when I think I bend over backwards too much for my clients, this happens. With another rush of adrenaline, I jump to my feet and pace again over the black and cream patterned rug on the floor.

I'm a professional. I can do this.

3

KATE

The first time I saw Hunter Morrissette was across the gym at the DeWitt Center at Bayard College. We were both working out. We were both freshmen. We both played hockey.

I had a hard time taking my eyes off him. To be honest, it's hard to explain why.

I mean, he wasn't ugly. He had a lot going for him—tall, ripped, athletic. There was certainly appeal about watching his biceps bulge as he lifted weights or his massive thighs flex when he squatted. But I was surrounded by fit male bodies, so it wasn't just that.

His eyes, deep-set beneath thick, straight eyebrows, were focused. His mouth was firm, his jaw set. He radiated intensity and determination. He had an air of maturity that other freshmen didn't have. Later I learned he was nineteen compared to my eighteen, but still, he seemed older even than that.

I found myself watching him from my treadmill. Curious about the fierceness and...okay, yes, attracted to it too.

The second time I met him was when he returned the pink lace panties I'd dropped on my way back to my dorm room from doing laundry. We lived in the same dorm—all the freshmen lived on West Campus.

He held them out to me, his face impassive. "You dropped these."

I stared, then heat flooded my face as I recognized the underwear. I reached out and plucked them from his fingers, trying to be nonchalant. "Thank you so much!" I added a flirty, "These are my favorite."

My smile was met with flinty aloofness. "Better be more careful with them, then." He turned and strode away.

My smile ebbed. Okay, Hunter Morrissette was an asshole.

Our paths crossed time and time again—we were in Economics class together. We played and practiced and worked out at the DeWitt Center. Watching the men's hockey team games was my Saturday night fun. We ate in the same dining hall and ended up eating at the same table most of the time as friendships formed between men and women athletes.

My best friend, Bryson James-Bolton, was also a hockey player. We're from Chicago and were ecstatic that we both got into Bayard. We started off eating together, and then girls from my team joined us and guys from his team joined us...including Hunter. We had a big group of jocks always sitting together and we all got to be friends.

Although Hunter was anything but friendly.

I came to see it wasn't just me. He was aloof and unsmiling with pretty much everyone. One day, someone dropped a tray in the dining hall. The loud clang and crash echoed through the room, startling everyone, heads whipping around. But Hunter jumped right out of his seat. His eyes got a panicked look in them as his hands curled into fists. He looked poised to actually bolt out of the room.

I stared at him and he met my eyes. Slowly, his hands relaxed and his face loosened. He dropped into his chair and shook his head. "Too much caffeine today," he said dryly. "That scared the shit out of me."

The others barely noticed it, but I kept watching him, observing the tension in his shoulders and the tightness of his mouth. I didn't know what to make of it and it made me curious.

Hunter rarely partied with us and didn't seem to have close friends, and yet more than once he came to our nine A.M. class with dark circles under his eyes and an exhausted droop to his sculpted lips. Yet he never missed class and was always at the gym later that afternoon pumping weights then hitting the ice for warmups and drill work. He was never one of the guys yukking it up or playing pranks, always serious and focused.

For some reason, it irritated me.

Not that I was a big partier, either. Life as a D1 athlete was a full-time job, leaving me little time for much else besides hockey and studying, never mind partying or even dating.

"Hey, Bridges," Bryson said to me one day at dinner late in late October. "That was an amazing goal the other night against Quinnipiac."

I beamed. "Thanks." I got the puck and skated in on their net, one on three, undressed one of their defensemen, and got the puck up and over the right shoulder of their goalie.

"You had a hot stick," Bryson added.

Sitting next to him, I slid him an affectionate smile. "Or maybe I'm just that good."

He leaned his shoulder into me. "Or that."

Hunter was watching us, his gaze flicking back and forth between me and Bryson. He probably thought we were together. I wanted to disabuse him of that idea. But it felt weird, and I didn't say anything.

In December, during exams, I embarrassed myself again in front of Hunter. I was stressed with hockey, practices, games, and studying. I'd pulled a couple of all-nighters and my head was messed up.

One day, I woke up and freaked out because I was missing my Economics exam. I jumped out of bed and ran around my room, grabbing clothes, yanking them on. I bolted out of my room and down the hall, my jeans unzipped, my shirt half-buttoned, trying to shove my arms into my jacket so I could sprint across campus. On my way to the elevator, I ran into Hunter and skidded to a stop.

"What are you doing here?" I screeched. "We have an exam!"

His eyebrows pulled together. "We just wrote that exam."

I stared at him. My brain was fuzzy and exhausted. Then recollection slammed into me like a slapshot. "Oh fuck." I pressed my hand to my forehead. "You're right."

I'd written the exam a few hours ago, came back here, and crashed.

Gesturing awkwardly toward my chest, he said, "You're exposing yourself, Katerade." He used one of the many nicknames people called me.

I looked down to see my shirt gaping open. I yanked it closed. "Whatever. Jesus." I slumped, my head dropping forward. "I did the exam, right? You saw me there?"

"Yeah." He paused. "You okay?"

"Just stressed." I took a deep breath and lifted my head. "And now embarrassed. I must have crashed so hard I didn't even know what day or time it was when I woke up. I thought I was missing the exam."

He lifted an eyebrow. "You think I'll tell people about this?"

"I know you will." I rolled my eyes. "I wouldn't blame you. It's comedy gold, to be honest."

Miracle of miracles, he smiled. "Don't worry, Katerade. I won't tell anyone. Your secret's safe with me."

As he walked away, I felt a melting sensation deep inside me. Maybe Hunter Morrissette wasn't such a jerk.

One day a bunch of us were sitting in the dining hall having lunch. Callum Booker was talking about the scouts who would be at the games that weekend. Callum was one of Bayard College's top freshman players, along with Bryson, and was hoping to be drafted. I didn't know where he was getting his advice—NCAA players weren't allowed to have an agent, but you could have an "advisor," who was sometimes an agent—but he was spouting off shit that didn't make sense.

"No," I finally said. "A two-way contract doesn't mean you're waiver-eligible. It just means you get paid a different salary if you're loaned out. Whether or not you have to clear waivers is determined by either how many games or seasons you've played, and there are limits depending on your age."

Everyone at the table stared at me. Callum laughed and rolled his eyes. "You don't know what you're talking about."

My blood heated and created a buzzing in my ears. I freakin' hated it when guys thought they knew more about hockey than me.

Bryson made a low sound of apprehension.

Callum's gaze slid over to Bryson. "What?"

"Don't you know who she is, man?" Bryson said.

Callum blinked and glanced back at me.

I sighed.

"What do you mean?" Callum asked.

"Her dad is Joe Bridges."

My dad wasn't that famous, but clearly Callum had heard of him. As had Hunter, by the lift of his eyebrows.

"The assistant GM of the Chicago Aces," Callum said slowly.

"Yep." Bryson grinned. "Don't question her hockey knowledge. She grew up in hockey arenas."

"Huh," Callum said. "Whatever." His face wore a look of annoyance.

Asshole.

I tamped down my annoyance. I'd seen it before. Guys hated it when I knew more about hockey than they did. They also hated it when I skated faster than them and got better marks in class.

I caught Hunter's eyes, which gleamed with amusement and...was that admiration? Did he actually like that I just busted Callum's balls?

Callum was a second-round draft pick that year. And now he's one of my clients.

In sophomore year, things were different. Bryson had also been drafted by the NHL and he was now back in Chicago playing for the Vegas farm team. I was beyond thrilled for him, but I missed him. Our group of friends had changed, with some of the players having left and freshmen joining the team, but Hunter and I were still there.

I found myself more and more impressed with Hunter's hockey skills. Also, his edge. Last year he'd been an okay player, kind of out of shape but with good hockey smarts. This year, he was faster and had developed a physicality to his play that made him hard to play against. He was now on the second line. He worked hard every shift, and he made unselfish plays that actually made my heart swell.

One night, one of our Dmen, Dwayne Jones, blocked a shot. It hit him in the side of the leg. He managed to get up, but he was obviously in pain, trying to skate but limping badly. When the whistle blew, Hunter went straight to Dwayne, and helped him get off the ice. Another time, Hunter had an easy shot on an empty net near the end of the game, but he passed the puck to Tyrone, who hadn't scored that year.

I thought about how hard Hunter worked off the ice too. He busted his ass every practice and never missed a workout. Despite his tendency to reclusiveness, he was becoming the guy everyone wanted to be around.

I found myself more and more attracted to him. I wanted to crack that steely façade. I wanted to see him smile. I wanted to see his O face.

Oh my God. What was I thinking?

It confused me because I still thought he had as much personality and excitement as a stick. On the other hand, as someone very competitive and a bit of a workaholic myself, I admired his intense focus.

I'd been invited to a frat party off campus on Thursday night. I was going to ask him to go with me. I skulked around the common room, trying to catch him at an opportune moment. I never saw him. I loitered after Stats class to try to talk to him. And it worked...I was walking toward him with a smile on my face when another girl approached him from behind, threw her arms around him and giggled.

He turned to her and kissed her. "Hey, babe. Ready for coffee?"

My stomach dropped like a rock all the way to my toes.

"Yes!"

He hadn't realized I was even going to talk to him, and they both left without a glance my way.

Fuuuuuck.

My shoulders slumped and a heaviness settled inside me.

Well, at least his girlfriend showed up before I totally humiliated myself by inviting him to the party.

It was for the best. I needed to focus on hockey and studying.

I got to know Hunter's girlfriend, Tandy. She became part of our group and I explained hockey to her as we watched the men's team play. I felt she was only interested in Hunter because he was a hockey player—but I kept those feelings to myself. Their relationship was none of my business. Although, I kind of threw up a little in my mouth one day when I overheard Hunter tell a couple of guys how cool it was that Tandy knew so much about hockey. Blergh.

Whatever. I shut down any feelings of attraction I'd had for Hunter. Nothing was ever going to happen between us, and that was fine. I had enough going on in my life.

4

KATE

I was lying on a mat using a foam roller on my quads, my face scrunched up with the discomfort while I was thinking about the paper I was working on for Expository Writing. I was arguing that federal student loan policies had contributed to widespread growth in college tuition. The paper was due Monday and I suddenly felt a huge, hot pressure swell up inside me. I'd just turned in another paper, had a test next week, and we were traveling to Canton this weekend. How the hell was I going to get it all done?

I pushed away the foam roller, flopped flat on my back and closed my eyes. Tears burned and leaked from the outer corners. I pressed my lips together, trying to get control of my emotions, but I felt so overwhelmed and stressed and exhausted.

"Hey."

My eyes popped open wide at the low male voice.

Hunter stood above me, eyeing me with concern. "Are you okay?"

I glanced around the gym and discovered we were there alone. Thank God no one else was witnessing my breakdown.

"I'm fine." I swiped my hands across my wet eyes and did a crunch to sit.

"You don't look fine." He crouched beside me, concern pulling his eyebrows down. "Did you hurt yourself?"

"No." I shook my head and tipped it back. "I'm just..." I covered my mouth. "It's a lot. That's all."

His eyes warmed with sympathy. "Yeah. It is."

"There's so much...it's such a slog...studying on the bus, or in the hotel...practices..."

He nodded. He totally got it. "We love what we do," he said. "But it's hard work."

"Yeah." I blew out a breath and touched my fingertips to the corners of my eyes to dash away a couple more tears. "Damn. I don't know why I started crying."

"You need some down time."

"I'll have down time when I die."

He snorted a laugh. "Come on." He stood and jerked his head. "I'm on my way to Bingo's. Come with me." He named one of his teammates who lived off campus. "Time for a little relaxation."

"I have a paper due Monday and a trip this weekend."

He reached down and grabbed my hands, pulling me up so easily my feet actually left the floor. His strength was...hot. "Okay. Let's make a plan for finishing it."

I blinked. "Um..."

He walked me through my schedule and what I needed to get done, and maybe I'd been overwhelmed and freaking out when I didn't really need to. And he was right—I needed a break.

"I can't go like this." I gestured at myself. I was a sweaty mess.

"Go shower and change. I'll wait for you."

I bit my lip. "Okay."

I knew he wasn't taking me on a date. He had a girlfriend. It was just friendship, and that was okay. I liked being friends with guys. There was no pressure.

So that was how I ended up hanging out with a bunch of hockey players, getting drunk on a Thursday afternoon. Was I bothered being the only girl there? Not a bit. I was a good hockey player all my life and at times played with boys' teams. I liked boys. I liked hanging around with boys.

We ordered pizza and someone went out for more beer. A bong came out. Things got a little raunchy, but not more than I could handle. The guys started asking me which of them I'd go out with, if they were available, which made me laugh. Then they wanted to know who was the best kisser and wanted me to try it with each of them. I laughed more. "You guys, that could be considered sexual harassment. Knock it off."

The only guy there who wasn't a hockey player was Henry. His twin brother Harris played hockey. Henry was a cute architecture major. So when they pushed me to say who I'd go out with, I pointed at Henry. "Him. He's not a hockey player. That's all I need to know."

Everyone laughed, including Henry, but a little while later he found me in the kitchen. "So. When are we going out?"

I smiled, drunk enough to go along with him. "Tomorrow night?"

"Sounds good to me. Give me your number."

"Maybe we should try kissing first. If it's not good, we won't waste our time."

"Makes sense."

And he crowded me against the counter and kissed me.

It was good.

Hunter walked in on us. "Hey, Katertot, you okay in here..." His voice trailed off.

I waved a hand at him behind Henry's back, telling him to go away. He disappeared. Henry and I made out for a while then rejoined the party.

Later that night, Hunter and I walked home together. We were both pretty drunk.

"So. You going out with Henry?" Hunter asked.

"Yeah. Tomorrow night."

He nodded. I sensed a tension in that nod and silence.

Hunter stopped walking.

"What?" I asked.

"Look." He gestured to our surroundings. "It's nice."

I gazed around. Snow drifted down from the pearly gray sky, piling onto black tree branches, sparkling beneath the streetlights. The world was hushed and white and twinkling...almost magical. And I wouldn't have even noticed if he hadn't stopped us.

I smiled at him. "It's beautiful."

"Yeah."

We start walking again. "Thanks for inviting me," I said, my hands in my jacket pockets. "That was just what I needed."

"Things get pretty intense sometimes."

"Yeah." I cast him a sidelong look. "You never seem bothered by it. Or wait...maybe it's more that you're *always* intense."

He grunted.

"You're a really good hockey player," I said. "You could play pro." I slant him another look. "How come you're not?"

"I didn't enter the draft."

"Um, yeah. Obviously. What about this year? There are scouts here all the time."

"I'm not interested in playing pro hockey," he muttered.

"Why not?"

He didn't answer for a moment and I got the feeling I was being nosy. But I was so intensely curious about him. I had been since the day I first saw him. Then he says, "I can't do it."

This time I didn't ask. I just waited.

"Did you hear about the Swift Current Warriors bush crash a couple of years ago?"

"Yes." My mind worked, trying to connect dots. I knew Hunter was Canadian, from Calgary. Did he...?

"I was on that bus."

I stopped walking and turned to stare at him.

"I played for the Warriors."

"Oh my God." I pressed my mittened hands over my mouth, my gaze fastened on his face. "Oh, Hunter."

He closed his eyes and his mouth firmed into a grim line. "I walked away without a scratch. I have no idea how. But…it messed up my head."

I nodded slowly, lowering my hands. My insides quivered. I could see how hard it was for him to tell me this. If he hadn't had a lot of beer, he probably wouldn't have. And I felt…honored…that he did so. "I can understand that."

"Yeah?"

I blinked. "Yeah." I waited for him to say more, if he wanted. I knew a lot of people were killed in that accident, and some seriously injured.

"I still don't understand why nothing happened to me." He inhaled a long breath through his nose. "I was supposed to enter the draft. Me and one of my best buddies were pegged to go first round. He did. But I just couldn't do it."

Pain shot through my heart. I was an athlete too. I knew what a big deal it was to be drafted into the NHL. I knew how guys prepared for years for that, especially guys who were being scouted and ranked and considered to be first round picks. For him to have missed out on that…I had no words. It was tragic. Heartbreaking.

He started walking again and I fell into step beside him, our arms brushing against each other. "After all the funerals, I took off and holed up in a cabin in Tofino. British Columbia," he added. "I didn't want to play hockey. I didn't want to see people. I didn't want to talk to anyone. I was fucked up."

I nodded.

"I stayed there for months. My parents were worried about me. Finally, they got me to start seeing a counselor."

"Oh, that's good."

"I didn't want to do it. But I also didn't want to live the rest of my life like that. I spent nearly a year going for counseling, and then I decided I did want to play hockey again. Just not pro hockey. And I got in here at Bayard."

My eyes stung and my chest ached. "Oh, Hunter." I slid my hand into his gloved hand and squeezed.

"I can't believe I'm telling you this."

We were all alone on a quiet street, no traffic, snow falling silently around us.

I couldn't believe it either. This private, reclusive guy was telling me about what happened to him. I hated that it happened to him, and I was touched that he told me this. "I'm glad you are. I...does anyone else know about this?"

"Nah. And don't say anything. I don't want people to feel sorry for me. Don't *you* feel sorry for me." His voice roughened.

"I..." I didn't even know what to say. Of course I felt sorry for him. He went through an unspeakable tragedy. But I didn't pity him.

"I don't like talking about it. People don't know what to say. It gets all weird and awkward."

I didn't want things to be weird and awkward between us. This made me see him in a different light. Thinking back to when I'd first met him and thought he was an asshole because he was so reserved and serious, shame curled in my gut. He'd been through so much, and I'd had no idea.

We were on campus, nearing the dorm.

"I won't say anything," I assured him. "But I *am* sorry that you went through something that horrendous. I'm also impressed that you dealt with it and now you're here."

He cleared his throat. "Thanks."

I couldn't stop thinking about what Hunter had told me over the next few days. It rattled me. I felt guilty for misjudging him. I felt silly about some of the things that upset me, when he'd been through something so awful. I felt stupid and shallow. I also felt intense admiration for Hunter.

The next week, I found out that Hunter and Tandy had broken up two days before that party. And yes, the thought crossed my mind...*had* Hunter invited me on a date to that party?

Nah.

What if I hadn't kissed Henry? What if Hunter had asked me if I was going to go out with Henry and I'd said no? Would our walk home have been different?

It was silly to think about that. By that point, I'd gone out with Henry and we'd had fun. Unlike other guys, Henry didn't have a problem with how competitive I was, or how I liked to be in control. I liked him, and our relationship continued until the end of that school year, when Henry graduated and went home to St. Louis. We knew things were ending. We went on a last date, spent one last night together. We both cried a little, and then life went on.

In our junior year, Hunter and I both started off single, but it wasn't long before he started seeing a girl named Colette. Sometimes I got her and Tandy mixed up. They sort of looked alike—cute, with long, bouncy blonde hair, extreme eyelashes and eyebrows, and lots of pink lip gloss. Hunter and I were firmly in the friend zone, but I got the feeling Colette didn't like me much.

One night Hunter and I were studying together at the library and ended up going out for coffee after.

"Colette won't like this," I told him as we settled into seats at Starbucks. I loosened the big scarf around my neck but kept it on because it was freezing outside and I was still cold. In here, it was warm and cozy, with dim golden lighting and soft jazz music playing.

"What? Why not?" He draped his jacket over the back of his chair, still standing.

"She doesn't like me." I didn't want to cause problems for him and Colette. But on the other hand, he was my friend and he should be able to hang out with whatever friends he wanted to.

His face scrunched up. "Bullshit."

"No, really. But it's okay." I waved a hand. "She's just being... possessive. She cares about you."

He frowned, then shook his head. "She likes you."

I shrugged.

"What do you want to drink?"

"Caffé misto." I reached for my purse.

"I got it. Anything to eat?"

"No, I'm good."

He headed over to the counter. Returning with our coffees and a plate of something, he asked, "Are you going to take that scarf off?" Amusement tipped up the corners of his mouth. He still didn't smile a lot, but more than last year. I felt he'd loosened up more than last year...socializing more with the guys he lived with, and with our small circle of friends.

"No. I'm still cold."

"You're always cold."

"Not when I'm soaked with sweat after a hard shift."

"Okay, true."

He was right, though. I had an electric blanket on my bed, wore thick socks and layers everywhere, and slept in flannel pjs.

"What are you eating?" I peered over at his plate.

"Salted caramel cake."

"Ah. Your fav." He loved anything caramel. "Why do you keep going out with puck bunnies?" Oh shit. I'd blurted that out without thinking.

He didn't take offense, even on their behalf. "You think Colette is a puck bunny?"

"Well, yeah."

To my amazement, he smiled. "Nothing wrong with bunnies."

My mouth fell open. I mean, he wasn't wrong, but...for some reason, I was surprised at Hunter. He didn't seem like the guys who used their jock status to bang every bunny they could.

"She's only interested in me because I'm a hockey player," he said easily. "I know it. It's fine. I'm not looking for more than that."

"Oh."

"And she's hot."

Again, not wrong. My spirits dipped. I didn't have fake eyelashes, highlighted hair, and I didn't wear much makeup. I wasn't "hot" like

Colette was. I swallowed a sigh. I could only be myself, and most of the time I was pretty happy with myself.

I accepted a bite of his cake. We talked hockey, which we both loved. We talked about classes, about our friends.

"You never talk much about your dad," he commented.

I shrugged. "He's not relevant." I paused. "That sounded terrible. I love my dad. But I don't want to be Joe Bridges' kid here."

"Oh yeah. I get that."

Just like I knew he didn't want to be the guy who was in the Swift Current bus crash.

"You must have gotten your love of hockey from him," he said.

"Yep. Me and my brother."

"How old is your brother?"

"He's sixteen. He's a really good player."

"Cool. Is he planning to come to Bayard?"

"Actually, I think he's more interested in golf than hockey."

"Huh. What do your parents think of that?"

"My mom is gone," I said quietly. "She passed away when I was sixteen."

"Oh shit. I'm sorry."

"Thanks. It was hard. She was a great hockey mom, totally sacrificing her own life to make sure Ryan and I got to practices and games and tournaments. And with Dad traveling so much, she was on her own a lot."

"That's great. What would we be without hockey moms?"

"Right? After Mom died, I tried to keep things going. Dad was away a lot, so I looked after Ryan and kept playing myself, and wow, it was a lot. We didn't appreciate Mom enough when she was here."

"That's probably true of all of us," he murmured. "Not appreciating what we have until it's too late."

"Yeah." I paused. He was speaking from experience, no doubt. More and more I felt a sense of connection with Hunter, especially since he'd shared his past with me. But things were getting heavy, so I changed the subject. "Anyway. Colette must be good for you. You seem a lot more relaxed this year. Last year you were pretty uptight."

His lips twitched as he lifted his coffee cup. "I'm always uptight."

"You're focused. Intense." I tilted my head. "You don't look as rough as you used to."

"Hey!" His head jerked back. "Thanks a lot."

I ignored his mock affront. "You don't have huge hockey bags under your eyes."

He made a choking sound. "Jesus."

"You looked like you partied all the time, but I knew you didn't." I eyed him curiously.

He scrubbed a hand across his face. "I had a lot of trouble sleeping last year."

"Ohhh."

"I still do, but it's better. Last year I used sleeping pills sometimes, but this year I haven't had to. I don't want to use drugs, but it's hard to function on zero sleep."

I nodded, my heart tripping. "That is true. I'm glad things are better for you."

"I had a lot of nightmares," he added quietly, lowering his gaze to the table. "The first year after the accident. They were tapering off, but starting college messed with me again."

"It's a lot of stress. You're not the only one with nightmares." I paused, then held up a hand. "Sorry. I'm not minimizing what you went through. I know it's more than just bad dreams."

He lifted his gaze and met my eyes. "The first bus trip we went on, I nearly lost it," he confessed.

Sitting very still, I studied his face. "I didn't know that."

He gave a jerky shake of his head. "I hid it. I didn't want anyone to know it. Except Coach. He knew. I'd done a bunch of desensitization things, even gone on bus rides before I came here to Bayard. But still…it was fucking brutal."

"Yeah."

"That first trip, I was trying to act calm, like nothing was wrong.

But when I went off on Juice for blocking the aisle, he said, 'Whoa, someone forgot his meds today' and I nearly punched him."

"Oh shit." I stared at him in dismay. "Asshole."

"People say stupid shit without thinking about it."

Although Hunter had confided in me and talked more about his ordeal, I didn't know exactly what he'd through. But I knew he was very mindful of who he talked to about this stuff. He didn't want to look weak in others' eyes. Again, I wished he didn't feel that way. I wished he didn't *have* to feel that way. I wished he could have been honest with his teammates about what he was going through. But I got why he didn't.

Friday night I went to a party at Jude's place, for his birthday. He and I'd been going out together for a couple of months. I liked him, but I wasn't crazy in love with him. Which seemed to be how I felt about most guys I went out with, *if* I found a guy who could handle me.

The party was loud and noisy and we were playing Drunk Jenga when Hunter arrived. A cheer went up upon seeing him step into the living room. He shook his head, one corner of his mouth lifted.

"Hey! You need a drink!" I called to him, jumping up.

"Yeah. I do." He looked at Jude. "Happy birthday, man."

"Thanks, Morry!" Jude stumbled over to Hunter to hug him. He was half wasted, but why not, it was his birthday.

I led the way to the kitchen to get Hunter a beer, bopping along to the music blasting from the speakers. I opened the fridge door, then paused. Looking over my shoulder, I asked, "Do you want beer? Or some of my Mexican punch?"

His eyebrows shot up. "Mexican punch?"

I pointed to the big bowl on the counter, now about half full of bright orange beverage.

"What's in it?" he asked doubtfully.

"Juice. And tequila. Lots of tequila. Grenadine. 7-Up. It's really good!"

"You're cute and all, but I'm not drinking that shit."

After a startled beat, I burst out laughing. "Okay, fine." I hand him a beer. "Why are you so late? And where's Colette?"

He rubbed that back of his neck. "We broke up."

My jaw came unhinged. "What? Why?"

He didn't meet my eyes and shuffled his feet. "It doesn't matter."

"You look pissed. What happened?" I was a little tipsy, but sober enough to read the look on his face.

He sighed. "You were right. She was steamed that I went for coffee with you the other night."

My eyes nearly popped right out of their sockets. "Are you shitting me?"

"I shit you not."

"For fuck's sake!" I glared at him, although it was Colette I was mad at. "That's just stupid! You can go for coffee with whoever you want!"

"That's what I told her."

I narrowed my eyes. "Did you dump her because of that?"

He hesitated, then nodded. "I'm not staying with someone who thinks she can tell me who I can be friends with."

Suddenly, it dawned on me that this happened because of me. My chest tightened and I swallowed thickly. "Ah, hell. I'm sorry, Hunter."

"It's okay. It's her problem."

"Yeah, but…I feel responsible."

He shook his head. "It's not your fault."

"We *are* friends." I was a little liquored up and I threw my arms around him to hug him. "And I'm sorry."

He hugged me back, probably just about knocked out by the alcohol on my breath, but gentleman that he was, he said nothing about that. "I told you—"

"I mean, I'm sorry that happened. You're such a good guy." My face was so close to his. I could see his beard stubble, the texture of his skin, and I could smell his clean, musky scent. Electricity prickled over my skin. I was consumed with the desire to press my lips to his cheek. His square jaw. His mouth.

My boyfriend was in the other room. What the hell was I doing?

I stepped back and stretched my mouth into a smile. "Come on. We'll cheer you up."

He followed me back to the living room where Jude had just pulled out a Jenga block that said *Make someone else drink.*

"Morry!" Jude shouted, pointing at Hunter. "Drink!"

Hunter lifted his beer and chugged the whole thing, everyone hooting and cheering him on. He finished with a grin and wiped the back of his hand across his mouth in a sexy move.

Gah. What was wrong with me?

5

KATE

In our senior year, neither Hunter nor I dated much. Hockey was intense that year because both the men's and women's teams were considered favorites to go to the Frozen Four. I was putting in extra time on the ice and so was Hunter. It was also the year we were graduating; recruiters were on campus to hire us for corporate jobs, and NHL scouts were at all the men's games.

There was only a small gang of us left who'd been together all through college.

After a study session one night, Hunter and I went back to his place for beers. His roommates were out, so we grabbed drinks and made ourselves comfy in the living room.

There were a couple of young guys on the team who were likely to get drafted. The NHL Central Scouting had them on their list of "Players to Watch" from each major league around North America. They also had Hunter on their list.

He kept dismissing their interest. For the last four years, he'd been adamant he wasn't interested in playing pro hockey. But I kept seeing flickers of excitement in his eyes, which he quickly extinguished with cynicism. His game had improved so much, I could see why scouts were interested.

"Did you meet with that scout from New Jersey?" I asked him.

"Yep." He took a pull from his beer.

"How did it go?"

He shrugged and studied the bottle in his hand. "Okay, I guess."

"You're so talkative." I rolled my eyes.

One corner of his mouth lifted. "What do you want me to say?"

"Tell me how you feel. What do you think is going to happen? Will they make an offer?"

"I don't know. I also talked to guys from Vancouver and St. Louis."

"It's so freakin' awesome that they're interested!"

"Eh. I'm almost twenty-three. That's pretty old to start in the NHL. I don't think there's much chance."

"I'm not so sure of that. You're very talented. And you've worked really hard. If they're watching Baz and Danny, they have to see that you're better than they are. More experienced."

"Experienced being a euphemism for old."

"Oh Jesus. You're not old."

He rubbed the back of his neck. "I'm not better than Danny. That kid's so fast and he has amazing hands."

He had a point.

He continued. "There was a better chance of being signed when they were scouting me back when I was eighteen. But I blew it."

My jaw went loose. "You didn't blow it! My God. That accident was not something you could control."

He didn't look at me. "There was no reason I couldn't have gone in the draft that year. Physically."

"Hunter. Mental illness is as real as physical illness, or injury. Again, it wasn't something you could control."

I hated that he felt that way, that he screwed up his chances of playing in the NHL, when what happened to him was a horrible tragedy.

"I know." He sighed. "But there's still a feeling about mental illness that you should just get over it."

I scrunched up my face because I knew he was right.

"And I'm probably being judged about that," he added.

"I'm sure the interviews you had with them showed them that you're okay now."

"Well. We'll see, I guess. What about you? Still planning on law school next year?"

"Yeah. Back to Chicago for a few years."

It had always been my plan to go to law school. Unlike the men's hockey players, there weren't many opportunities for women after college. I'd always known that, though. I knew I was never going to play in the Olympics or play professionally. But I did know I wanted to stay in the game. I'd interned with different teams during summers, and I hoped to help manage a team, like my dad, some day. Which was why law school was my goal. But I was nearing the end of my hockey career, and dammit, I was going to miss it. So, so, much.

I knew Hunter would too, if he didn't get any offers. He'd have a business degree, though, and he was thinking about jobs in sports management, which he'd do great at. He was a talented athlete, but he was also smart as hell.

"Have you got someone to give you advice? About contracts?"

He grinned. "You."

I rolled my eyes. "As if."

"No really, you know more than anyone I know."

"I doubt that. But I'm happy to help you look at things, when it happens."

"If it happens."

I ignored that. "Do you want me to talk to my dad about it?"

"Jesus! No!"

"I mean, maybe he could recommend someone to act as your advisor."

"Eh. We'll cross that stream when we get to it."

"When it comes to an SPC, it's not as complicated," I went on, referring to a Standard Player Contract. "It sets out how much a team can pay you based on the salary cap. But then there are bonuses to negotiate. A signing bonus. A performance bonus."

"Christ." He rubbed his jaw.

"A performance bonus is a great way for you to prove to them you can play in the NHL. You work your ass off and get rewarded."

"Yeah." He shifted in his seat.

"You don't want to talk about this."

He lifted his head and grimaced. "Nope."

"You need to be prepared."

"Prepared to be disappointed." His cocky smile was meant to indicate he didn't care, but it didn't fool me. He cared. He cared a lot.

When he was on the ice, he was totally confident. And he had reason to be. Somehow, I knew this was going to happen for him. I'd been around hockey my whole life. I'd watched my dad scout players. I could be biased because Hunter was a friend, but on some level I knew it wasn't that.

"Frozen Four this weekend," Hunter comments. "For you."

"Yeah." I suck in a breath and make a terrified face.

He laughs.

"Then for you guys in two weeks."

"Yep."

No pressure at all. Finals, scouts, and a NCAA Division I Ice Hockey Tournament. No big deal. "We got this," I tell him confidently.

He meets my eyes with a half-smile. "We definitely do."

It was a great year for Bayard hockey. The women won our championship, and two weeks later, so did the men. Hunter won the Hoby Baker award, which is given to the top men's player. It was an incredible high—the championships, the award, the celebrations, graduating from college. Those are some of the best memories of my life.

To celebrate, a bunch of us went on a trip to Cancun before we headed off in all different directions, some of us for the summer, some for the rest of our lives—four days of sun, surf and tequila. It was like a dream, with the sunshine and sand and palm trees. After so much stress, we all needed to let loose. Luckily, we were staying in an all-adult singles place that had a reputation for great partying, so our noisy beach volleyball games, all-night dancing and drinking, and nursing painful hangovers beneath sunglasses and hats while sipping Bloody Marys next to the pool didn't cause any real problems.

During the day there were pool parties involving suds and inflatable pineapples and flamingoes, beer pong, and hobbie cat and windsurfing lessons. There were even topless optional areas, and after enough drinks, all of us girls daringly shed our bikini tops. The sun on my bare boobs felt glorious.

The vibe shifted when the guys joined us. I think the other girls enjoyed the fact that they'd shocked the boys, who gamely tried to pretend everything was normal. I was only conscious of Hunter. I stretched out on my lounge chair, but from behind my big sunglasses I kept glancing his way. Except he wore sunglasses too so I couldn't see if he was looking at me.

But I knew he was. I just knew. I felt it. I felt the sizzle over my skin, the weight of his gaze on me like a touch.

When we decided to play volleyball in the pool, we put our tops back on.

At night we danced at parties with pumping music by DJs and live musicians, often still in our swimsuits, downing tropical cocktails and shots.

While we were there, Hunter was on his phone constantly. Everyone kept bugging him to put it away, and a few times he disappeared to take a call. He didn't say what was going on, but I had my suspicions.

On our second last night, my roommate Harley, one of my closest friends from the team, disappeared with Hunter's roommate Kyle. They weren't the only ones who'd hooked up on the trip. We were all healthy, fit, and ready to blow off steam. Danny and Heather hooked up, Bingo and Gina, Harv and Nerida.

Hunter and I did shots with the others in the bar, danced together, me in my black bikini top, flowered sarong knotted below my navel, and silver sandals. Hunter's black pants sat low on his hips, narrow suspenders someone had given him attached to them and stretched over his bare torso. It would have been a ridiculous look, but Hunter had a spectacular chest and shoulders, broad and muscled, tapering down to his six-pack abs, and besides, everyone there was dressed in over-the-top, revealing outfits. I'd never seen him so loose and playful, his smile open and easy as he boogied down.

Everyone else had paired up, so Hunter and I moved together and started grinding to a throbbing tune. We were both laughing…trying to be as outrageous as we could, but with each other it was hilarious.

Until it wasn't.

The music changed to a slower tempo and we turned to face each other. I draped my arms over his shoulders, a little breathless from dancing and laughing, and he clasped my hips. Our eyes met. Our feet barely moved. Heat washed down through me. The air around us buzzed with awareness, and my heart thudded in my chest.

We moved to 'Ride It' by Regard. Then 'Bad Thing.' He looked at my mouth and my breath stalled in my chest. Desire swirled inside me, thick and hot, settling into an ache between my legs. Our gazes caught and held as we swayed to the music.

Yes, I was drunk. Yes, I was floating. But I was also completely, totally aware of what was happening. And I wanted it.

Pressing against each other, feeling his erection, his hands on my hips sliding the sarong up my thighs, his eyes searched mine as if trying to find the answer to a question.

I slowly nodded.

We left the party and went to the dark beach, feet scuffing on the sandy path through the palm trees. The lounge chairs had all been pulled back from the water and were arranged in neat rows beneath the trees. The music faded away behind us, mingling with the whisper of waves onto the shore. I kicked off my sandals and we walked toward the water, the sand cool and soft on the soles of my feet. The ocean stretched out vast and dark, stars glimmering in the cobalt sky.

"Tomorrow's our last day," I remarked wistfully.

"Yep. It's been fun, though."

"So much fun."

For some reason I was struck in the chest by the fact that when we left here, I didn't know when I would ever see Hunter again. I was filled with an urgent alarm. Turning to him, I grabbed his shoulders. "Hunter."

"Katertot."

We stared at each other in the moonlight...and then we were kissing. My hands slid into his hair, that thick wavy hair I'd always wanted to touch. His hands pulled me tight against him, his erection against my belly, which was flip-flopping with lust. My breasts ached and I pressed them against him. He groaned.

Our mouths devoured each other, wet and messy, tongues licking and sliding. I felt wild and desperate and I wanted to feel him against me everywhere. "Hunter."

"Yeah. I know." His mouth slid down to my neck and he pulled my skin into his mouth, hard enough to make me gasp. I loved it. My head fell back, and he sucked along my throat, then glided his tongue over me. I hung from his shoulders, my legs weak, my pussy aching.

"I need more. I need you."

"This is crazy."

"I know. But..." I pulled back and stared into his eyes, which were heavy-lidded and dark. This man...holy shit. I'd known him for nearly four years. We'd been friends. Confidantes. Now...I felt something more than that swelling up inside me, huge and hot. And I needed to show him. I needed to show him how I felt. "I want you."

"I want you too." Another rumble rose in his chest and he tangled his fist in my hair, pulled my head to him for another deep kiss. I melted into him, and then he picked me up and carried me back across the sand.

"Where are we going?"

"Here." He stopped at a lounge chair hidden in the shadows of the palm trees and lowered me onto it.

"Impressive," I murmured. "I'm no lightweight."

"Phhht." He came down beside me, sliding an arm beneath my shoulders, and his mouth opened on mine. I couldn't get enough, kissing him, pressing against him, sliding my bare leg up over his hip.

His cock pressed into my pussy right where I needed it, but just not… quite… enough. I rocked into him, seeking more.

"Oh, Christ." He opened his mouth on my jaw. "Kate…" He kissed down my throat then between my breasts, and I arched my back, my breasts swelling, my nipples hard. "So fucking beautiful." He turned his mouth to the inner curve of one breast to kiss me there, then the other, and sparks exploded inside me when he tugged the cup of my bikini top down from one breast, exposing me. My nipple tingled in the night air and as Hunter's lips closed over it, my entire body went up in flames. A soft cry escaped me as he sucked on the tender tip, a ribbon of sensation unfurling from my breast to my pussy, and I rolled my hips against his needfully. He moved to the other breast, pulling it free from my top, sucking then catching it between his teeth, making my body vibrate with electricity.

"Oh God." My hands moved. "This…" I tried to work open the fastener of his pants, finally pulling it free, then groping his zipper.

"I'll do it," he gritted out. We shifted ourselves so he could open his zipper and then his cock was free.

My heart hammered, my hands curled around him, and oh God, he was beautiful, thick and hard, the skin soft and thin.

He made a strangled noise. "What if someone comes?"

I fumbled with the knot of my sarong and then tugged it off me. I draped the big square of fabric over us. All that was between us was my bathing suit bottom.

"I don't have a condom," he muttered. "*Fuck.*"

"I'm on the pill. I got tested…not long ago. You can pull out."

"Argh." He sounded choked again. "Okay."

His fingers slipped into my bikini bottom and tugged it aside and then he was touching me…*there.*

I let out a soft cry, every nerve ending in my body jumping with pleasure. Heat flowed through my veins. His big, blunt fingers felt so sinfully good, gliding along sensitive, slick flesh.

"You're so wet," he mumbled, then kissed me. "So wet and soft."

His fingertips brushed over my clit and electricity jolted me.

Then we heard noises.

Someone was coming down the path.

We both froze.

"Shhh." He nuzzled my ear. "It's okay."

I nodded. We were deep in the shadows, and if they did see us, it would look like we were making out. They couldn't see anything. My heart hammered and my pussy clenched with unfulfilled need.

The people didn't notice us, and their voices faded away as they strolled in the opposite direction.

"All good." Hunter brushed his mouth over mine. His body vibrated against me, his cock straining in my hand as I stroked him. "I wanna fuck you."

"Oh God. I need you inside me."

It was awkward and bumbling, but also hot and thrilling. The risk of being caught added an edge to the excitement. With my suit yanked to the side, he pushed inside me.

Heat rushed through me, my body tightening around him. I made a soft, strangled noise as he withdrew then slid forward again, deeper, stretching me, filling me. I pulled my knee higher on his hip as he moved against me, inside me, his face buried in the side of my neck. He slid his hand down to my ass and gripped me there, holding me for his thrusts.

We couldn't move a lot, we couldn't make noise; it was strained and yet so damn erotic. I felt myself get wetter and wetter as he moved faster. We both panted and swallowed the noises we wanted to make, our bodies bumping and grinding. I needed pressure on my clit and I tilted my pelvis.

"Okay?" Hunter murmured in my ear.

"Yes…" I felt the spark of my orgasm deep inside me, caught it, let it build. I squeezed and clenched his thick shaft and his chest rumbled. "There…oh God…"

Unbearable pleasure built, twisting, spiraling up. I dug my fingers into his back, holding on as I went over, jerking, shivering. I pressed my mouth to his shoulder to stop the noises.

"Fuck, Kate, that was hot. I'm close…"

I couldn't speak, just hung on as he pounded in and out in short, shallow strokes and then he pulled out, gave his cock a few fast jerks and came on my hip. He wasn't loud, but his gasps of pleasure filled my head and saturated me with satisfaction.

We clung together for long, trembling moments, my legs enervated, my heart still pounding.

"Holy fuck," he muttered. "Holy, holy, fuck."

"I know."

"We just had sex on the beach."

I couldn't stifle my giggle. "Yes. Yes, we did."

He relaxed back onto the lounger, pulling me half on top of him. In the near dark I could make out his smile. "Can't wait to tell the guys."

"What!" My head jerked back.

His teeth flashed white and he pulled me back to him. "Kidding. Jesus. I'm not telling anyone about this."

I huffed. He'd always been so serious and he had such a dry sense of humor, sometimes it was hard to know he was joking

Then he peered at me. "Are you?"

"No!"

"I want to do it again. I mean…" He kissed me. "I want to do *you* again. All goddamn night."

A thrill ran through me. He felt the same! This was wild, but it felt right and perfect and…about time. "Let's go."

I was sticky and sweaty, and I peeled myself away from him to stand on the sand. I tugged my swimsuit back into place and tied the sarong around my hips again as Hunter zipped up. Then he took my hand and we sprinted back to the resort.

"Let's go this way." Hunter pointed to the path on our left.

"Good idea." Then we didn't have to go past the bar where we'd left the others.

"Whose room?"

"Good question." We both had roommates. Except…they'd left together earlier and hadn't been seen since. "Try yours."

As soon as Hunter opened the door, we knew this was a mistake. Harley and Kyle were stretched out naked on one of the beds, asleep.

Our eyes met and we backed out. "Well, my room then," I said cheerfully. I started down the hall and rounded the corner, both of us still nearly running.

I opened the door and flicked on a light. "At least we know no one's here!"

"True that." Hunter pushed the door shut, clicked the privacy lock, reached for me with an evil glint in his eyes, and tossed me onto the bed.

When I woke up in the morning, Hunter was gone. It wasn't until hours later I got a text message from him telling me about the offer he'd gotten from the New Jersey Storm, and how they wanted him there right away for their playoff run.

I felt small and crushed. I waited for more texts, about when we'd see each other again, but that never happened.

Apparently, he didn't feel the same as me.

6

HUNTER

Present Day
New York City

The café Kate suggested is bright and sunny, with banquette seats lining both long walls, and a few tables in the middle. I get there first and the hostess seats me at a table for two in front of the window. The tables on either side are empty, which I'm happy about so we can have some privacy.

The last month has been rough. I've been worried about Vern and worried about my career. I flew up to Toronto to see him and I felt like I'd taken a hard hit into the boards, seeing how much thinner and weaker he was. It scared the shit out of me.

And dammit, it seems like the stress has brought back my insomnia. I haven't been sleeping. I can't focus. I'm jumpy and irritable. I can't handle the worry and the uncertainty. I fucking hate this. I hate feeling so weak and out of control. It pisses me off.

I take off my jacket and request a coffee while I wait for Kate, then pick up the menu to have a look.

I don't see the menu, though.

I can't believe I had the guts to call her.

I haven't seen her in years. The last time I saw her was that night in Cancun. We texted a few times after that, but I never actually saw her again. I tried not to think too much about what had happened between us and how I'd bolted. I'd had no choice, but still…I told myself it was for the best. It was one wild night, and things would have been awkward the next day. I was the guy who went out with puck bunnies, not because I was a jock and I could get the hottest girls, but because I was happy to be used. There were no worries about getting too involved or committed.

When it became evident that Vern wasn't going to be working again any time soon and I needed a new agent, the first name that came to mind was Kate. I know lots of other agents, lots of good agents, but I couldn't stop thinking that she was the one I wanted to work with.

Kate's one of the few people in the world who knows exactly how messed up I am. And she never judged me for it. The idea of working with someone who doesn't get me ramps up my anxiety.

"Hi."

I look up and see her standing next to the table. My heart slams against my sternum and my mouth goes dry.

Fuck, she's still beautiful. Her dark hair is shorter now, brushing her shoulders, cut in a layered, sophisticated style, and highlighted with caramel. She's wearing an ivory blazer with a matching silky top beneath it, narrow black pants, and beige heels.

I rise to my feet to greet her, my face breaking into a big smile. She came. She's here.

I go for a hug, just a casual one, holding her shoulders. "So good to see you again."

"You too!" She draws back, sets her big leather purse on the floor, and takes the chair opposite me. She sounds friendly, but I'm not convinced. We were friends for years and I know her. I can see the flicker of her eyes and the pinch of her pretty mouth. "How have you been?"

I'm a mess. "I'm okay," I say, even though she's the one person I could be honest with. "A little disturbed about what's happened to Vern."

"Is he going to be okay?"

I shake my head. "Hard to say. After the surgery, they said it went well, but then he had some kind of complications and got really sick again. He was in the hospital for quite a while."

"That's terrible." Her face softens with sympathy. "He's the same age as my dad."

"How is your dad?"

"Good! Still in Chicago. Ian Yarish retired this year and Dad's the GM now."

"I heard that." I pause. "And you? How are you doing?" I drop my gaze to her left hand. No ring. I probably would have heard if she got married. Maybe. "Husband? Kids?"

She laughs, but it's a little stiff. "Uh, no. You?"

"Nope."

Our eyes meet. And hold. She drops her gaze first.

"And business?" I ask. "How's the agent business?"

Her lips curve up into a wry smile. "It's...interesting."

"That sounds...unclear."

Her smile deepens. "Yeah. I mean, it's *interesting*. I end up doing a lot of things I didn't expect to. But I really do love negotiating a good deal for my clients and then helping them navigate this bizarre world after that's done."

"That's great. I knew you'd be good at it."

Her eyelashes flutter down, then back up. "Thanks."

The waitress returns to take our lunch order. I get a cheeseburger and Kate orders shrimp dumplings. I take the chance to study her more as she orders. Her skin glows with health and energy. Her long bangs fall across her eyes in a sexy sweep, and my gaze lingers on the shadow beneath her full bottom lip that always made me think of biting that lip.

Get that thought out of your head, Morrissette.

Once the waitress has gone, Kate picks up her coffee cup.

"Tell me about how you became an agent," I say.

"Well. You know I interned with different teams during my summers."

"Thanks to your dad."

She rolls her eyes. "Come on. Part of the business is who you know. A *big* part. And I needed all the help I could get. Honestly, I thought I wanted to be a GM like my dad. But he kept telling me I was 'too player focused,' and I realized I *wanted* to be player focused."

I nod. I can totally see that.

"Dad thought maybe I should work for the players' union, but I decided to go work at a sports management agency." She pauses and drops her gaze. "It wasn't the best experience. So I went out on my own. I had a couple of clients who came with me, luckily."

"Callum."

"Yeah. He's one of them."

"I hear Van Halston is going to sign with you."

"I heard that rumor, too."

I laugh. "He's going to go first in the draft. Great client."

"I guess we'll see."

"Wow. You're cagey."

For the first time, she laughs. "Cagey? I prefer to call it discreet."

"I guess it's good to know that my secrets are safe with you."

She gazes across the table at me. The heat that builds around us tells me we're both thinking of the same "secret."

"Absolutely," she says quietly. "I would definitely want you to know that. One thing I commit to is that I will never break your trust in me."

"Do people give you a hard time because you're a woman?"

Her face shutters. "Oh sure. Every woman in a male dominated business goes through that."

She's not being totally open with me. I know her well enough to see that.

She straightens her shoulders and forces a smile. "But I hate it when someone tells me I can't do something, so I just work harder."

"That's my Katertot."

A smile flickers on her lips. "I think my hockey background helps my credibility. They know I'm knowledgeable about the business and understand this world."

"There's no doubt about that," I say quietly.

After a beat, she says, "Thanks. Usually, once we start talking hockey and they see I know what I'm talking about, it's just business. Being an athlete, I'm aggressive enough to negotiate contracts. But being a woman, I also have a...nurturing side." She makes a face, and I know she's thinking of her dad and her brother. "Some of these young guys need that, and honestly negotiating contracts is a small part of what I do for my clients."

She probably looks after them like she looked after her dad and her brother. I want her looking after me.

No. Not like *that*.

Hell. I can't let my mind go to the things she could do for me...

Our lunch arrives. When we're settled and the waitress has left us, I pick up a French fry.

"Most of my job is managing their lives once those contracts are done," Kate continues. "Especially the young guys. There's incredible pressure on them, from the media, their teams, their families. Pressure they put on themselves. Sometimes there aren't a lot of people they can turn to. I'm someone they can turn to."

I nod, taking in her words.

"Also, as an agent, I don't only negotiate contracts. I also look for marketing opportunities. You don't have a wife and kids, but that's something else I keep in mind when I'm making deals for players—their family, their commitment to the community."

I nod. I like everything I'm hearing from her. But then, I was sold on her before she even sat down at the table. "How long have you been in New York?"

"Just over a year."

"D'you like it here?"

"I love it. It's busy and noisy and hectic, but exhilarating. I feel like I'm in the center of the world. And since my clients are spread out over the continent, that's a good thing."

"Yeah. I like it too. I mean, I live in New Jersey, but it's so close. I have a great apartment there."

"What are your plans for the summer? Going home to Calgary?"

"Yeah. At some point. I needed to deal with this first."

"Of course. How's your family?"

"They're good." She met my parents when they visited me at Bayard College. My little sister Arianna had been obsessed with Kate because she played college hockey. "Arianna's at Bayard now."

"Oh, no way! That's amazing!"

Her happiness unfurls something warm in my chest. "Yeah. She just finished her junior year."

"Playing hockey, I assume?"

"Of course." I grin. "When I tell her you're my agent now, she'll go nuts."

"We haven't agreed yet, remember? Don't jump the gun. What's she doing for the summer?"

"She's back in Calgary. She's got a summer job as a camp counselor."

"Fantastic."

"I'll probably go to Tofino for a while, too. Do some surfing. I love it there."

"Right. I'm sure it's beautiful." She bites her lip and looks at me directly. "How've you been with your PTSD?"

Trust her to come right out and ask about it. Things are changing with respect to mental health, but a lot of people are still uncomfortable talking about it. I exhale slowly. "I was doing great until this happened with Vern."

"Oh no." Her forehead creases. "I'm sorry."

"I guess it's the uncertainty, not knowing what's happening with him. Also a new contract and where I'll play, and then suddenly not having an agent."

She touches her fingertips to her lips.

"But I'm dealing with it. I don't want you signing me because you feel sorry for me."

She drops her hand and rolls her eyes. "As if. I'm a businesswoman, Hunter."

"Right."

"And look at you." She waves a hand. "You're a professional hockey player in the NHL. You had your doubts...but you did it."

My chest warms. "Yeah. I did." Big thanks to her.

"So." She's finished her lunch and pushes the plate to the side, leaning forward. "You need an agent."

"Yep. Like I mentioned on the phone, Vern's not going to be working for a while. If ever." I grimace. "And I'm a UFA as of June thirtieth."

She nods.

I know I don't have to explain things to her. I've never questioned her hockey knowledge, or her knowledge about the business of hockey.

"There are fifteen guys on the team with finished contracts. They're going to sign Crusher and Alfie as soon as they can. They're not going to sign me again."

"You don't know that."

I shake my head. "I'm being realistic. They won't have enough cap space left to sign me for what I want." I lean forward. "I've proven myself the last four years. I want more money and a longer contract term. They've been giving me one-year terms since I signed with them. I want more than that."

She nods thoughtfully. "I agree."

My eyebrows lift.

She hitches one slim shoulder. "I did my research before meeting today."

Satisfaction spreads through my chest. Yeah. I knew she'd do that. And she agrees with me.

"Have you considered any other agents?" she asks.

"I have." I pause. "But you were the first one I called."

"Oh."

"Yesterday I talked to a couple of guys after I phoned you. I didn't get the feeling from them they think I deserve much more money than I've gotten the last couple of years."

"That's bullshit."

I blink. She keeps her face expressionless even as she utters the expletive. She's good.

"You finished the season third in the league in hits last season. You set a team franchise record for most hits in a season. You're a shot-blocking machine—eighty-five last season."

I grin. "Yeah."

"Also, you upped your offensive game with a career high in goals, assists and points." She reels off the numbers from memory.

I sit back in my chair and cross my arms.

"Why are you laughing?" she asks coolly.

"I'm not laughing. I'm impressed. You're amazing. But then...I already knew that."

Our eyes meet again, this time with a little crackle of heat between us.

Man, I have to watch what I say. Anything suggestive brings back memories of Cancun.

"Thank you." Her tone is detached. Professional. She drops her gaze. "I did some research on comparable players."

I nod. That's one way agents establish a player's value—what other similar players are getting paid.

"I see you as similar to a Jönsson. Also Denby. Maybe Girard in Montreal."

I contemplate those names. "I'm better than Girard."

"You're more physical," she says with a nod.

Oh Christ. She had to say that. Heat flows south, thinking about being physical with her. I battle to maintain my composure.

"I've researched the team, too," she continues. "Whatever Al Feroze gets, you can be sure Cunningham will be looking for something similar."

"Yeah."

She purses her lips. "I could see those two eating half the team's cap space. Let's say locking up those two costs the team fourteen million. That leave them with twelve million if the cap goes up to its projected levels for next season."

"That's not much."

"Agreed."

"Have you got thought of other teams that would be interested?"

"Oh yeah." A little smirk graces her pretty lips. "Have you?"

"Hell. I don't know. Rumor has it the Golden Eagles are looking for third line winger."

"Third line." She taps her lips. "Yeah, I've heard that, too." She tilts her head. "Are you sure you want to work with me?"

I hold her gaze steadily. Things might be a bit weird between us, but there's nobody I'd trust more with my career than Kate. "Yes."

"I can give you references. You can talk to some of my other clients."

I doubt that will change my mind, but it's probably a good idea to do due diligence. "Okay."

She sucks her bottom lip between her teeth in a rare display of vulnerability. "Hunter…"

Heat slides through my veins. "Yeah?"

For a long moment she doesn't reply. Finally, she says, "I don't know if this is a good idea. After what we've discussed today, we should both think about it."

Shit. I don't need to think about it. But I don't want to seem desperate either. Even though I am. "Okay."

"I totally trust her."

I'm on the phone with Kevin Beaven, one of Kate's clients in New York. He plays for the Bears.

"That's good." I move to the window and stare out at the Hudson River.

"Yeah. She's always up front with me. I think she has more integrity than a lot of people in the business. She's not trying to be all 'Jerry Maguire'—she's just herself. She gets the job done. She's been great for my career. And honestly, she's been great for my life. She knows hockey and gives me advice on that, but she gives me life advice too when I do dumb shit."

I smile. "I heard about your dumb shit."

I sense his discomfort. "She bailed me out of fucking jail, man."

I chuckle. It's not funny, but...

"I was an idiot," he adds. "Don't be an idiot like me."

"I'll try. We all do dumb shit at some point." Like not entering the draft when you were supposed to go first round.

"Anyway, I don't hesitate to recommend her to you. She'll work her ass off for you."

I won't mention what a nice ass it is, because that would be dick-ish. I am, however, thinking it. "Thanks. I appreciate your honesty."

"No problem. Good luck, man."

"Thanks."

I end the call, pull my earbuds out, and drop them and my phone onto the kitchen counter. I've called two of the three names Kate sent me. I don't need to call the third. Beaven and Hulsey both confirmed my instincts about Kate. I want her.

I mean, I want her working for me.

I have to get past what happened between us, though. We were *friends*. So one night we got a little drunk on a hot tropical vacation with lots of skin showing—holy *fuck*, she went *topless*—and got carried away. It didn't mean anything. It was a bunch of kids letting off steam after a long college year.

It's like we're different people now. Back then, Kate was sporty and fun and sort of girl-next-door. She rarely wore makeup, her long hair was usually in a ponytail, her usual outfits were jeans and Chucks. Seeing her yesterday was jaw-dropping. She looks the same…but sophisticated. Professional. And brain-cell-incinerating hot.

I'm different too. I've been doing so much better. I still have the occasional nightmare, and it's only been the past year that I get on the team bus without that sharp flash of memory, but I've felt a lot more confident. I may have screwed up years ago, but I've worked my tail off and I've gotten where I want. Almost. This contract will put me where I want to be. Secure. Validated.

And I need Kate to do that, so I have to keep my shit together.

I send her a text message, telling her I talked to her references and I'd still like to sign with her.

When she doesn't reply immediately, I get changed and go to the gym in the building to work out. That's always been the best way of dealing with stress and anxiety for me. An hour later, sweating and panting, I return to my apartment. Of course I check my phone first.

Still nothing.

KATE

I never make mistakes. Except that one night…

Am I really going to do this? Agree to be part of Hunter's life again, after what happened?

Oh my God, I was so awkward yesterday. When I saw Hunter in the restaurant, I was a big stew of emotions. I was nervous, for sure. But also…happy. A joyful sense of fullness spread through my chest, reminding me how much I missed him. But I tried to hide how happy I was, tried to be professional. Instead, I came across as stiff and amateurish.

I was hurt about how things ended, but when I heard from him what had happened, I couldn't blame him. I blamed myself for catching feelings when we were only friends, and then for one night, friends with benefits.

He looks good. A little more mature, with dark gold beard stubble, his thick wavy hair cut in a tousled style with neat sideburns, his body a little heavier. Is it possible his shoulders are broader? He was wearing a blue and white checked shirt over dark-wash jeans, the soft cotton of his shirt fitted to his shoulders. I wanted to run my hands over that soft cotton.

His eyes held the same focused intensity, the same brooding look of someone who's experienced a lot of pain and guards his heart from feeling it again.

When he leaned in to hug me, I breathed in his scent. He smelled the same—the same shampoo or body wash he used back in college, clean yet musky and warm. That scent alone was enough to melt my ovaries, never mind how hot he looked. And that only added to my awkwardness—he still affects me.

Okay, I need to put things in perspective. I was hurt when he left without saying goodbye, and without even a hint that maybe we could try to be together. I'd gotten sex confused with feelings. That was all it was—sex. So we spent the night boffing our brains out. Big deal. We were drunk and horny and that night clearly wasn't supposed to mean anything to either of us. It was just sexy fun and games at the end of a wild vacation.

It was years ago. We've both been with different people since then. Okay, I have, and I assume he has. I haven't met anyone that I've wanted to spend the rest of my life with, but that's life. I have no trouble getting dates on dating apps and I could go out with someone this weekend if I want. In fact, I should do that.

This is business. And, like I told Hunter, I'm a businesswoman and I'll make this decision considering the alternatives, the pros and cons of each, and consequences of a decision to represent him or not. I sit down at my desk and actually write things out, then I read over my notes.

It's a no brainer, as far as business goes. I just need to leave out my feelings.

I slouch in my chair. I think about Tarek Bennani at PSM where I started my career. I think about the demeaning things he said and did to me. I think about the helpless fury I felt nearly every day I worked for him. I think about my decision to leave there and go out on my own and prove to him and the rest of the management at the company that he was a sexist asshole and I could do this job better than him, and with more integrity than him, all day long.

I want Hunter Morrissette as my client.

With a client like Hunter, I'll be a *real agent*. I almost laugh at myself for that thought, but sometimes I still feel like I'm pretending to be an agent and soon people are going to find out I'm faking it.

My other clients came with me from PSM. Hunter would be the first player I've signed on my own. This is *big*.

And I have to be honest with myself—I knew I wanted to take him on as a client from the moment he called. I've been prolonging this because I'm letting my emotions take over. That stops right now.

Hunter texted me yesterday, following up. I haven't replied yet.

I straighten and reach for my phone, and open the app. I type in my response. *I've given this careful consideration, and I'm happy to offer you representation.*

Then I straighten my shoulders and open the file I've already created for Hunter on my computer. I have work to do.

Two days later, I'm at Hunter's apartment building in Hoboken. The doorman calls up and then waves me to the elevators. When I knock on Hunter's door, he flings it open.

"Hi." He beams at me.

"Hi, Hunter. How are you?" I ignore how good he looks in a pair of softly faded jeans and a navy Henley.

"Great. Great. Come in." He steps aside and hold the door for me. "We can sit over here." He leads the way into the living room.

"Nice view." I cross the patterned rug and sit on one of the two big couches. He takes a seat opposite me. The view is all blue—blue sky, blue river, even the skyscrapers on the other side of the Hudson River appear blue.

"Thanks. I like living here. I'm going to miss it."

I don't try to reassure him that he may not have to leave, because we both know that he likely will have to. "We'll find you a great place to live, wherever you end up," I say calmly.

He nods.

I spread out some papers on the table and go through them with Hunter. He seems uninterested and I sit back. "You should be paying more attention to these."

He blinks. "You said I could trust you." Our eyes meet and heat fills my chest. "I do trust you, Kate."

"Well, that's good, but even so, it's your career. You shouldn't trust anyone but yourself."

We resume reviewing the contract, then Hunter signs and we're done. Yay.

He sits back. "Thank you. This is a big load off my mind."

I hate it that this situation has been messing with his mind. And even though it's a business decision that's beneficial for my bottom line, it makes me feel good that I'm helping him. I gather up the papers, slip them into a folder and slide it back into my bag. "Good. That's what I'm here for."

"Did you really bail Beaven out of jail?"

I blink, keeping my face neutral. "Did he tell you that?"

"Yeah." He shakes his head, chuckling. "You won't have to do that for me, I promise."

I try to stop my smile. "Good to know. I've gotten some strange requests, though, so don't get too cocky."

"Okay. Here's a request. Come downstairs and have a drink with me in the bar. It's happy hour."

Hunter's request makes me freeze.

Have a drink with him? Jeez, I still haven't recovered from yesterday's lunch with him.

I stuff papers into my big purse, pretending to rearrange them and taking my time. I stand. I need an excuse. I don't have one. I don't know what to say. It would be ridiculous to say we should keep things professional; I have dinner and drinks with clients all the time. But Hunter's different than all my other clients. He's seen me naked.

And more.

I resist the urge to wipe my brow as sweat breaks out on it.

He's waiting for an answer.

"I don't know if that would be a good idea," I finally say.

His eyes flicker, but his expression doesn't change. He lifts his chin. "We're friends, Kate."

"I-I know." I clutch my purse with both hands.

"Let's have a drink. We have years of catching up to do."

A small, sharp knife twists in my heart. We wouldn't have to catch up if he'd felt the same about me as I felt for him. "I don't have time today." I rush the words out. "I'm sorry. Things are so busy right now. But I'll take a rain check on that!" I smile brightly and head to the door. "I'll touch base with you in the next few days about how things are going." I beeline toward the door.

He follows me, nodding. "Sure. Okay."

"Talk soon!" I wave a hand, and bolt.

As I wait for the elevator, I tip my head back. Oh my God. What an idiot I am. I should have been prepared for that.

The doors slide open and I step in.

He wants to be friends.

I thought I got my head wrapped around the fact that he would be my client. I thought I convinced myself that I could do this without my feelings getting mixed up in it. I wanted another client, one who's going to make me big money and boost my reputation as an agent. I convinced myself I could do this.

And I just lost it.

Fuck!

I let out a long, slow breath as the elevator descends. Okay. We don't need to be best buddies like we were in college. But we *do* need to be friends. It's a business relationship, for sure, but I'm pretty involved in my clients' lives and I'll have to be involved in Hunter's.

Out on the street, I pause. I need to get myself together. Which way am I going?

I start down the street, thinking I'm heading toward Hoboken Station, the way I came. It's a bit of a walk, but that's okay, I need to move. And think.

At the first corner, I realize I turned the wrong way. Dammit! I do an about face and retrace my steps.

I have to be able to handle this. I just have to. I've been able to handle a lot of things in my short career—sexism, discrimination, harassment. Being broke. Being laughed at. This is *nothing*.

By the time I'm on the train zipping along under the Hudson River, I'm calmer. More confident. This will be fine. I'll have a drink with Hunter when I have things to discuss with him, and it'll be fine.

I hadn't planned on going to the gym today, but a workout would probably be a good idea. Then I'm going to go home and drink a six pack of Easy Street Wheat Beer.

I spend the next week doing research and making a lot of phone calls.

On Thursday, I make myself head to the gym. I'm not as active right now as I am when I'm coaching hockey, and staying in shape is important to me. I joined Steam Gym when I moved to New York. I didn't want some fancy place with weird classes; I wanted old school weights and machines. Steam Gym fits the bill—concrete block walls, cement pillars, basic lighting. I have to admit I've gotten hooked on their HIIT classes, though.

This is where I met my friend Soledad. We're both single, close in age, we love working out, and we've gotten to be friends.

I push inside the gym and greet Kaley, the receptionist/trainer, then hike into the women's change room. Doesn't look like Soledad is here yet, but I'll ride a bike until she shows up and class starts. I change into shorts and sports bra, and lace up my shoes.

I pause in front of a mirror to slip a headband on. My hair's not long enough to put in a ponytail anymore, barely brushing my shoulders, but this keeps it out of my face.

I swing my arms and hop as I make my way through the gym to the row of bikes. Muscled guys are pumping iron and doing pullups. I'm used to working out with guys, so I barely notice them.

I've been pedaling for about ten minutes when someone taps my shoulder. I turn to see Soledad. "Hiiii!"

"Hi!"

I slide off the bike and we hug and exchange some chat as we stroll toward the classroom. We enter to find our instructor Elbis is preparing for class. "Hey, ladies." His smile flashes in his dark brown face. "You ready to sweat?"

"Be gentle with us," Soledad says with a laugh.

Soon we're warming up, moving side to side, then skating, then squatting.

"Squeeze those glutes!" Elbis yells. "Shoulders back!"

I focus on my form, concentrating on the moves, knowing that physical activity will help me deal mentally. It always has. I love the heat in my muscles that becomes a burn, the moisture that gathers on my skin, the feeling of strength I get.

By the time we're doing our last set of London Bridges, elbows and toes on the mat, pelvis shifting from side to side, my heart is pumping fast and I'm drenched. I love it.

"Five...four...three...two...one...and done!"

Soledad and I high five each other then shake out our legs. We follow Elbis through the cool down then stagger out of class.

"Jesus," Soledad gasps, guzzling water from her bottle.

"I know." I too gulp down water. "That was good."

"You're a maniac."

"Yeah." I laugh, swiping the back of my hand across my forehead.

After showering and changing, Soledad and I stand side by side at the mirror fixing our hair and makeup as she tells me about her day. She works as an interior designer at a local firm.

"It was nearly a disaster," she says. "The upholsterer was holding our furniture hostage."

"What? How can they do that? Didn't you pay the bill?"

"We don't usually pay in advance." She rolls her eyes. "They were having cash flow problems and the people who work there hadn't been paid in weeks. So they held the stuff hostage. I needed that furniture today. The client's having a big party this weekend. So I did arrange to pay our bill in advance but I made sure that the guy's employees got paid and they delivered our stuff this afternoon."

"Whew!"

"No kidding."

We sling out bags over our shoulders and leave the gym onto the now dark street.

"Incognito?" I say.

"Okay!"

We often go there after a workout. It's close and they have great cocktails and good food that isn't wildly expensive. We approach the red-neon-lit building. They have a nice rooftop patio in the summer, but it's still a bit chilly for that. Inside, the place is long and narrow, with brick walls and dark wood. We pass the bar against one wall and take a table for two.

"I need to see the hockey game," I tell the server immediately.

She nods. "We've got the Penguins' game right there." She points.

"Perfect."

Knowing me, Soledad lets me take the chair facing the big screen. She shakes her head, smiling.

"It's my business," I tell her, also smiling.

"I know, I know. I think it's cool."

I already know what I want, so I don't bother looking at the menu, instead fixing my attention on the TV screen. Penguins are up by one near the end of the first period.

"Who are you cheering for?" Soledad asks.

"You know I don't cheer for any one team."

"How can you not? You have to cheer for someone."

"I want my guys to do well." I don't have that many clients in the NHL yet, but one of them is playing in this game. "Jason plays for Carolina. I want him to play well. If they win, they're on to round two. Against the Bears. Who one of my other clients plays for."

We order our drinks and food, a Buffalo chicken salad for me, a barbecue whiskey burger for Soledad, along with two margaritas and a basket of chips to start.

"So…I have a big new client," I tell her when we have our drinks.

"Oh yeah? Who is it?"

"Hunter Morrissette. He plays for the New Jersey Storm."

"Oh, wow! That's great news! Congratulations!"

"Thanks." I bite my lip. "It is great…but I'm having some misgivings."

Her forehead creases. "Why?"

"I knew him in college. We were…friends." I look down at my drink. "And for one night, we were more than friends."

Soledad makes a small noise and I look up to see her wide dark eyes. "Whoa."

"Yeah."

"One night?" She sinks her teeth into her bottom lip.

"One night in Cancun." I give a dry laugh. "That sounds like a movie."

"X-rated, I assume."

"Oh yeah." I roll my eyes. "We drank a lot of cerveza and tequila and…hormones kind of took over."

She lifts one shoulder. "That happens."

"It wasn't just us, true. But…" I stop, not sure where I'm going or how much I want to say.

She munches on a chip, watching me.

"I really liked Hunter." Again, I look down. "When I first met him, I had a little crush on him."

"Ah."

"Then I thought he was a jerk. He was so…moody. He never smiled. He didn't party. He barely talked to anyone."

She nods.

"But I got to know him better and realized he wasn't that bad. Except then he had a girlfriend. So."

"Just friends."

"Yeah. There was one time…" I stop. "Well. Nothing ever

happened. I had a couple of boyfriends, he had a few girlfriends. Then in Cancun, it was just us, and some of our teammates."

"So he obviously was attracted to you, too."

I make a face. "Who knows? We were all wearing skimpy clothes and drunk. If it wasn't me, it would have been one of the other girls." I scoop up some salsa with a chip.

"Ohhhh, Kate."

"What?"

"That bothers you?"

"No."

I can tell she knows I'm lying by her little snort. "It was more than hot vacation sex for you."

"Women can have hot vacation sex with no strings attached just as easily as men can."

"Sure. Theoretically. But we're talking about you."

I sigh. "Okay, you're right. I kind of read more into that night than was really there. I realized my feelings for him had changed from friendship to...well, something more. But the next day he left. We never even talked."

"Oh no." Her eyebrows slope downward.

"At first I was...disappointed." That's not quite the right word. Hurt... angry... heartbroken? Nah. But I was sad. "But he had a good reason. When he texted me to tell me he'd been offered a contract by the New Jersey Storm, I understood. He'd been on the phone the whole trip, so I figured he was making some kind of deal. The Storm were in the playoffs, and they wanted him there right away. And I was happy about that for him, because he wasn't sure he could do it, in his situation." I explain briefly how the draft works and that he was older than most guys are when they enter the NHL.

"How was it seeing him again? Do you still have feelings for him?"

I don't answer. I should say no, of course not. But I'd be lying. Again. "I guess I do. I'm just not sure what those feelings are."

"You want to look after him. Like you look after everyone."

I blink at her. "He's my client. That's what I do."

She nods. "But do you also want to bang all your clients?"

I choke. "No!"

"You want to bang *him*."

"Thanks for clarifying exactly how fucked I am."

She laughs softly. "Sorry."

"I need him as a client. He's the first client I've signed on my own. Plus, it'll be the biggest contract I've negotiated. It'll be great for my reputation, as well as my bank account."

"And…?"

I frown. "And what?"

She lifts one shoulder. "I feel like there's more."

"Oh." I suck on my bottom lip briefly. "Okay, I guess there is. I feel like he needs me, too." I pause. "He, uh, went through some stuff after the bus crash." I can't tell her Hunter's story; that's private. "Stuff he shared with me back in college. And I want to help him with this."

She smiles. "Then do it."

Sounds so easy. I just hope I can, without my feelings for him messing things up.

8

KATE

One of the many calls I make is to my dad. I need to talk business with him, but also talking to Hunter about Vern's heart attack rattled me, because they're about the same age and my dad's not exactly one to look after himself.

I'm pretty sure the Aces aren't going to be interested in Hunter, based on what I know about their roster situation, but it's worth putting feelers out.

"Katy! How are you?'"

"I'm good! How are you?"

"Eh, doing okay. Busy."

"Are you eating right?"

He chuckles. "Probably not."

"Dad!" I huff a sigh.

"It's fine, it's fine. I've been doing better." He pauses. "I, uh, I've been seeing someone. She likes to eat healthy."

I freeze like a snow sculpture in Winnipeg in February. "What?"

He's seeing someone? Whoa! My dad's been a widower for ten years. This is the first time I've heard him mention anyone, although if I'm being realistic, I'm sure he's been with women.

"Her name is Jenelle. She's really nice."

I don't know how to handle this. But it's Dad and I want him to be happy. "That's so great, Dad. Is this…serious?"

He pauses. "Maybe. Yeah."

Oh wow. "She must be fantastic."

"Yeah. She kind of is." The happiness in his voice relaxes me. "You can meet her some time and see for yourself."

"Okay. Sure. So…she's making you eat healthy?"

He laughs. "Yeah, as much as she can."

"Have you been to the doctor for a checkup this year?"

"Yes." I sense his eye roll.

"How was your cholesterol?"

After a beat, he says, "Why are you asking that?"

"Did you hear about Vern Tayhan?"

"Ohhhh. Yeah. That's awful."

"I'm worried about you. You're the same age as him."

"My cholesterol is fine." His tone softens. "I've even been working out."

"Oh." I blink. "Okay, that's good." Surprising, but good. Is this more of Jenelle's influence? Huh. "Does Ryan know about Jenelle?"

"No. I haven't heard from him for a while." Dad sounds disappointed. "I text him sometimes and all I get back is a couple of words."

"Men," I mutter.

We chat a bit more, then I say, "I need to talk business with you."

"Sure." He sounds curious.

"I have a new client. Hunter Morrissette."

"That's great, Katy! Another client! He's a good player."

"Yes. He was one of Vern's clients, and he's a UFA this year, so he needed a new agent."

"Yeah, I guess so."

"So I'm talking to you…agent to GM…about whether you have any interest in him."

"Our forward lines are pretty set for next season. There are a couple of contracts I'll be working on over the summer, but I don't anticipate things changing much."

"I figured that. Just thought I'd ask!"

"But you know, this could be the perfect time for him to enter the marketplace," he says encouragingly. "After the year he's had, there are definitely going to be teams interested. In fact..." He pauses. "Give Brad Julian a call."

The manager of the New York Bears. "He's on my list."

"Tell him I said hi."

I smile. Dad and Brad Julian are friends going all the way back to their playing careers, although they're rivals now. "I will. Thanks, Dad."

"Good luck, Katy."

After I end the call, I have to stand and walk around. I pretty much expected that business outcome, but sweet baby Jesus on toast, I didn't expect to hear my dad has a girlfriend!

And it sounds like she's looking after him. Which has always been my role, since Mom died. But it's good. All good. Definitely good. I do need to meet her though. Dad's not a hockey player anymore, but for some reason I'm concerned this Jenelle is after him because of who he is.

Okay. I need to focus on work.

No, first I need to call my little brother and give him hell.

He doesn't answer, per usual, so I shoot him a text message. *CALL DAD YOU LITTLE SHIT HE HAS NEWS.*

By the next week, I've left messages, sent emails, and made follow up calls. I've felt out Bob Goodaker, the GM of Hunter's current team, and he's very complimentary toward Hunter but noncommittal. I've pitched my new client to several other GMs and like Dad said, there's interest. There's lots of time and I know sometimes all the pieces have to fall into place before a deal can be done.

I've also scored a meeting with Brad Julian, since he's here in New York. Face to face is always better.

In Mr. Julian's office, located adjacent to the Apex Center where the Bears play, he greets me with a big smile and a firm handshake. "Great to see you, Kate."

"Thanks."

"Have a seat." He gestures at a table in the corner of the room. I sit facing the window that overlooks Sixth Avenue, with a glimpse of the Empire State Building between other edifices. That view still gives me a thrill, as a relatively recent transplant to the city.

"How's your dad?" Brad takes a seat across from me and relaxes into it.

"He's great." I want to blurt out, *He has a girlfriend!!!* But I keep that to myself.

"So you've been here in New York how long? A year?"

"A little over a year, yes."

After some small talk, Brad turns the meeting to business. I make my pitch and we have a good discussion. "He's not a flashy guy," I say. "But he's very useful in the facets of the game that aren't flashy. He kills penalties and blocks shots. Some guys aren't as good at that as others, but Hunter's good at it. Really good. He wins puck battles. He goes to the net. He knows his assignments and he does what it takes to get those things done."

"He's definitely what we used to call gritty."

Brad's got a great poker face, but I'm good at reading people and I sense genuine interest. We throw around a few numbers and of course he's low balling me. He talks about some of the pieces he needs to move into place, which I totally get.

"Let's keep in touch," Brad says as we finish up.

I pick up my purse and stroll to the door. "I will. I've had considerable interest from other teams."

"Oh, Kate. You have to say that."

I laugh. "I do. But in this case, it's true."

I feel good about that discussion, reflecting on it as I stroll along Sixth Avenue. I consider taking the subway home, but it's a nice afternoon so I keep walking, window shopping. Impulsively, I pop into Zara to check out spring clothes. I quickly fall in love with a short, flowy dress in my favorite shades of blue. I rarely wear dresses, but this one is so pretty. I can afford a new dress…

I try it on and love it even more. Okay, sold.

I also end up with a pair of strappy sandals. They have a nice heel, not too high, but pretty.

I swing my bag as I continue strolling downtown, making another stop at a market to pick up a few things I need—cheese, coffee, a big salad for dinner. Then I turn and go a couple of blocks out of my way so I can pass by Washington Square Park, all pretty and green and cool, filled with people lying on the grass and kids playing. I stop at the dog park and scan the area. Oh, there they are!

I spot Milo and Rosie. They're usually here at this time of day, which is often when I go for a run if I don't have meetings. I love dogs, and I've stopped by to pet them so many times, they know me now. Probably because I bring treats.

I fish the plastic bag out of my purse and go into the park to greet them. They bound toward me as soon as I call them. I wave at their owners, sitting on a bench over by the fence, and they wave back.

I make them sit and give them the treats. Milo likes crunchy ones, Rosie prefers soft ones. Then I rub their heads. "You are so good," I say. "Are you having fun?"

They bounce up and down then take off, Rosie chasing Milo, running for the pure joy of it. There's one more dog I sometimes see here, but it looks like Lucky's not here today.

I leave the park and trace my steps back along the sidewalk toward my place.

I need to update Hunter on what I've been doing. I know he's anxious about this situation. So maybe it's time to take him up on that offer of a drink and go over a few things. Unless he's gone back to Calgary? He didn't say exactly when he was leaving, and he doesn't need to be here.

I wait until I'm in my apartment with my shoes kicked off to call him.

"Hey, Kate."

"Hi. How are you?"

"I'm okay. You?"

"Good, good. Are you still in town?"

"Uh, yeah."

"Okay. I thought you might have gone home to Calgary. You said you were going to."

"I am, but I kind of wanted to stay and get this sorted out."

"It might not happen that quickly," I caution him. "You need to go ahead and live your life. Go see your family. Go surfing."

"Yeah. I guess."

"Well, since you're here, I thought we could meet up and go over a few things. I can update you on what I've been doing."

"Yeah." His tone becomes more enthusiastic. "Sure. Tonight? Where?"

I smile. "Tonight's fine. Are you okay coming to Manhattan?"

"Of course."

We discuss his route and I suggest meeting at the Golden Bottle Tequileria. He takes note of it and we agree to see each other there at seven.

Okay.

A little squiggle works through my belly at the idea of seeing Hunter again.

He's a client. Calm your tits, girl.

My tits are a little excited. Pressing my hands to my boobs, I sit at my desk and stare at my computer. I've got a bunch of emails to deal with and I need to update my spreadsheets. I've been focused a lot on Hunter, but he's not my only client whose contract is up, and I'm still eager to sign Van Halston, so I have to stay on that.

After a couple hours more work, I head to the bedroom to change and get ready. My new dress is still in the shopping bag. I should wear it. Why not?

I hang it up, but it's not the kind of fabric that creases so I think it's okay. I've never been one to wear a lot of makeup, but I put on eyeshadow, mascara, and blush earlier for my meeting and I think it still looks okay. I swipe a brush over a highlighter compact and light up my cheekbones a little, then smooth on lip gloss. I brush and fluff my hair, change into the dress, and even slip on the new sandals. I think I can handle walking a few blocks in these heels.

About a half hour later I'm at the Golden Bottle in Hell's Kitchen. Hunter is standing inside the entrance waiting for me. His eyes brighten when he sees me, his face creasing up into a smile. "Hey!"

"Hi." I smile too, stepping inside.

His gaze wanders downward, taking in my dress and bare legs. He blinks. "You look...fantastic."

"Thanks." Repeating the compliment sounds fake, so I don't, but he does look good in a black button-down shirt over dark jeans, topped with a black leather jacket.

The hostess arrives with a smile and I gather Hunter has already spoken to her since she takes us straight back to a table. The noise at the front of the restaurant near the bar is raucous, but back here it's quieter. I hang up my light coat and take a seat at the table for two. The place is dark, with lots of worn wood, exposed bricks, and ornate gold chandeliers providing a little light.

"Remember that tequila tasting we did in Cancun?" Hunter says as we pick up menus.

The air goes static against my skin. I keep my eyes on the menu as my insides tighten. I don't want to remember Cancun!

Why the hell did I pick a Mexican place? Damn, I'm an idiot.

"Yes," I say calmly. "That was very educational."

He laughs. "We all got hammered."

"That was pretty much the entire trip," I say dryly.

"I do remember some of what we learned." He studies the menu. "Let's get the Casamigos."

"Mmm. Okay." I need to stay sober. This is a business meeting. But I can handle a shot of tequila, I guess.

Only, when he orders and the drinks arrive, they're not just a shot. They're a glassful.

"It's sipping tequila." Hunter lifts his glass to admire the amber liquid.

"Right." I take a deep breath and sip. "Oh." I let the taste spread over my palate. "It's smooth."

He nods with satisfaction. "Yeah."

"I taste...caramel and vanilla."

"That's why I like it. Also, oak."

I take another sip. "Yes."

Our eyes meet, sharing amusement at our tasting notes.

We figure out what to eat, starting with a trio of guacamoles and chips, then we're left alone.

"Okay," Hunter says. "What's happening?"

I grin. "Don't get excited. This is a slow process. But I'm working, I assure you. I've spent hours on the phone, and today I met with Brad Julian."

His face falls. "Brad Julian? From the Bears?"

"Yes."

He stares at me. "I'm not playing for that team."

9

KATE

What?

I stare back at Hunter. Controlling my expression, I ask evenly, "What do you mean?"

"I mean, I'm not playing for that team. Ever."

"Oh." I nod slowly, gathering my thoughts. "You didn't mention that earlier. You said you were open to anything."

He scowls. "I didn't think I'd end up there."

I adjust my lips into a tiny, calm smile. "To be honest, it seems like a perfect fit."

"No." He jerks his head from side to side. "I can't play there."

I take a leisurely sip of my tequila, hoping my composure will influence Hunter. Right now, he makes a pressure cooker look calm, color sliding into his cheeks, his eyes flashing. "Okay. Tell me why."

"I just can't."

I tip my head to one side, letting him see my skepticism. Then I lean forward. "Hunter. It's me. Kate. You can talk to me."

I see his internal struggle. He gulps back a mouthful of tequila that makes his eyes water. Then he shakes his head and sets the glass down on the wood table with a clack. "Tell me who else you've talked to."

I pause for a moment. I see he's avoiding talking about whatever is bothering him about playing with the Bears. How hard should I push? Maybe this isn't the time.

So I tell him about my other conversations. Hunter listens, settling down, and asks a few questions. Our chips and guacamole arrive in the middle of our discussion, and we pause briefly as the waitress sets them in front of us, then carry on.

"Just those teams, huh?" he asks as I finish.

I pick up a chip. "Vegas seemed interested, but I don't think seriously. Their top three lines are solid and they have a lot of talent on their farm team. Unless something changes. You never know."

"Yeah." He purses his lips.

"You're not happy."

"No, I am!" He jerks his head up. "I mean, sort of." He takes a deep breath, scoops up some guac with a chip and eats it. I do the same as I wait for him to say more. "I guess I'm disappointed that nobody's jumping on me."

I lift an eyebrow and he barks out a reluctant laugh.

"That *is* disappointing," I murmur, glad I got a chuckle out of him. "But I did warn you this won't be quick. We can't sign with anyone else until July first. After talking to you and getting your thoughts about the teams and what they might offer, I'll go back to them and talk more."

He nods. "Okay. I'm interested in Long Beach. And Toronto."

"We need to talk about the differences between signing with an American team and a Canadian team."

"Right."

I pull out my chart of income taxes paid by NHL city.

"Jesus Christ." Hunter jerks his head back. "What the fuck is that?"

I smile. "It's a helpful tool I made. Let's have a look." I go through the tax differences. "A three-million-dollar contract in Long Beach will give you more net salary than a three-million-dollar contract in Toronto."

"Fuck."

"But there's more to it than that. Every NHL player is paid in

American dollars, including those in Canadian cities. So you can make up the tax gap by being paid in US funds."

"Depending what the dollar's like."

I smile. "Right. Some of your business courses coming back to you?"

He grins. "Maybe I did learn something in college."

"The teams will be looking at it differently though. They'll use the tax implications to justify why you can take a lower salary, so the team has more money to spend on other players, because your net salary will still be the same as someone who makes more in higher taxed cities."

He frowns. "That's bullshit."

I shrug. "It's what they'll try. I'm not saying I'd go along with that."

His face relaxes for the first time since I mentioned the Bears. "Christ, you're smart, Kate."

His words make my chest heat up, and the warmth flows into my cheeks. "Thank you. This is my job now."

"It's why I hired you."

"That's right. So. We also have to consider the cost of living in different cities."

We continue our discussion through dinner, and when we're done eating, I pull out my laptop and show Hunter the numbers I've come up with on my spreadsheet. "It's more than numbers, obviously. You want to play for a team where you're a good fit, and that's a lot of intangibles. Things like the coach, who you'd play with, what their expectations of you are."

"Right."

"Okay. I'm ready to follow up with these teams. I'll keep you posted."

"Okay, great."

"You can head home to Calgary, you know. You don't have to be here."

"Yeah, you said." His voice holds an edge as if he feels insulted.

"I'm not trying to get rid of you," I say with a laugh. To be honest, if he leaves it'll be better for my focus, but I also feel a tiny twinge of disappointment at the thought of him not being here. Hunter's brought a little spark of excitement into my life. I love my work, but the buzz of negotiating and making a deal isn't quite the same as the tingle of flirting with a hot guy.

It has to be enough, though. I'm totally focused on building my career and I don't need sexy tingles and sparks in my life. Especially from Hunter.

"What have you been doing with all your spare time now the season's done?" I ask him.

"Working out, mostly. A few of the guys are still around and we've gone golfing, and boating. Speaking of golf, how's your brother?"

"He's a jerk."

Hunter laughs. "Okay."

I smile. "He's fine, as far as I know. I don't hear from him much. He's on the PGA tour. I think he plays in Florida this week. He's always traveling, it's hard to keep track of him."

"I'm surprised you're not *his* agent."

"We talked about it, actually. But I know nothing about pro golf."

"The job of an agent is probably the same."

"Yeah…but I think Ryan was tired of listening to his big sister. I've been riding his ass since our mom died, and he's done with that."

Hunter's smile is sympathetic. "Just like that, they've grown up and left the nest."

That makes me laugh. "Yeah. And now apparently I don't even need to worry about my dad. He's got a girlfriend."

"Really. Good for him."

"It's…something to adjust to. But yes, it is good for him."

"This is the first time he's had a relationship?"

"Yeah." One corner of my mouth lifts. "It was a surprise."

"It can't be that much of a surprise. He's not that old. It makes sense he'd want to…" He stops.

I lift an eyebrow.

"Er…lay some pipe?"

I choke.

"Dip the schnitzel? Visit Mount Pleasant?"

I fall back in my chair, wheezing with laughter. "What! Oh my God."

He grins.

"We're talking about my father!" I swipe a tear escaping from eye. "Please. No more."

"Sorry."

He doesn't sound sorry. He's watching me with amusement and a heated look in his eyes. My belly does a flippety thing even though I'm still giggling. I haven't laughed like this in a while.

"You always did kill me with your sense of humor," I say. "You seem so serious and intense and then something hilarious comes out of your mouth. I think it's even funnier because it's so unexpected."

"Believe me, I was happy to discover I still had a sense of humor."

"I bet you were." I shake my head. I still get a little pang thinking of what he went through years ago, but he's come so far. "Thanks for the laugh."

"You're welcome. Anyway, apart from the sex, does it bother you that your dad might love someone else?"

I drop my gaze. "It's been ten years since my mom died. That's a long time. I worked with a guy whose wife died and six months later he was with someone new." I wrinkle my nose. "That didn't sit right. But Dad's been on his own a long time."

"You haven't met her?"

"Nope. Just found out last week. I have to make a trip to Chicago and check her out."

He grins and shakes his head. "You haven't changed."

"What?" My head pulls back. "What does that mean?"

"You're still looking after everybody."

"Oh. Well." I play with my water glass. "I guess I don't need to anymore."

"It's good to care."

"Oh please." I toss my head with an eye roll. "It's just that men are such helpless babies."

"Uh-huh. Thanks."

"Okay, not you."

Our eyes meet and the air shimmers between us. I've sure never thought of Hunter as a helpless baby.

He's a man. Grown up, big, more mature and responsible than he should have been at nineteen, when I met him, and now he's even bigger. More confident. More vital. He's a man in his prime.

I squeeze my thighs together on the pulse I feel low down inside me. Damn.

"Another drink?" Hunter asks.

We finished our tequila a while ago. I feel pleasantly mellow but not drunk. I shouldn't but… "Okay."

Hunter signals the waitress with the confidence of a multi-million-dollar pro athlete, which he is not…*yet*. But I'm going to make him that. Because he deserves it.

"What would you like?" he asks me.

"I'll have a margarita this time. On the rocks."

"Another Casamigos," he requests for himself.

The waitress departs.

"So." Hunter folds his arms on the table. "What do you do for fun in New York?"

"I work a lot."

"That's no fun."

"Yes, it is! I love my work. And I'm just starting out, so I have to bust my butt. Come on…you love your job, too."

"Sure."

"What do *you* do for fun?" I lift my chin. "In college, you were Mr. Serious."

"Ha. And you weren't?"

My head jerks involuntarily. "What?"

"You were just as focused as I was. You took everything seriously—hockey, school, all our friends' problems."

I let that sink in. "I guess I did." I didn't think much about how people saw me. I always thought Hunter was no-nonsense and focused, but I didn't think I came across like that too. "But not all the time."

His smile is achingly gorgeous. "No. Not all the time."

Oh yeah…Cancun.

I pull my bottom lip in between my teeth briefly.

The waitress arrives with our drinks and I take a gulp of my margarita. "Yum." I lick some salt that sticks to my lips, catching Hunter watching me, his eyes hot. My heart bumps. I swallow another tangy mouthful.

"There's a lot to do for fun here," Hunter continues the conversation easily. "It's New York."

"True. Well, I hang out with my friends. My friend, Soledad, and I workout at the gym together. We both love going to the theater. And in the winter, I coach a girls' hockey team."

His eyes widen. "Really?"

"Yeah." I smile, because this is part of my life, apart from my career, I do feel passionate about. "I wanted to get involved and make sure girls have opportunities to play."

"That's fantastic." He tips his head. "Do you ever play?"

"Oh sure. It's always great to get on the ice."

"Yeah." He pauses. "Do you miss it?"

So much. But I smile. "Of course."

He narrows his eyes knowingly. "I missed it too, when I wasn't playing. It's such a big part of me."

"I know." I pause. "Have you been watching the playoffs?"

"I didn't want to at first, but yeah, I've been watching some."

"I try to watch my clients. The Bears are out now." I sigh on behalf of Kevin. "I'm missing the St. Louis game tonight."

"Who's your client?"

"Callum Booker. Remember him?"

"Oh yeah." He laughs. "I can't believe you signed him as a client. He was so insulted when you knew more than him."

83

I grin. "Right? It's good to have the know-it-all working for you though."

"We can go somewhere else and watch the game, if you want."

I check the time on my phone. How can I say no to hockey? "Okay." I toss back the rest of my margarita. When the waitress brings the check, there's a bit of a skirmish between Hunter and me over who will pay.

"No, I'm paying," I say firmly. "It's a business meeting."

"I'm not letting you pay."

"I'm paying." I fix him with a stare.

He gives me my stare back, then smiles. "Okay. Thank you."

I'm glad he doesn't think it's a threat to his masculinity to have me pay for dinner.

Once that's taken care of, we head out onto the dark street.

"I think I know a place a couple of blocks away," Hunter says, setting his hand on my lower back to direct me down the street. We cross at the intersection and turn right at the next corner and he stops in front of a pub that looks like an upscale sports bar.

We step inside and immediately see the game on the big TVs mounted on every wall and pillar.

"You were right!" I let out a delighted laugh as we head toward a couple of stools at the long bar. Hunter pulls out one and holds it for me to hop onto. I find the hook under the granite bar top to hang my purse on and settle into my seat while Hunter sits next to me. He picks up a menu card and studies it.

A smiling bartender approaches us. "What can I get you?"

"Oh." I blink. "I'd like a beer."

"We have lots of that." He winks at me.

I laugh and peer over at the menu Hunter has. "Anything that's not IPA."

"I recommend our What the Hell's Lager," the man says.

"Sounds good."

"I'll have the same," Hunter says, pushing the card across the counter.

We both look up to the TV. There are only about six minutes left in the second period and Dallas is up two-one. We watch one of the Dallas players do a spinorama to avoid a Dman and get a shot on goal, and we both make the same impressed noise. I glance sideways at Hunter in amusement and our eyes lock. There's no question that we both love hockey and that's a strong bond between us.

Our beers arrive, deliciously cold and bitter.

"Who are you cheering for?" I ask Hunter.

He shrugs. "I don't really care. I think St. Louis is a good team. They should win."

I nod. "I don't disagree."

We watch silently, and in the last minute of the period, St. Louis gets the puck. The player breaks for the Dallas net while two Dmen chase him. Hunter and I (and a few other patrons in the bar) let out a cheer that explodes when he scores. I turn to Hunter and he lifts his hand for a high five.

"Tied it up!" I say.

During the intermission, we dissect the brief part of the game we saw.

"Callum doesn't seem to be getting a lot of ice time," Hunter comments.

"Yeah." I make a yikes face. "He's a fourth line winger. He's got potential."

"He's young."

"Yes. All my clients are young."

"Except me."

I eye him. "Well, I do believe you are my oldest client, but I'd hardly say twenty-six is old."

"Seriously? All your clients are younger than me?"

I push my lips out. "I'm a new agent. I don't even have that many clients."

"You will." He lifts his beer to his lips and swallows.

"I appreciate the vote of confidence." I say it casually, but deep inside, it moves me. Because I haven't had a lot of votes of confidence.

Even my dad is hesitant about me being an agent, and my experience at Pinnacle Sports Management did nothing to build my confidence. In fact, it was the opposite.

He hitches one shoulder. "I know you. You're smart, knowledgeable, tough."

I nod. The word tough is exactly what I want to hear. That's how I want people to see me. When my mom died, Dad and Ryan didn't need to see me helpless and crying. I had to step up and take care of things. My hockey teammates needed me to be strong and dependable. My clients need me to be fierce on their behalf.

At the same time, I feel a faint longing deep in my heart to be seen as something other than tough...to be seen as soft. Attractive. Even...sexy.

But those things are what got me in trouble and I can't go there again.

"Thanks." I say it matter-of-factly and lift my beer to him in a toast.

10

HUNTER

For some reason, I get the feeling that Kate didn't like being called tough. Maybe because she's a woman, and that sounds…masculine? But she's a feminist and she'd take my head off with a hockey stick if I said that. Maybe tough is the wrong word. I probably should have said strong. Tenacious. Smart. Yeah, those are better words.

The moment has passed though, as the game resumes. We order another round of drinks for the last period, cheering as St. Louis takes the lead. When Dallas pulls their goalie and throws everything they've got at the St. Louis net, we're on the edges of our seats. I don't even care who wins, but it's fun watching Kate cheer on Callum's team, fun getting swept up in the fervor.

I wish it was me on the ice, still in the playoffs.

Oh well. There's always next year.

Down to the last seconds, one last shot on goal, St. Louis makes the save…and they win.

Kate throws her hands in the air with a cheer.

She always was competitive. And loyal. I remember her coming to my games at Bayard and loudly cheering us on. I always liked it when she was there. Even more than I cared if my girlfriends were there.

Kate's eyes sparkle as she picks up her nearly empty beer glass and tosses it back. "That was fun."

"Not as much fun as playing, but yeah…it was."

"I guess I should get going."

I don't want the evening to end, but this was supposed to be a business dinner. I mean, it *was* a business dinner, as she so clearly emphasized when it came time to pay. So I nod and finish my own beer, then settle up the bill with the bartender. This time, I'm paying and Kate acquiesces gracefully.

"How are you getting home?" I ask out on the street. "Do you need a cab or an Uber?"

"I'll take the subway."

I frown. "It's late."

"It's fine." She shakes her head with a tiny eye roll, and I smile. "I do it all the time. How about you?"

"Uber. Let me walk you the station at least, and I'll call a car from there."

"Okay." She pulls out her phone and studies the map, then points. "There's a station a few blocks away."

We set out along Nineth Avenue. It's gotten cooler, and I eye her light jacket. "Are you warm enough?"

"I'm fine."

"Are you sure? You're always cold."

Her eyes widen. "You remember that."

"Sure." Of course I remember that.

She looks so pretty in the floaty, flowery dress that matches her blue eyes. I like seeing her legs.

Don't think about her legs. Don't think about the rest of her body. Which is absolutely smoking hot. I'm a jerk. She's my agent. But I've seen her naked and I'll never forget that if I live to be six hundred years old.

"Um…" Kate stops. "This is Forty-eighth Street."

"Yeah."

"Shit!" She pulls out her phone again. "I turned the wrong way."

I frown bemusedly and take the phone from her hand. "Yep. You did."

We turn and back track.

"I'm sorry," she mumbles. "I have a terrible sense of direction and for some reason this city confuses me."

"How can it confuse you? It's a grid. Mostly."

"I know, but I always get my directions turned around. I've added a lot of steps to some days because I went the wrong way."

I shake my head, smiling. "I think we're good now."

We pass Forty-second Street and I pause, taking Kate's elbow and drawing her out of the crowds of people still thronging the sidewalk. "Look."

She follows my gesture. The street is bright as daylight—lit with dazzling neon in shades of pink, scarlet, green and white, taillights of cars glowing red. Towers glitter above us against the dark sky. Energy pulses around us, dynamic and vibrant.

"It's beautiful," she says, eyes wide. "Chaotic...excessive...but beautiful."

"Yeah." We stay there for a moment, taking in the vibe. It fills me with electricity.

She turns her face up to me. "Thanks."

"For what?"

"For making me stop and look." She wrinkles her nose. "I'm always in a rush, always going somewhere, doing something. Sometimes I don't pay attention to things like that."

"I remember." I smile wryly, recalling that snowy night back in college when we walked home from a party. I see a shared recollection in her eyes. "It's good to slow down and take a minute to enjoy something beautiful."

When we arrive at the stairs down to the station, we pause at the green railing. "Thanks for all you're doing for me," I say. "I appreciate it."

"It's my job," she says lightly. "I'll check in with you again next week. I may not have much to tell you, but I think it's good to keep the lines of communication open. And call me if you have any questions at all."

I hate that she's talking to me in such businesslike tone. And I don't know why I hate it. "Sure. Well. We'll talk soon."

"Yes."

"Thanks for dinner, too."

"My pleasure."

Neither of us is making a move. Just spewing out banalities. Like we've never kissed until we couldn't breathe. Like we've never banged our brains out. On a beach, no less. Christ. My dick thickens remembering that. I have to stop thinking about that.

"Good night." I take a step back. "Send me a naked selfie when you get home so I know you got there safely."

Her eyes widen and her mouth hangs open. Then she laughs. "Hunter!"

I grin, trying to keep things light despite the tension now crackling around us. "Just kidding. But seriously. Text me. I'm worried you might get on the wrong train."

Her mouth opens on an outraged protest but then she meets my eyes and sees I'm teasing. She shakes her head. "I know which train to get on."

"Text me."

She huffs. "Fine. Good night." With a wave she turns and jogs down the steps.

I watch her hair bounce, her skirt fluttering around her thighs. Then she disappears.

I turn to the street. There are taxis everywhere and I stride to the curb to hail one to take me home.

She texts me before I'm even home. And even sends a naked photo —of her bare feet.

I grin as I text back. *Sexy feet.*

Oh Christ. She's not some chick I've been sexting with. She's my agent. She's…Kate.

I had fun tonight. It was even fun talking business with her. She impressed me so much, and that was fucking hot. Even hotter than seeing her in a dress with bare legs. Then watching a game with her…

also fun. She's so animated and passionate about hockey. You gotta love that, right?

I mean, not *love*. Not that kind of love.

Her turning the wrong way and getting us lost should have been annoying. Instead, it was amusing. It's cool seeing perfect, in control Kate with a tiny little flaw. Which she hates. But that's who she is. She's almost perfect, and I'm...not.

KATE

After our discussion at the Golden Bottle last night, I do some research. I'm curious about why Hunter doesn't want to play for the Bears. They have a new coach who's been pretty successful so far and seems popular with the team. Bears' management has a reputation for being supportive of their players. The roster is pretty damn good. I study it, looking for a clue about Hunter's objections, then on a hunch I google the Swift Current Warriors bus crash.

And a piece of the puzzle falls into place.

I didn't realize that Easton Millar and Josh Heller were also on that bus when it crashed. They've both joined the team in the last couple of seasons. Hunter must know them. But what I don't understand is why he doesn't want to play with them.

So, it's a piece of the puzzle but not the complete picture. Do I need to know? Of course I do.

The more research I do, the more people I talk to, the more I learn about each team's situation, the more it seems like the Bears would be a great place for Hunter. Somehow, I have to convince him of that. And to do that, I need to know what's going on with him.

I spend a bunch of time on the phone, talking to connections at various teams and a few other agents. There are all kinds of rumors, and I know better than to trust rumors, but usually rumors start for a reason. The Golden Eagles are apparently in serious talks with another winger's agent. The Leafs are supposedly meeting with John Waring. This prompts me to make a few more calls to stay on the radar and make sure they remember Hunter's on the market and has what they need.

And I call my dad again, to check in. Because that's what I do, even if he does have someone in his life who's apparently monitoring his meals and activity. I don't know if she knows what a workaholic Dad is, or that he loves fettuccine alfredo and prime rib and deep-fried anything, all things he should avoid. I don't know if she really cares.

We chat for a while, a little about business, and then about Jenelle. Wonder of wonders, Ryan called Dad after I bugged him to, so that's good. Ryan's flying around between North and South Carolina and Texas, but he's going to try to get to Chicago for a few days between tournaments, and Dad suggests I come home then too.

"I'll definitely try," I tell him. "Just give me a bit of notice to book a flight."

"I will. Okay, take care Katy."

"You take care, too, Dad. Love you."

Then I text Ryan to ask him to let me know his plans about going home. I add, *What do you think about Dad having a girlfriend?*

As usual, his reply comes hours later. *It's cool.*

Also as usual, the minimal words required. I sigh. We all have good relationships and grew even closer after Mom died, so I know it's not that he doesn't want to talk to us. It's just him and his busy schedule.

Soledad and I go out Friday night to see a new Broadway play, A Life of Truth and Lies. We both love it, and I leave the theater feeling uplifted. We walk a few blocks down Seventh Avenue to go to a thirtieth-floor rooftop cocktail lounge. The drinks are super expensive, but the spectacular, sparkly view of the city is worth it and it's fun spending time with her yakking about all kinds of things.

I'd love to talk more about Hunter, but tonight I keep my thoughts and mixed-up feelings to myself.

11

HUNTER

I don't know why I'm doing this, other than the fact that I have nothing else to do.

Kate told me to go home to Calgary, and I will at some point, but right now I want to be here. So I agree to go with Hakim to some kind of kids' picnic thing in Central Park, which is a fundraiser for Langmore Children's Hospital.

I like kids. And kids usually like me. So maybe it'll be fun.

It's Sunday afternoon, a bright, warm day in May. The park is green and shaded with the soft light unique to Central Park. Hakim and I find the event, already swarming with kids and parents and...oh sweet Jesus. Mascots.

I feel the blood drain out of my face. Sweat breaks out on my back and my feet stop moving.

Hakim jerks his head around. "What? What are you doing?"

"Nothing." I swallow. I don't tell people about my fear. So far, I've managed to avoid the Storm mascot at any events we've done and nobody's noticed that I duck out when he's around. "I sort of don't feel well."

He frowns. "Suck it up, buttercup. Come on." He slaps my shoulder then gives me a shove along the path.

I eye the mascots across the field. My gut clenches. I'll stay far away from them. Jesus.

I get involved with a game of golf frisbee with a bunch of kids. A few of them are hockey fans and are excited to meet me. I'm not a star like our team captain or our top scorer, but fans like me because I'm a physical player and I come through with the odd clutch goal.

I flick my wrist and send the plastic disc sailing, to land right in a basket. I pump my arms in the air and cheer. Then I help one little dude who doesn't know how to throw a frisbee. We get it close enough to bounce off the edge of a basket. I high five him. "Super close, buddy!"

I look up to see a mascot approaching. It's Mr. Met. Sweat breaks out under my Storm T-shirt. The urge to run is real.

I take my frisbee and move to another group of kids as Mr. Met jokes around with some of the others. Fuck. I swipe my hand across my forehead.

"I have to move on now," I tell the kids a little while later. "You keep practicing, Mick, you're going to be great at this sport."

I hightail it across the grass to a food truck. I'm not even a little bit hungry, but I can hide out there for a while. I wonder if they have beer.

No such luck. But I grab a lemonade slushie and gulp some down. I survey the crowd. There are no mascots over at one crowd I see preparing for some other activity. So I walk over there and introduce myself. There are two guys who turn out to be baseball players, Gord Delman and Antonio Reyes. Their girlfriends are there too, Ellie and Nira, who are busy filling water balloons.

"We're playing water balloon dodgeball!" a little girl tells me excitedly.

"We're gonna get wet!" another kid yells.

I laugh. "I'm not gonna get wet. You won't get *me* with one of those balloons."

They all jeer me.

Of course, when the game starts, I make a show out of trying to dodge their balloons, letting them hit me. Soon my jeans and shirt are soaked and the kids are gleeful. The balloon I take in the face isn't one I wanted; I didn't see that one coming. I shake water out of my eyes and hair and swipe at my face. Nira hands me a towel, grinning.

I hear a voice behind me. "Hunter?"

That sounds like Kate. I turn quickly, then stumble back. It's the New York Bears mascot.

A bear, naturally. Wearing a hockey jersey. But the face...Jesus fucking Christ. The eyes are evil and that big smile with teeth showing is creepy as fuck.

I save myself from falling on my ass on the grass.

The bear lifts a hand and does a circular wave at me.

What the fuck?

"It's Orson!" a couple of boys cry, running at the bear to throw their arms around its legs.

They're better men than me.

My shirt is already wet, which is actually good so people can't see the sweat soaking through it. My armpits prickle and my legs feel weak. I rub my mouth. I have to get out of here.

Since Orson is distracting the kids, I bolt back toward the food truck. There was a big trash can there I can puke in if I need to.

"Hunter!"

I don't turn to see who's calling me, although weirdly it sounds like Kate again.

At the food truck, I keep an eye out from a distance. I spot one of the Bears players talking to Orson. Hey, that's Kevin Beaven, one of Kate's clients. One of the guys I talked to about her. As long as they stay over there, I'm good. Also, I warily watch the big black and white spotted Dalmatian with a huge black firefighter hat, and the giant Pikachu. I suck air into my lungs and hope my heart slows down before I have a heart attack worse than Vern's.

How the hell did I get myself into this? Fucking Hakim. He owes me big time.

I order a hot dog, mostly for something to do so I don't look like an idiot, and I'm holding it in my hands when I see Orson bouncing toward me. Fuck no.

I look wildly around for an escape route. I start to move but Orson calls, "Hunter!"

I'm so fucked up right now. I stare at the goddamn bear running toward me. That bloodcurdling smile. Those spine-chilling eyes.

I toss my hotdog into the trash can, turn and start run-walking across the park, probably looking like a five year old about to pee his pants. I glance over my shoulder to see Orson in pursuit, now running, if you can call it that, the bear lumbering over the grass, waving his arms.

I nearly crash into a family, not watching where I'm going. "Sorry, sorry!"

I dart around them and glance back again just in time to see Orson trip over his big paws, er, feet…whatever…and go flying flat on the ground. I can hear the "oomph" from here.

A bunch of kids watching break into laughter, no doubt thinking this is part of Orson's schtick. This is my chance to escape. But I pause. There's a person in there (which makes it extra freaky, in my opinion).

I watch Orson struggle to get up in the bulky costume, rolling around on the ground. Kids are screaming with laughter. Fuuuuuck me.

Heaving a sigh, I turn and jog back to the bear to help him up. *I can do this. I can do this.*

"Thank you!" Goddammit, that sounds like Kate.

What. The. Fuck.

I gape. "Kate?"

Orson's hands go to the head of the costume to lift it off. Only it won't come off.

My mouth drops open. My heart is still racing.

"Oh shit." The voice inside the head comes out muffled, but it's… Kate. "I can't get this off. And my shoulder hurts."

"Oh hell." Did she hurt herself when she fell? "Are you okay?"

"I don't know. Help me!"

"I can't." I can't get close enough to that disturbing face to help her. But it's Kate.

"What?" Her voice is a muffled screech. "Hunter! I'm stuck in here! It's bad enough barely being able to breath and...and I fell." She lets out what sounds like a small sob. "I'm going to suffocate if I can't get this off!"

People are still watching. If she takes the head off here, kids could be freaked out.

If she doesn't take the head off, *I'll* be freaked out. Okay, I already am.

"This way." Swallowing, I take her paw and tug her toward the road. There's a big rock outcropping on the other side. If we can get behind it, we'll be hidden from the picnic.

Orson can't move as fast as I'd like so I'm practically dragging... her? ...along. Once behind the big rocks, I stop. "Okay, let's get this off you."

She starts tugging at the head again. "I can't." She sounds like she's crying.

Kate doesn't cry. Except for that one time in college I found her in the gym, overwhelmed and tearful, and she nearly broke my goddamn heart that I tried to wall up.

I can't look at the bear face, so I step behind her and feel around the neck of the costume, trying to loosen it. I have no idea how this thing works. But I manage to pry something loose and between us we wrestle off the head.

Kate appears, her face red and wet, her hair limp and plastered to her head. "Oh my God, thank you!"

"Are you hurt?"

"I-I don't know." She sniffs and rolls her head around. "My shoulder hurts, but I think I'm okay."

I stare at her. "Why? Why are you in this ghoulish costume?"

"Ghoulish?" She gapes back at me. "It's not ghoulish, it's cute! The kids love it."

"It's creepy," I mutter, dropping my gaze.

"Is that…why you were running away?"

"I wasn't running away."

"That's what it looked like. Or maybe you were running from *me?*" She plants her paws on her hips.

"No! I didn't know it was you."

"Then you were running from Orson. Jesus, Hunter."

"Forget about that. Why are you doing this?"

"Kevin asked me to. He arranged it with the Bears, but the guy who was supposed to be inside this got sick. He'd promised the organizers he'd bring Orson, and he needed someone who'd fit in the costume. Apparently, the usual dude isn't that big." She holds her arms out. "Fits perfectly."

My head moves slowly side to side as I take this in. "This is what you do for clients."

She starts laughing. And laughing. She bends over, she's laughing so hard, swiping tears from her eyes. "Yes," she says. "This is the wildest thing yet."

Well, it's good that she's laughing now instead of crying. When I saw her tear-streaked face, I got that tight feeling in my chest that I had that day in the gym years ago. I wish I could laugh too, except I'm freaked out, embarrassed, and still pissed that I even came to this shindig.

Kate straightens, smiling. "Okay. Damn. I can't believe this. I need to get out of here."

"Um. Okay." I look around. I'm only too happy to escape. "How did you get here?"

"I met Kevin at the Apex Center to get the costume and he drove us here."

"Okay. Let's get out of here. My car's parked just off Fifth Avenue."

"I can't leave with this." She gestures at herself. "Apparently it's worth a lot of money."

I roll my eyes. "I should kidnap it and never give it back."

"What do you have against Orson? Oh…is it because he's the competition?"

"Yeah. That's it. Beaven can come pick up the costume from you. I'd say he owes you."

She purses her lips. "Oh, he definitely does."

"Take it off. Take it all off."

Our eyes meet and we both burst out laughing.

"I can't. I don't have shoes. Kevin has my shoes."

"Are you…naked under there?" I arch an eyebrow.

"Wouldn't you like to know."

"Oh, I would," I mutter under my breath. "Okay, let's go."

At least without the disturbing face I think I can handle this. Seeing Kate's pretty head on the shoulders of the bear is somewhat reassuring. I lead the way out of the park and across Fifth Avenue to my car and we climb in. "Home?" I ask.

"Yes, please. I live in Greenwich Village. Go all the way down Fifth and I'll tell you when to turn."

I fire off a quick text message to Hakim to let him know I bailed, then pull out and make the turn onto Fifth.

"Um, can you hurry?" she asks. "I have to go to the bathroom."

"Jesus." I glance at her. "I'll try."

It's not that long of a drive. Once we're on her street she says, "Finding a parking spot here will be impossible."

"I can let you out, if you need to…go."

She bites her lip. "Wait! There's a spot." She points.

I crank the wheel to turn. After an impressive feat of parallel parking, I help her out of the car and across the street. She leads the way around the corner and inside to her second-floor apartment.

We walk into the bright and sunny apartment. Being a corner unit, it has lots of windows, and the décor is light and airy, all pale gray and white. "Cute place," I say.

"Thanks. It's tiny but I love the neighborhood."

"It looks like you."

She gives me a skeptical look.

"Organized. Tidy. Modern."

She gives me a long, impassive look. "That's me, huh? Tidy?"

Shit. There I go again. I called her tough that night and I think she was insulted. Now I've done it again.

"Well, not right now," I admit, eyeing her sweaty hair and face.

That probably didn't make it better.

"You're not wrong." She sighs and sets the bear head on the small island. "Okay, help me get this off. I really need to pee now."

We wrestle her out of the costume, and I try not to notice that I'm touching her. Under the getup, she's wearing a thin tank top and a pair of tiny, tight black shorts. I swallow hard.

One hand grazes her bare arm. Then her thigh. I hear her sharp intake of breath and my gaze lands on her nipples, now hard and poking against her bra and tank top. Christ.

I kneel to help her step out of the costume. She sets a hand on my shoulder for balance and lifts one long, sleek leg. I want to run my hands up and down her leg so badly my palms tingle. My dick is pushing aggressively against the fly of my jeans.

I look up at her. She's watching me, her lips parted, her eyes pupils dilated. A flush stains her cheeks and she catches her bottom lip between her teeth.

Daringly, I set my hands on her calf and she pulls the other foot free of the fur garment. I slide my hands around the back of her firmly muscled calves, and then up to the backs of her knees. She shivers. "Hunter..."

She's not stopping me. I glide my hands up the backs of her thighs, then over the little shorts to cup her ass. I straighten my legs and stand, pulling her closer. Bending my head, we're nearly nose to nose. Her eyelashes flutter. Our mouths are so close... "Kate."

She pulls back, her eyes full of regret. "Hunter. We can't do this."

I close my eyes at the stab of disappointment. "Right. Right. Sorry."

"Also, I still have to go to the bathroom." She darts away from me and into the bathroom, slamming the door shut.

I lean against her kitchen island, sweating, breathing hard. My heart is galloping. Jesus. I fucked up. Why did I touch her like that? What the fuck is wrong with me?

I cover my eyes with one hand.

I hear water running. Then the door opens. Kate appears. She stands in front of the door, still damp-haired and rosy-cheeked.

Our eyes meet.

I open my mouth to apologize again, but she says, "I need a shower. I feel gross from that damn bear costume."

"Go ahead."

"Help yourself to a drink from the fridge. I think I have a few beers. I'll be quick."

"No rush."

The first thing I do is turn the bear head around so I can't see the face. Then I mosey around, peering out the windows through leafy branches onto the street below. The sidewalks are busy, with little shops and cafes nearby. Turning, I check out her place. It's definitely neat and organized, unlike my and Hakim's place some days. Her work desk is carefully arranged, the kitchen is spotless. I open her fridge and study the contents. Lots of healthy things, including a number of orderly containers stacked on shelves. And yes, there's beer. Just what I need.

I pull one out, pop the top and take a long pull. Jesus.

I almost kissed Kate.

I collapse onto her gray couch and fall back into the many cushions that line the back. Part of the couch extends into a lounge chair, and I lift my legs onto the couch too, stretching them out.

I admit that since I left Cancun, and Bayard, my life has been full of hockey. I had something to prove and I was determined to do it. I thought about Kate, sure. But she was in Chicago going to law school and living her own life. I missed her, but it was just the way things were.

Seeing her again, though, brought back all those memories. She was kind of a bossy know it all when it came to hockey, but then I got to know her better and I saw that she really did know it all. That makes me smile. Also, she cared a lot about people. Her bossiness was actually leadership on the team and her teammates respected her for that. And so did I. I remember being so attracted to her, but she was always with another guy and nothing ever came of it. Until that night.

I can do hockey. I *can't* do relationships. I'm so fucked up, no one will ever love me. I learned that a long time ago. Plus, now she's my agent, basically working for me. Although it's not the kind of business relationship where there can be a conflict; it'll just make things awkward. Maybe.

Then again, Kate already knows how messed up I am. That's exactly why I wanted her for my agent. Except…she's probably going to want to know why I was running away from her in the park earlier. What the hell am I going to tell her? She's smart enough to know that I wasn't running away from Orson because he's the mascot of another team. My mind churns, but I come up with no bullshit. Maybe she won't ask. Maybe I should have dropped her off and left her here and never seen her again. Yeah. No. As if that would work, now she's my agent.

Fuck.

She steps out of the bathroom along with a small cloud of steam. A scent drifts over that reminds me of a field of flowers in the sun. But what truly gets my attention is the towel that's wrapped around Kate's perfect body.

Her long, toned legs are on display, along with bare arms and shoulders. The guy downstairs takes note of the curves and hint of cleavage where the towel is tucked in. I swallow a noise that rises in my throat.

"Just have to get dressed!" she calls as she zips in bare feet from bathroom to bedroom.

I make a quick adjustment in my jeans and tip the beer bottle to my lips for a big gulp. Christ.

She returns a few minutes later dressed in a pair of cropped leggings and a short, loose sweatshirt. Her hair's still damp and her face is bare and clean. Today she's not that sophisticated New York businesswoman I've seen since we met up again. She's college Kate—casual, athletic, and so fucking hot it's a wonder my pants aren't on fire all over again.

"I'm sorry," I say. "Sorry I touched you like that." I shake my head. "No excuses."

Her lips lift into a soft smile. "Okay."

"Are you all right after that fall?"

"Oh. Yeah. My right shoulder feels a little sore." She rolls her shoulders back, which sticks out her tits. "But I think I'm okay."

Jesus. It's hot in here.

"How are you doing?" She looks over at me. "Need another drink?"

Oh hell yeah. "Beer me up."

She laughs. "I could use one too." She pads to the fridge, still barefoot, and pulls out two more bottles.

Sitting forward to set my empty on the small round coffee table, I try not to stare as she walks back toward me. "Thanks." I take the one she offers, and she drops onto the couch a short distance away from me. She stretches her legs out in front of her, crossed at the ankles. Her toenails are polished a shimmery rosy color. She has pretty feet.

"That was a wild afternoon," she says with a sigh. "Thank you for rescuing me."

I run my tongue over my teeth. "You're welcome. I can't believe you did that."

"It was for a good cause. I'm a sucker for getting a smile from kids."

"You like kids?"

"Sure. Doesn't everyone?"

"No."

She arches an eyebrow. "You don't like kids?"

"*I* do. But some people don't. I always get a kick out of the little fans. I was having fun—" I stop short.

She doesn't say anything, watching me as she takes a sip of her beer.

"It was fun," I say lamely.

"What was going on with you? Why were you trying to get away from me? I mean, from Orson."

I take another swig of lager. "I wasn't." I try the lie again.

"Bullshit." Her gaze is steady.

12

HUNTER

Aw fuck. She's always the one I spill my guts to. She's one of the few people who knows how messed up I was after the accident. She comes across as cool and serious. But when I told her about my PTSD, she didn't get all weird. She didn't judge me. And she's kept her word to not tell anyone else.

I don't tell people about it because I think they'll see me differently. Weak. Damaged. Pathetic. And I've never told anyone else about my stupid fears for the same reason.

The truth is, I *am* damaged. I know it. I just don't want others to know it.

Except Kate already does. And she's still here...I mean, I'm still here...ugh. Might as well tell her every damn thing.

"I have this sort of strange phobia," I finally say.

She cocks her head. "A phobia?"

"Yeah. A fear of mascots. It's called masklophobia."

Her faces scrunches up into a "Whut?" look. She blinks. And blinks again. Then she says, "Oh."

She's not laughing.

"I've never heard of that," she continues slowly, pulling her legs up onto the couch and tucking them under her. "I guess it's like a fear of clowns? I've heard of people who are terrified of clowns."

"Yeah, I don't like clowns much either." I rub my chin. "But mostly mascots."

She nods. "Do you know why? Did something happen that was traumatic?" Her eyebrows pinch together. "This isn't because of your PTSD from the accident, is it?"

"No, it's been since I was a kid. The first time I saw a someone in a costume like that, it was the Easter Bunny. I barely remember it, but I do remember how fucking creepy he looked and it scared the hell out of me, because he was talking but his mouth wasn't moving. My mom says I tried to run away, but everyone laughed and chased me, and that scared me even more."

"Aw." Her eyes shine with sympathy. "How old were you?"

"I think five. Mostly, I just avoid them. It's not like mascots are a big part of my life."

"Except hockey mascots."

"Yeah." I make a face. "I had no idea when Hakim asked me to come with him that there'd be a bunch of them at that picnic. Or that one of them would chase me."

She laughs softly. "I'm sorry."

I grin. "It is kind of funny."

"Not so funny when I fell on my face." She grimaces. "But I think the costume protected me."

"That was why I went back to you. I was worried you were hurt."

"But you didn't know it was me."

"I kept hearing your voice. I couldn't believe it was you in there." I start chucking. "Christ. I can't believe this. It's actually hilarious."

"It's good you can laugh about it." She smiles. "And then I got stuck in the costume."

"Maybe having to rescue a mascot will help me overcome my phobia."

"Ha! You're welcome."

Our eyes meet in a burst of heat. I swear I see sparks in my peripheral vision.

"Oh shit!" She bolts upright.

I start. "What?"

"I don't have my phone! I gave it to Kevin to hold for me." She reaches out and grips my arm so tightly I swear there'll be bruises there.

"Oh. We'll get it. I'll call him."

The look of utter panic on her face has me biting back a smile. "Now. Do it now."

"Calm down. It'll be fine."

"My phone! It's my life!"

I pull out my phone. I have Kevin's number from when I called him as a reference. It rings a couple of times, then he answers. "Morrissette. What's up?"

"Hey. I have your team mascot. I'm holding it for ransom." I meet Kate's eyes, which widen. Then she bites her bottom lip, smiling.

Silence. "What the fuck?"

"I need Kate's cell phone, her shoes, a dozen beers, and an extra-large pizza delivered to her place within the next hour, or you'll never see Orson again."

Kate cracks up, falling sideways on the couch.

"No anchovies on the pizza," I add. "Do you have the address?"

"Uh…no."

I look at Kate and she shouts it out.

"Got that?"

"What is even happening?" Kevin sounds confused. "Are you serious?"

"Serious as a shootout in sudden death OT."

"Okay, that's serious."

"Yeah. Also, you owe Kate."

"Ha. I guess I do. Okay. See you soon."

I end the call and set my phone down. "There. It'll be here soon."

"I'm being held for ransom?" Her eyes twinkle.

"No. Not you. Orson." I jerk my head at the costume. "I'll set that motherfucker on fire if Beaven doesn't show up."

"Hunter." She cackles more. "You won't do that."

"Hey. You know my little secret now. You know I'll do it."

She shakes her head, still shaking with laughter. "You're nuts."

"True, but I own it."

"Wait, I didn't mean—"

"I know." I smile. I'm fucked up, but I can still joke around. "So. This is a nice apartment."

"Thanks. It's small, but it's a great location. Finding a place in New York wasn't easy."

"I've heard that."

"It's nothing like your luxury digs."

"Eh. It's a hotel. With apartments. I need a roommate to afford it."

"You won't after you sign your next contract."

I have to smile. "I like your confidence."

"I am confident." She tosses her hair. "I'm good at my job." Then she mutters under her breath, "Even though some didn't think so."

I frown. "Who didn't think so?"

"Long story." She waves a hand.

"We have time."

She gives me a look. She doesn't want to talk about it. I get that. I can respect that. Even though somehow I always end up spilling my guts with her.

"Any more news of your dad's girlfriend?"

"Nope. I talked to my brother about it. He's all, whatever. Men."

"Yeah, men and women are definitely different. Thank God."

Her eyebrows snap together. "What does that mean?"

"I mean thank God we're different. I *like* how women are different —soft, nice smelling…what is that shower gel you use, by the way?"

She blinks.

Uh-oh. Getting too personal? I definitely appreciated all her differences that night in Cancun. Repeatedly. All night long.

Ahem.

"Never mind. Also, women are much stronger than men. Probably smarter. And you can multi-task."

She chokes on a little laugh and her frown clears. "Okay."

"Look at your many talents." I wave a hand at Orson's head over on the counter. "You can whip up a killer spreadsheet, negotiate like a shark, then dress up and charm little kids."

"I do indeed have many talents."

When Kevin arrives, Hakim is with him. Somehow, they found out they'd both been ditched.

Kevin hands Kate her phone and a bag with some clothes in it and sets a dozen beers on the counter. Hakim carries two big pizza boxes that smell fantastic.

"Two pizzas?" I raise my eyebrows.

"We're joining you," Hakim says. "You owe us after that bailsky."

Fuck him. I mean, I guess it was kind of rude. But I'm annoyed that they're crashing my time with Kate. "We had a costume crisis."

"I fell," Kate says, deflecting any attention from the fact that she was chasing me. "I hurt my shoulder and I couldn't get back up, and then I couldn't get my head off."

Kevin's lips twitch. "That is a crisis."

"Also, I had to go to the bathroom." Kate moves into her little kitchen and opens a cupboard. She pulls out four plates. "Urgently."

"Okay, okay. No overshares." Kevin waves a hand.

"I guess you two don't know each other." I introduce Kate and Hakim as we serve ourselves pizza and open beers. Then we all settle in Kate's little living room to dig in.

"Great pizza," I say between mouthfuls. "I'm starving."

"Hopefully the event was a success," Kate says. "It seemed like lots of people there, and the kids were having fun."

"They were having fun pelting me with water balloons." Luckily, I'm dry now.

"What could be more fun?" Hakim says.

"I agree. Water balloons are the best."

"So, Kate." Kevin points at her. "Tell us the latest gossip on trades."

She grins. "I don't gossip."

"But you probably know everything," Hakim says.

"She does," I affirm. "But she won't tell you."

"Damn."

I can see they're only joking. Half-joking.

Kate's at ease, laughing and bantering with us. It reminds me of that day I found her crying and took her to Bingo's place to cheer her up. She was the only girl there and she fit right in. That was also the day I was going to...*fuck*. Forget that.

When we're done with the pizza, we lounge around with another beer. Then Hakim says, "I guess you can drive me home now that we're both here."

"Sure," I say with all the enthusiasm of a guy about to get his balls waxed. "Let's go."

KATE

What a day.

Looks like everyone's leaving, including Hunter. Damn.

I argue with the guys over the leftover pizza and convince them to take it. I have my meals planned and prepared for the next week, so I don't need it.

As they leave, Hunter catches my eye and holds it. I give a half-smile, which he returns, a thread of connection drawing out between us.

"We'll talk next week," he says.

I nod.

When they're gone, I load the dishwasher and wipe the counters. And think.

I have a lot to think about.

We almost kissed. He had his hands on my ass. And I liked it.

He apologized, but the truth was, if he'd kissed me, I probably would have kissed him back. Yikes. That attraction is still there, and still strong. But he's my client.

Then he told me about his phobia.

My heart aches for the little boy who was laughed at because of it. He's such a contradiction—big, tough hockey player on the ice, but off the ice a guy with hidden wounds and layers of sensitivity that he feels he has to hide. I understand why he feels that way. The world's view of masculinity is toxic. I wish it weren't so. And oh my God...my heart...I love it that he feels comfortable enough with me to be honest.

I close my eyes briefly, my hands gripping the edge of my counter.

I can't have feelings for this man.

Shaking my head, I turn.

I hoped I'd have a chance to talk to him about Josh Heller and Easton Millar. After he opened up about the mascot phobia, I thought maybe he was in a mood to share. But then Hakim and Kevin crashed our party.

I sigh and sit on my couch.

I'll see him again, obviously. It'll have to wait until then.

It's Sunday night. I took a day off to cavort in the park in a bear costume, then eat pizza and drink beer with hockey players, something I've missed so much. I'm not going to work now. I'm going to watch more episodes of The Office, which I'm addicted to, have another beer, and go to bed early.

When I check my phone in the morning, there's a text from Hunter, sent last night around eleven, when I was already sleeping.

We were friends in college. We're still friends. Right?

I smile, then push out my bottom lip. What are we doing? I rest my elbows on my island and lean on them, my phone in both hands.

I'm filled with longing. I'm not even sure what for. For Hunter? For Hunter's wondrous wang? For his friendship? Or...something else?

I message him back. *Of course.*

His reply comes quickly. *Dinner tonight?*

I don't know what we're doing, but I do know I want to see him again. *Sure.*

I add, *I can make dinner here.*

That would be great. What time?

Seven?

A thumbs-up emoji arrives.

Now I have to go shopping. I made my meals ahead for this week —it keeps me from eating junk because I'm too lazy to cook—but I'd rather serve Hunter something that will wow him. Hmm.

Hunter likes beef. I ate with him enough times to know that. And I have a great bistro steak recipe. I fling open my fridge door to do inventory. I have nothing I need except beef stock, so I make a short shopping list and soon I'm hiking down Sixth Avenue to the little gourmet grocery store. I select steaks, little potatoes, fresh thyme, a bunch of spinach, and a bottle of red wine. I pause at the bakery counter, eyeing pastries. Dessert? I should have something to offer.

Overwhelmed with delicious choices, I finally request two squares of chocolate caramel slice, then head back home. Okay, I have work to do.

Van Halston has emailed me to let me know he's back in Chicago and wants to meet in early June. He suggests a couple of dates. I pull up my calendar. That would be perfect! I could visit Dad and meet Jenelle. I don't know if Ryan will be there that weekend, but his schedule is ridiculous, and I have to meet with Van. He's going to be an NHL superstar one day, and I want to be his agent. I want to guide his career. That would be such a fucking rush.

I let him know I'll be there. Then I book a flight. And email Dad and Ryan.

I have to convince Van I'm the best one to represent him. Having a client like Hunter definitely helps.

I check in on a bunch of things I'm working on, including Hunter's contract. I track the news of trades and signings, analyzing how this affects my clients and their various teams.

Then it's time to clean up and start dinner.

I get the steaks out of the fridge and season them with salt and pepper. I clean the potatoes and toss them with a mixture of olive oil and fresh thyme. I chop shallots and wash the spinach, which I'll lightly sauté with a bit of garlic and olive oil. That only takes minutes.

Then I jump in the shower. My hair's still a disaster from yesterday, so I shampoo and blow dry it with my round brush to smooth and flip up the layers. A little eyeshadow and mascara, a bit of highlighter on my cheekbones and I'm good. I pull on a pair of ripped jeans and a black T-shirt that says YES I DO PLAY LIKE A GIRL, TRY TO KEEP UP. I'm not going to make it weird by dressing up.

I pour myself a glass of the red wine. I need some of it for the sauce for the steak, so I have to open it. I'm scrolling through social media on my phone when Hunter arrives.

My heart bumps as I open the door and see him. Goddamn, I could climb him like a ladder. "Hi."

"Hi." He smiles, eyes crinkling up and walks in. "I brought wine."

"Oh good. Wine is good." I take the bottle from him and can't stop smiling as I carry the wine to the kitchen. "Would you like a glass? I have some open."

"Sure. Thanks."

I pour and hand him a glass and we sit on my couch. I keep a safe distance between us so I don't accidentally end up in his lap.

"How was your day?" he asks.

"Busy. Hey, guess what?"

"What?"

I hesitate. "Okay, I'm telling you this as a friend. It's not public."

"Got it."

"Van Halston wants to meet with me again."

"That's great! Does that mean…?"

"I hope so!" I sip my wine. "He's in Chicago and wants to meet up there, which is perfect because I can see my dad and meet his girlfriend." I wrinkle my nose.

"What was that look for? You shouldn't judge her before you've met her."

"I'm not judging her. I mean, I sort of am. I just want her to be good enough for my dad." Then I remember Calgary. "When are you going home?"

"I haven't decided yet." He shrugs. "Hakim's still here, so we're working out together and hanging out and…" He meets my eyes. "You're here."

I bite my lip. This makes my heart swell up in my chest, because I like him being here too. I nod. "I am." I told him he could go back to Calgary and we'd stay in touch. "Don't let that stop you from seeing your family."

"Lots of time."

"True. The playoffs aren't even over. That's when I expect things will heat up on the free agency market."

He nods. "Yeah." He drinks his wine. "I hate being in limbo like this."

"I know. Believe me, if I could ink a deal tomorrow, I would."

"I know." He holds my gaze. "I trust you, Kate."

"Thank you." My heart bumps.

"What's for dinner?"

"Dinner? Um…steak."

"I'll help you cook."

"Okay. Let's do it."

We take our wine to my tiny kitchen and start cooking. Hunter seems to know his way around a kitchen, getting the potatoes in the oven to roast, peeling and mincing garlic. We chat as we cook and move around each other in the kitchen. It's easy and fun, but also every time he brushes an arm against me reaching for something or bumps into me as I move to the stove, heat and sparks flash through me. Must keep my hands to myself and not feel up all his muscles.

I heat up the skillet to sear the steaks before popping them into the oven to finish them. As I cook the spinach, Hunter makes the red wine sauce for the steak.

"You seem to enjoy cooking," I comment.

"I do. I also like eating."

"Me too."

Soon we're sitting on the two stools at my little island with our dinners and more wine. Hunter cuts a piece of steak and pops it into his mouth. "Fantastic."

"Oh good."

"I hated spinach when I was a kid." He picks up some on his fork. "But now I actually like it."

"I always liked it. And it's so healthy."

"Yeah. I still try to eat like our nutritionist taught us in college."

"She was wise. I have to admit, I'm not as dedicated as I was, now I'm not playing. I do enjoy a big bowl of popcorn or potato chips once in a while."

"Once in a while is fine. I'm not saying I *never* eat junk."

"How about dessert? I got these amazing caramel chocolate squares."

"My weakness. Caramel anything."

I smile. "I do recall that."

There are things I don't know about Hunter...all the things he's done since college, his new friends, the women he's been with. But the things I do know about him make this so much easier than being with a stranger. We're comfortable with each other...but also a little on edge, with unintended heated looks and sizzling touches.

How is this happening?

There's a hockey game tonight. Conference finals. I turn on the TV to see what's happening and we both get comfortable on opposite ends of my couch to watch. Except I keep glancing at him, taking in his profile as he watches TV, the drape of his shirt over his hard-packed abs, his long legs. A couple of times, I catch him looking at me and my skin heats.

We drink wine, talk about the game using shorthand, and finishing each other's sentences. I like being friends with Hunter. I really do. But damn, it's hard not to think about being naked with him.

13

HUNTER

"Thanks for dinner." I'm about to leave even though I'd rather stay and wrap my arms around Kate and kiss her senseless.

"You're welcome. This was fun."

"It was."

She arranges her face into a neutral expression. "Could we get together again Wednesday?"

"Sounds good.

I leave her apartment and find my car where I parked it in a lot a few blocks away. As I drive home, I can't stop thinking about Kate.

After I told her about my phobia yesterday, I felt like such a dork. But as usual, she didn't judge me, just accepted it. Everyone's afraid of something, right? I remember in college the fake snakes in the cooler trick that totally freaked out Bingo when he went to grab a bottle of water. He's terrified of snakes. He was crying, he was so scared.

Mascots aren't even my biggest fear. My biggest fears are too big to even name.

Kate is amazing. Beautiful. Sexy. Smart. Caring. Driven. She loves hockey as much as I do. I love spending time with her. I do want to be her friend. I guess it's best we keep things like that, but fuck, I had a hard on the entire time I was at her place. It doesn't help that I remember exactly what fucking her was like. She's physical and sensual and enjoyed it as much as I did.

But that's in the past, and I guess it has to stay there.

When I get to the apartment, Hakim is sprawled on my couch playing Super Smash Brothers. He glances up at me. "Hey. Where were you?"

"Went out for dinner."

"Ah." He focuses on the big screen TV. "With Kate?"

"Yeah. How'd you know?"

He smirks, not looking at me. "Not a tough guess. You two were practically setting off the smoke alarms yesterday every time you looked at each other."

"What? Fuck off."

"Fucking your agent isn't going to get you a bigger contract."

My eyes bug out of my head. "What did you just say?"

Hakim grimaces. "Uh…"

I pin him with a laser gaze.

"Sorry."

"That's not what this is. We're just friends."

"Just reminding of you that little fact."

"I know that, asshole. Get off my couch."

"Sit on mine."

"Fuck sake." With an exaggerated sigh, I stretch out on his couch, grabbing a cushion for my head. I stare up at the ceiling. *Thanks, Hakim, for reminding me…we're just friends.*

"You wanna golf tomorrow?" I ask Hakim.

"Sure."

I think about naked Kate. I think about her mouth. I think about how her long legs wrapped around me, and… Fuck, I'm getting another stiffy.

"I'm going to bed," I announce, rolling off the couch before Hakim notices my boner.

"Okay."

A man of few words.

In my bedroom, I can give in to thoughts of Kate. Kissing Kate. Fucking Kate. Kate's mouth on my cock. I let out a groan as I take hold of my dick and jerk it. I've been doing this a lot lately, thinking about Kate.

I have to stop thinking about her like this. She's my agent, as Hakim helpfully pointed out. I need to focus on my goal—getting that big, new contract.

Kate made a reservation at a restaurant near her place, so I meet her at her apartment and we walk the few blocks to Sasha's. The narrow street bustles with pedestrian traffic, parked cars lining each side. Older, non-descript buildings create an urban tunnel of brick that's somehow charming.

Sasha's is a tiny place with dim lighting, a marble bar, and very close tables. Sensual music floats and mingles with the chatter of voices and clink of glass and cutlery. It's…intimate. Sexy.

We take our seats at the table for two. The candle on the table gilds Kate's skin, and she's showing excellent skin tonight—a sleeveless black top with a wide neckline. Her lips gleam pink and her long bangs emphasize big, shadowy eyes.

Our waitress recommends the Negroni, the cocktail special, so what the hell, we both order that and check out the menu until she arrives with our drinks.

"I am not eating beef tongue," Kate mutters, her forehead furrowed.

"Oh, come on. But wait…what the hell is tatsoi?"

"I don't know and I don't care, if it comes on a tongue I'm not eating it."

"That sounded dirty."

She looks up blinking, then grins. "Yeah, it did."

"You're cute."

She looks up at me, a little smile playing on her lips. "Okay. Have you eaten tongue?"

"Hell no."

Our Negronis arrive and we each take a sip. Kate's eyes widen. "That's strong."

"I can get you drunk and take advantage of you." I pause. "Wait. That's a joke."

"I know." She smiles and rolls her eyes.

I tell her about my afternoon golfing. "So Hakim got frustrated because he sliced a stroke, like a hundred and fifty yards from the pin, and when he took his next shot it went into a bunch of geese. They were pissed and came straight for him."

"Oh no!"

"It was hilarious, he was yelling and running away from a bunch of geese. Those fuckers can be mean."

"And huge, some of them!"

"Yeah. At home, we called them cobra chickens."

A laugh bursts out of her.

"They didn't get him luckily, but we were all dying laughing."

We order our meals, duck confit for me and scallops for her, and talk more as we eat, then decide to share a dessert. Kate pushes her fork into the brownie with mascarpone ice cream and says, "So. Can we talk business for a few minutes?"

"Of course."

"Is the reason you don't want to play for the Bears because Easton Millar and Josh Heller are there?"

I freeze solid. I stare at the brownie, my fork hovering above it. Slowly I lower my fork to the plate. I lift my eyes to meet Kate's. As usual, her face is neutral, her eyes warm as she waits for my response. My chest rises and falls with each quick breath.

My jaw tightens. "Why do you ask that?"

I know that's not an answer.

"I need to know what's going on," she says. "As your agent."

This is agent Kate. Not fun, flirty, *friend* Kate. Okay. This is what we have to do.

"Obviously you know they played with me in Swift Current."

"Yes." She slowly cuts off another piece of brownie with the side of her fork.

"I don't want to be reminded of the accident."

She nods. "I understand that. But playing on the same team as them—"

"I don't want to." I cut into her sentence abruptly.

Her eyes flicker. "I think there could be a great opportunity for you there."

I narrow my eyes at her. "Did you talk to them again?"

"Yes."

"Fuck." I glare. "I told you I don't want to play for that team. Why would you even give them the idea I might?'

"It's called negotiating," she says dryly. "The more interest, the better."

I shake my head. "Okay, I don't know your job, but…I'm not going there."

"Okay, this is your friend Kate talking now, not your agent. Tell me why."

"You know why." I'm afraid seeing them every day will trigger my PTSD. Do I have to spell it out to her? Christ.

"You're afraid."

Hearing her say it like that makes me defensive. Never mind I know goddamn well I'm afraid. I don't want the whole world to know.

"Are you running away from it?" she asks softly.

There definitely was a time when I wanted to erase the accident from my past. I wanted to build big walls around the PTSD and deny its existence. Therapy helped me realize I couldn't just pretend it never happened. I've been doing well, but seeing Easton and Josh… Jesus. They were my best friends. We were always together, on and off the ice. We were the best players on the team, all three of us supposed to play in the NHL.

The year after the accident was a mess for me, but I knew Easton got drafted that spring. It's hard to describe the bitterness I felt about that, sitting in my cottage in Tofino, and then the dark shame that stained me because I wasn't happy for my friend.

I also knew Josh had been badly injured and was in the hospital for a long time. By the time he got drafted the next year, I was in a better place, getting ready to go away to college to play hockey because at least it was hockey. I was glad he'd recovered well enough to play again, but it still hurt. My two best friends made it there without me.

We've never talked since the accident. I see them when I play against them, a few times a year, but I act like they're opponents I don't know. I play my toughest games against them.

Playing with them on a team would be totally different.

"I'm not running away," I say. "I'm making the best decision I can for my mental health. And you should know that."

Her chin jerks down, barely, but I see her reaction. She's got a great poker face, but that got her. A curl of guilt twists in my gut.

"I don't think I *do* know that," she says coolly. "I'm not convinced this would be a bad move for you."

Fire blazes through my chest. "It's not up to you," I bite out. "It's up to me."

She swallows. Drops her gaze briefly. Then lifts her chin. "Yes. You're right." She sets down her fork. "I think I'm ready to go now."

I stare at her for a few seconds. The air around us is heavy. "Okay. Sure."

I catch the waitress's eye and take care of the check, then we leave. Out on the street, Kate walks briskly.

"Kate."

She doesn't stop. "What?"

"You're going the wrong way."

She halts. Her head goes back as she looks skyward. "Seriously?"

"Um, yeah."

She lets out a little growl, turns and marches back toward me, then past me.

It'd be funny, except she's pissed and I'm pissed and this isn't the time to tease her about her bad sense of direction. So I catch up to her.

Neither of us say much until we get to her place. She stops at her door. "Thank you for dinner." She looks up and meets my eyes. The reserve there feels like a punch in the gut. "I think it would be better if we keep our relationship business from here on."

Now, I'm really pissed. I cross my arms and my back teeth grind together. I'm afraid I'm going to say something I'll regret, so I snap, "No."

Her eyebrows fly up. "What?"

"No." I scowl. "We're both angry. Let's call it a night and sleep on things and talk tomorrow."

Her lips pinch together and she stares at me like she can't believe I'm saying that. Finally, she says, "Okay. Fine. Good night, Hunter."

"Night."

I make sure she gets into her building, then turn and stalk down the sidewalk. My hands curl into fists and my shoulders hunch up around my ears.

Shit.

Fuck.

Damn.

My gut feels like there's a boulder lodged in it. I drive home, yelling at the traffic and impatiently changing lanes. When I get there, Hakim is out, thankfully, so I can slam things around in the apartment, like the door when I stomp inside and the fridge door after I grab a beer.

Slouched on the couch, I stare out the big windows at the glittering view of Manhattan across the river.

Goddammit.

Now I'm thinking about Josh and Easton. I don't want to think about them. I've avoided thinking about them for years and it's been working fine.

I knew I should have tried to go see Josh in the hospital after the accident, but I just couldn't. Hell, I couldn't get out of bed some days. And Easton...well, he'd clearly moved on.

If I don't get that contract I deserve, everything I've done up till now is a waste. If I don't get that contract, I'll be back where I started —my life and career fucked up.

Just because Kate's my agent doesn't give her the right to tell me what to do with my life. I can fuck things up well enough on my own. And I know that playing for the Bears will fuck me up. I know what's best for me. I've made it this far—through college, into the NHL, and now I'm right on the edge of signing the kind of contract I want—I can't relapse.

She wants to keep our relationship business. So what? Now we can't even be friends?

I feel like I just took a hard cross check. I groan and lean my head back onto the cushions.

Was it a mistake signing with Kate as my agent? I wanted her because I know she's good at what she does.

No. That's not the only reason. I could find a bunch of good agents if that was all I wanted. I wanted *her*. It's always been more than friendship with her. She gets me. In college, she was the one person I could confide in, and not be looked at differently. When Vern had his heart attack and I worried about losing him, she was who I needed. Kate.

And yet, for the first time it seems like she doesn't really understand me. That's why I'm so angry. Okay, I guess I'm actually more hurt than angry. Goddammit.

I can't fire her. I need her. I need a contract. And like she pointed out when we first met, there's more to the player-agent relationship than contracts. My agent is part of my life. And...fuck it, I want it to be her. I don't *want* to fire her.

Doing that would be the shittiest douchehole move in the history of doucheholes.

Or maybe I am a douchehole anyway. Because...fuck...I care about her. And I don't want to lose her.

14

KATE

I'm doing my job. The job he hired me to do. And he questions my judgment?

That stung when he said I should know better. That this was about his mental health.

I understand that.

Am I pushing for something he shouldn't do? Would it truly be harmful for him to play for that team, with those two players?

I trudge into my bedroom, kick off my ballet flats, and throw myself on the bed.

I'm not a psychologist. Maybe I should be listening to him. He knows himself and what's best for him.

Yes, I think I can negotiate a damn good contract with the Bears. I can sense their interest in him, and based on their recent moves, he'd be an excellent forward for them. Isn't that what Hunter wants?

There are other options. If he wants me to forget about the Bears, I can do that. I'm not as confident in offers we might get from Long Beach and Toronto, but I can bust my butt to try to get the best deal for him I can.

I roll onto my stomach, squeezing my eyes shut. I'm his agent, but I don't want to lose him as a friend. A lump constricts my throat. I want to pick up the phone and call him and apologize, but I know I'll cry and it pains me to admit it, but he was right. We both need some time.

So I get ready for bed and crawl under the covers. It's impossible to shut off my mind. I keep going over and over our conversation. I could have handled it differently. Maybe I could have avoided getting him upset. I know that a lot of men don't respond well to strong women. That got me in trouble at Pinnacle. Guys in college who couldn't handle dating me, who were pissed off because I knew more about hockey than they did and didn't try to hide it.

But Hunter's not like that.

Or is he?

He wasn't like that in college. He was proud of me for being captain of the women's team. He never got annoyed at me for being bossy or knowledgeable. He liked it.

But now it's his life, maybe he feels differently.

I get up, have a drink of water, attempt to read a book for a while to distract me. This time when I go back to bed, I manage to fall asleep, but when I wake up in the morning, I feel exhausted.

But calmer.

I have work to do. Phone calls to make. There are a couple of other young guys in the draft this year I've been talking to. I arrange meetings in Newark the week of the draft. I know they'll be talking to a bunch of agents. They aren't going to be signing multi-million-dollar contracts, but that's okay. It's a long game and signing them now will pay off down the road.

Shortly after lunch, I check my phone and there's a text from Hunter. My heart caroms in my chest at seeing his name.

Hey. Can I come over tonight to talk?

Relief spills through me like water in a fountain and every muscle in my body goes soft and weak. I slump in my chair, my head bent forward. I guess I didn't even realize that I'd been terrified he might take me up on my offer to end our friendship. Or worse…fire me as his agent.

I suck air into my lungs and tip my head back. That could be what he wants to talk about.

If so, I have to give him credit for being mature enough to do it face to face.

I text him back. *Yes. What time?* Should I offer dinner?

7 okay? I'll bring food.

My breathing goes shaky. *Okay thanks. See you then.*

Now I have to fucking concentrate for the rest of the day. Ha. *Good luck with that, Bridges.*

Hunter arrives a few minutes after seven. His thick waves are tousled, the stubble on his chin and jaw a bit rough, and shadows under his eyes indicate he's as tired as I am. He's wearing jeans and a T-shirt and he's carrying a big bag from Shake Shack that smells incredible. It also makes me laugh.

"What's so funny?"

"I love Shake Shack."

He smiles but I can see the guardedness behind it. "Good."

"Also, I'm starving."

He sets the bag on the island and turns to me. "I'm sorry about last night."

I gaze up at him. He holds my gaze, his eyes steady and warm.

At this moment, I feel calm. Reassured. Safe. "I'm sorry, too."

"Let's eat and then talk more."

"Okay."

We devour our burgers and fries and lemonade. My stomach was a mass of knots before he got here, but now I really am hungry. I haven't eaten all day.

"Two burgers?" I lift an eyebrow at him as he unwraps another one.

"I'm a growing boy."

"Ha ha."

"Well, some parts of me are growing." He winks.

"Oh my God." I roll my eyes, even though heat flashes through me and I'm happy he's relaxed enough to make dirty jokes.

I gather up the wrappers from my meal and shove them into the bag, then slurp down the rest of my lemonade as he finishes his second burger. Then we move to my couch.

"Okay," he begins. "Again, I'm sorry. I overreacted." His eyes tighten. "I was triggered."

"I know. And I'm sorry I did that. You were right. I should have known. I should have listened the first time you told me."

"I need to communicate better without getting all worked up."

"I truly believe that it would be a good move for you, and not just for the money or the term, but because of the fit with the team. I think it would be an opportunity for you to shine." I shake my head. "But I shouldn't be pushing you to do something you don't want to do. You know yourself. I won't talk to the Bears anymore. We'll find something else."

He sits silently for long moments, chewing on his bottom lip. Finally, he says, "Okay. I appreciate that."

If there's a twinge of disappointment deep inside me, I push it away. I guess a small part of me was hoping he'd try to get past this. But it's okay. I'm a good agent and I'll figure this out.

"We both got emotional last night," he says. "I'll try to do better."

"Me too."

HUNTER

We go to a sports bar to watch a playoff game. Kate's friend Soledad and a few other friends of theirs join us. I bring Hakim and Disco Dan with me. It's a festive atmosphere in the bar, with all the TVs playing the game, lots of cheering, groaning and yelling.

"That was fucking hooking!"

"Oh, come on, offside, man!"

"Get off your knees, ref! You're blowing the game!"

That one gets a roar of laughter from everyone in the bar.

"I have to remember that one," I say to Kate.

"Sure. That'll get you a misconduct." She shoots me an amused glance and we both laugh.

I haven't experienced a game in this kind of atmosphere and it's fun. Also fun because I'm with Kate.

During an intermission, I say, "Hey, I talked to Vern today."

"Oh! Did you? How is he?"

"He's doing okay. I told him you had things under control."

She grins. "Yikes."

"His wife wants him to retire. He wants to keep working."

"He's not that old."

"Yeah. Anyway, we talked for a while. It was good to hear his voice."

"I'm glad you talked to him."

"I guess I didn't even realize how worried about him I was. He sounded more like his old self, complaining about his low-fat diet and not being allowed to drink Dr. Pepper. I'm so glad he's going to be okay."

I watch Kate talk and laugh with her friends. I chat with Soledad, happy to meet her after all I've heard about her from Kate. I watch Dan and Soledad flirt.

Kate and I have been hanging out, even working out together once at her gym and once at mine. We've gone for walks and she introduced me to a bunch of dogs—Rosie, Milo, and Lucky—at Washington Square Park, which was unexpected but cute. Not many people introduce you to their dog friends. We've talked about all kinds of shit and had a lot of laughs. I still struggle not to touch her and yeah, sometimes I fantasize a little at night when I'm alone, but that's harmless. Right? When I slip up and make some kind of dirty innuendo, she just rolls her eyes. Although sometimes she blushes.

Life feels good.

We take an Uber back to her place.

"That was fun tonight," I say, sitting in the back seat of the car.

"Mmm. It was."

"It reminded me of college."

"Yeah. Except you never partied with us in college."

I snort. "Yes, I did."

She smiles. "Not at first. You weren't very friendly."

I think about that. I remember how hard it was starting college. "I wasn't *un*friendly. It was just...hard."

"Was it?" She shifts to face me better.

"Hell yeah. I was nineteen, a year older than the other freshmen. I'd already lived away from my parents for years, but that was a whole new environment. And after what I'd been through, everyone seemed young and foolish. I wasn't into partying. I was there to prove to myself I could still play hockey."

Her lips push out in a tiny pout. "I didn't understand that at the time."

"I know." I nudge her shoulder with mine.

"For the record, I did realize you weren't an asshole fairly quickly." She pauses. "I may have had a little crush on you."

I don't move. I gaze into her gorgeous blue eyes, shadowy in the darkness. I clear my throat. "You did?"

One corner of her mouth lifts. "Yeah. I almost asked you out once." Her eyelashes lower. "But you were going out with Tandy."

My heart squeezes. "Ah. Fuck."

Her eyelashes lift again. "Why?"

"Because...I liked you, too."

Her eyebrows pull together. "Then why did you go out with Tandy?"

"I thought you were with Bryson."

Her lips part. "We were just friends!"

"Yeah, I found that out later."

"Oh my God." She stares at me.

"Then…that day we went to Bingo's, after I found you in the gym…"

"Blubbering."

I roll my eyes. "You were overwhelmed. I hated seeing you cry. You were always so strong. It killed me."

She blinks.

"I was going to ask you out…but I found you in the kitchen kissing that architecture fuckface."

She chokes and lowers her forehead to her hands, her shoulders shaking. "Henry."

"Yeah."

Then she lifts her head, sobering. "You know…I sort of hoped you were asking me to that party because you liked me…but I thought we were just friends, and…"

"I know."

"And then you started dating Colette."

"Yeah."

"Another puck bunny you didn't really care about."

"Yep."

Her eyes widen and her lips part. "Hunter…"

My smile goes crooked as she puts things together. "Yeah."

She swallows. "You broke up with her because of me. Because she didn't want you to be friends with me."

I nod sadly. "You were right. She didn't like you. But it was because she was jealous. She thought I had feelings for you."

Her breath catches.

The words are on my lips. I shouldn't say them. But hell. We're confessing all kinds of shit. I hold Kate's gaze and brush my fingertips over her cheek. "She wasn't wrong."

She stares at me, her eyes growing shiny. The silence between us stretches out. "Oh, Hunter. Really?"

"Really."

"Oh my God. How could we have been so stupid?"

I shrug. "I don't know. It happened. And then…"

131

"Cancun," she finishes for me.

"Yeah."

"But…you left. You didn't even tell me you were going, or say good-bye, or…" She stops. Her chin quivers.

"I know. I didn't have a lot of time, though. The only flight that day left early and I had to get to New Jersey."

She nods slowly. "I figured that out. But I…was hurt."

"Aw, fuck." I stare at her in dismay. "Really? I thought we were both just wasted and having fun."

"I know." She bites her bottom lip. "But I realized…I wanted more."

"Fuck me." I let my head drop back and stare up at the roof of the car.

She curls her fingers over my hand and squeezes. "I was happy for you. I understood why you left."

"You were going back to Chicago to go to law school."

"Yeah." The word pulses with regret.

I turn my head and our eyes meet again. "Kate."

"Hunter."

The air pulses around us. "Is it too late?"

She pulls her lip between her teeth again. "It's not too late. But… this might not be the best time."

I give a tiny nod. "I get what you're saying. But after those years that we wasted on other people, when we really wanted each other… let's not do that again."

She stares back at me. "What does that mean?"

"Can we…try?"

She pulls in a shaky breath and dips her head. "I want to…try."

I cup her cheek and peer into her eyes. "Me too."

We barely get inside her condo and she's in my arms, her arms wound around my neck, and our mouths crash together.

I make a low noise as I crush her to me, devouring her mouth, sliding my tongue inside, tasting her. She whimpers, opening to me, her tongue playing with mine.

My dick presses into her eagerly and she arches closer. I slide my mouth to her cheek, her jaw, then her throat as her head falls back.

"Oh God."

I suck gently on delicate skin, then lick her. "You're gorgeous." I nip her shoulder.

My hands go to her tight little ass again and I hoist her up. She immediately wraps her legs around me. I walk to the door of her bedroom and push it fully open with one foot.

Nice big bed, right there. It's a small room, only a couple of steps until we fall onto the mattress together, arms and legs twined around each other, kissing desperately, hands roaming everywhere.

Oh fuck. Oh Jesus. She feels fucking amazing, her mouth hot and wet and delicious, her taut body arching and pressing into me. Her hands slide under my T-shirt and up my back, sending tingles shooting down my spine to my balls. I roll her under me, pinning her to the bed, and she parts her legs so that I fit perfectly between them, my aching cock against her soft center.

After more long kisses, I push up and grab the hem of her top. Watching her face, I draw it up and over her head. She lifts to help me, then lays beneath me in a beige lace bra with barely-there cups. Another groan rumbles its way up from my chest as I study her sweet cleavage and firmly-muscled torso. Desperate for more, I bend to plant a hot, open-mouthed kiss between her tits, breathing in the scent of her skin.

My stubble scrapes over the inner curves of her breasts and I kiss her nipples through her bra. Her hips move on the bed, her back arching, and she reaches behind her to flick open the fastener.

"Thank you," I murmur, tugging the lace away from her.

Now her perfect breasts are bare and sweet mother of fuck...I may have seen them before, but right now, I'm just in total fucking awe.

My entire body is on fire. Electricity tightens every nerve ending.

"Kate." I close my eyes briefly. "I want to fuck you so bad." I open my eyes to peer into hers. "But...I want to make sure..."

15

KATE

I hold Hunter's gaze evenly. "I'm sure." I lift a hand and place it on his cheek.

Relief washes over his face, which is extremely gratifying. He wants me too.

He makes quick work of getting off my jeans and thong, tossing them aside. On his knees, he reaches behind his neck and pulls his T-shirt off. I press my hands to his bare chest, a freakin' work of art. When I rub my hands over his pecs, his eyelids grow heavy. I like that.

I lower my hands to his jeans and open the button and then the fly. His cock is an enormous bulge in his boxers and a shiver of excitement runs through me.

He grabs his wallet and retrieves a condom before rolling over to kick off his jeans.

"Oh, good thinking." I pluck it from his fingers, eager to touch him and put the condom on.

Now we're both naked. My gaze slides over him, from carved pecs to ridged abs to the thick but neat dark hair above his cock. His beautiful, thick, long cock with its perfectly ridged crown and pulsing veins. He moves back between my legs, on his knees, his thigh muscles solid and bunched.

I touch him, licking my lips, which makes his eyes flare hot. Curling my fingers around his shaft, I stroke him, once, twice, reveling in the heat and virility beneath my hand. "So beautiful," I whisper. I want to taste him. Suck him. But my pussy is pulsing and aching with need. I need him to fuck me.

I open the package and carefully roll the condom on. His jaw is clenched when I look up at him. I smile. "You okay, Morrissette?"

His lips twitch. "I won't be for long if you keep touching me like that."

I brush my fingers over his taut balls, eliciting a sharp hiss from him. He nudges my thighs farther apart with his knees and I drop my arms, lie back, and gaze up at him. His face is tight, his eyes blazing. His body is an inverted V against the faint filtering through the blinds on my window, broad shoulders, narrow hips. I want to touch him everywhere. I feel overwhelmed with the need swelling inside me, as if I can never get enough of him.

"You're beautiful," he rasps. He trails a finger between my breasts. "Perfect. Sweet." And he leans down to suck a nipple into his mouth.

A jolt of sensation shoots through me. My back arches and a cry falls from my lips.

He tugs and licks and nips the sensitive tip, covering my other tit with his hand, squeezing then plucking that nipple. I'm a whore for breast play, my nipples so sensitive, and having both of them toyed with at the same time sends aching pulls of longing to my womb.

He shifts his mouth to my other breast, pinches the wet nipple as he sucks the other and I'm on sensory overload. My inner muscles clamp down hard with desire, my clit pulsing.

"Oh God!" I cry. "That's so good..." I make some unintelligible noises as he plays with me for long, stretched out moments until I'm throbbing with sweet, mindless, desperate need. "I need you...inside me...please."

"Mmm." He kisses his way down my stomach, nuzzles the triangle of dark hair on my mound, then pushes my thighs apart with his big hands to study me. "You're ready."

"Oh my God, I'm beyond ready! I'm dying."

He laughs softly, parting me with his thumbs. "Oh yeah. You're ready. Look how wet and swollen you are. Gorgeous."

His words only inflame me more.

When he lowers his head and licks me, I nearly shoot up off the bed. I grab his head and hold on. "Hunter…"

"Mmm. So sweet." His hands hold my hips as he licks more, probes with his tongue, then slides it over my clit.

"Aaaaah!"

He teases and tastes and tongues me until I'm vibrating. I feel my orgasm hovering on the edges, but I need more…

"Fill me up. Fuck me."

"Yeah." Satisfaction thickens his voice as he moves again, closer, taking his cock in his hand to slide the head up and down through my wet pussy. I tip my hips up to give him access and he prods gently at my opening, then pushes in. "Fuck, Kate…"

My eyes are heavy but I watch his face, the way his eyelids lower, his mouth firms, his jaw contracts. Then he looks back at me. Our eyes meet and something sharp and sweet pierces me.

My lungs constrict. I lick my lips, our gazes locked on each other. He penetrates me deeper, stretching me, filling me, so completely and intimately I can't breathe. Can't think.

We've done this before. So long ago, though, it's almost like we're two different people now. And yet we're the same.

He stretches out over me, big and heavy, his elbows on the mattress, his hands smoothing the hair back from my forehead as he kisses me. I hook my ankles at the small of his back and wrap my arms around him. Our mouths join, cling, and part, again and again as he touches my face, then kisses my jaw and my neck. I release my ankles and smooth my hands up and down his sides, enjoying the feel of his muscles and warm skin. He pulls back to stare down at me, and I smile and slide my fingers through his thick hair.

He moves inside me, slowly, easing out and then back in. It's delicious friction as he glides over sensitive nerve endings and then as he pushes deep, he hits a spot inside me that's almost unbearably lovely. Our mouths barely touch as we move together, slowly at first. Then he pushes up onto straight arms and drives in harder. Faster. The bed bounces in an erotic rhythm.

I grab his thighs, then his waist, watching his face tighten. God. *God*. He's beautiful, so vital and strong. Sensation pulls tight inside me, coiling, and I tilt my pelvis more so he presses my clit on every downstroke. It only takes a few strokes and I'm blowing up, that hot spiral inside me bursting open, flooding my body with pleasure. It washes down my legs, making them weak, and my heart pounds. I can't stop the noises I make as I come so hard I'm blind, gripping Hunter's shoulders and hanging on as if I'm unwinding so fast I'll fly away.

He presses a hard kiss to my mouth as shudders wrack me, then a gentler, lingering kiss. He pushes back onto his knees, holding my legs as he drives into me, his face intent and focused, his mouth open as his own orgasm breaks over him. He shouts, his head falling back, his body tensing as he holds himself deep inside me and pulses. I squeeze him with my inner muscles, and he groans.

Seconds later he stretches out beside me, pulling me into my side so he's still inside me. I hook a leg over his hip and bury my face in his neck, both of us still breathing hard, still vibrating.

I struggle for words. Not usually a problem for me.

Hunter's hand cups the back of my head in a gesture that's surprisingly tender and makes my heart ping. "Wow."

"Mmmhmm." That was definitely a wow.

He shifts and uses his fingers to tilt my chin up so he can see my eyes. "You okay?"

"Oh, hell yeah."

His lips curve into a sexy smile. "Okay, good. That was phenomenal."

"Brain scrambling."

"Mind melting."

I smile too. "Yeah."

He brushes his knuckles over my cheek. "I missed you, Katertot."

His words and the nickname bring an unexpected sting to the corners of my eyes. I blink them back. "I missed you, too."

"I know you sort of work for me now...but it doesn't feel like that. It feels like you have the power."

I turn my head slowly side to side. "I like to think of it as a partnership."

He purses his lips. "Yeah. That's a good way to think of it. Partners. And...I'm not cutting out this time."

"What does that mean?" Might as well be up front here.

"I mean...I like being with you. Spending time with you. Laughing with you." He dips his head to rub his nose alongside mine. "Fucking you."

I press my lips together. "That sounds like..." I stop. "That sounds like a relationship."

"Yeah. It does." He clears his throat.

"Is that okay?" I search his face. He's the one who went out with the girls who only wanted to date hockey players so he wouldn't get too attached. "Is that what we're trying?"

When he asked me in the car if we could try this, I had to think. I like Hunter. I liked him years ago. I probably loved him. I know it's taking a risk. But maybe we can do this. So I said yes. But is this truly what *he* wants?

"Yeah. That is what we're trying." He kisses my forehead so tenderly and my heart melts in my chest.

Now we've admitted our feelings for each other, we can't get enough of the sexy times. I'm not complaining.

But that's not all it is. It's still fun going for a walk with him or sitting on a patio and people watching. And it's still hockey season—

tonight's the Stanley Cup final. St. Louis versus Boston. Hunter thinks St. Louis should win. I'm still cheering for Callum.

We watch the game at my place, eating pizza and drinking a beer on the couch, pretending that we're providing the color commentary, each of us trying to outdo the other with the dirty hockey talk.

"Look at that penetration!" Hunter calls.

I snort laugh. Moments later, I get my own chance. "Zach Zelinsky takes a pounding!"

Hunter grins. "Good one."

Then the real announcer chimes in with, "Colbert slides his hands down the shaft when he needs to."

"Did you hear that?" I crack up, falling against Hunter's big chest which is also shaking with laughter.

I get the next one. "That's a long shift. Melburn and Treiber need to get off."

"Ha!" Hunter guffaws. "Jesus, you always make me laugh." He pauses. "Also, super horny."

"Hunter!"

"It's true." He kisses my nose.

"Well." I shift against him suggestively. "You're not the only one."

St. Louis wins the game and we both watch the celebrations and sadness with the same feelings of recognition and envy. We've both been winners and I know Hunter would love to win again, hoisting that beautiful big silver cup.

And when it's all over, he takes my glass from my hand, sets it on the table with his own, and pulls me onto his lap. With a hand in my hair he kisses me—long, deep, wet kisses that go on and on. Heat builds inside me. I want him so much, I'm dying. Licks of electricity race over my nerve endings.

"I like this shirt." With a half-smile on his face, he touches the lettering on my T-shirt that says DON'T PUCK WITH ME. "But it's coming off."

I lift my arms as he pulls it up and over my head. "It's okay. You can puck with me if you want."

He grins. "I want." He admires my sheer demi-bra, tracing a finger from between my breasts down over my abs. Sensation skitters through me, my already-hard nipples tightening even more. He opens the button of my jeans, lowers the fly and holds my hips so I'm tight against his erection as he kisses my throat, my chest, the inner curves of each breast. He bites one nipple through the sheer fabric, giving me a jolt of exquisite pleasure.

I reach behind me to undo my bra and let it fall so he can touch my aching breasts and he obliges with a low groan of appreciation, cupping them, sucking, licking. He kisses all around the outer curves and it's torturous and erotic.

I rub my pussy over his cock, our jeans a barrier between us. I want to touch him. Taste him.

I slide off him and down to my knees on the floor between his spread thighs, my fingers going eagerly to his jeans to open them. Just as quickly, he whips his shirt off over his head and then lifts his hips to help me pull his jeans and boxers down.

"Kate...Christ..."

I take him in my hands and hold him, admiring the crown and the fullness of his balls. I bend my head to gently kiss the tip. Thick, liquid desire swirls inside me.

Another groan rumbles in his chest and his fingers slide into my hair, firm but so gentle. My mouth longs for him and I swirl my tongue around the head, tracing the ridge, going lower to get him nice and wet. Then I open my mouth on him and slide my lips down to meet the edge of my hand.

He tastes clean and male. The scent of his skin is musky and the feel of him inside my mouth, alive and virile, turns me on almost to the point of pain. I squeeze my thighs together.

"Fuck that's good..."

I slide my lips and my hand up and down, lick around him, suck harder.

"Touch my balls," he begs in a low voice. "Oh yeah...like that."

I curl my fingers around him and gently squeeze, caress him with my fingertips, then lift my mouth off his shaft and sink lower to lick the tender skin of his sac. Daringly, I suck one testicle into my mouth, then the other.

His hips are lifting, his hands tightening in my hair, and he makes tortured noises that I think are pleasure. I nip at his inner thigh, kiss his groin, then suck on him again until he starts thrusting up into my mouth.

He stops. "Jesus," he gasps. "Come here. Want to fuck you."

I'm eager for that too. I scramble back onto the couch to straddle him, but he takes hold of my waist, stands and lifts me like I'm a bag of potatoes. He sets me on my knees on the couch, facing the wall. Ohhhhh…

I lean on the back of the sofa as he slides a hand between my thighs and encounters wetness. "Oh yeah. There we go…so fucking wet."

I suck on my bottom lip and close my eyes as he plays there, pushing my legs wider, lifting my hips so my back is arched. As I hear rustling noises, I peek over my shoulder to see him rolling on a condom, and then he's pushing at my entrance. He takes his time, inching in and out until he's fully seated, his groin against my ass.

"So tight." He grips my hips. "So wet."

I rest my head on the couch. "Fuck me." That liquid desire is converging in an unrelenting ache between my legs.

"Oh yeah." He slides out in a delicious pull. "Look at this ass. Jesus, Kate. You're fucking perfect." His hands cup my cheeks and squeezes, and I tighten around him, earning another rough noise. "Perfect." Then he grasps my waist and slams into me.

I cry out. I grip the couch as he bangs me with fast hard strokes, air propelled out of my lungs as he penetrates so deeply I can't breathe. I push up and twist to look at him. His face is carved, but his mouth is soft and sensual. He's watching his cock slide in and out of me but lifts his gaze to my face as I turn. He reaches up to cup my cheek, his thumb brushing my mouth, and I open and suck it in. His eyes blaze.

I release him and lower my head again. He trails his fingers between my ass cheeks in a shockingly forbidden move that thrills me to my core. I gasp and quiver, pushing my ass back against him faster and faster.

"Yeah," he growls. "I like that...fuck me back."

I need to come. I reach between my legs to find my clit and rub in a tight circle over it.

"Fuck yeah. Come, baby. Do that...I'm close..."

"Me too. God, Hunter, your cock...this is so deep. I'm there..."

The spiraling sweetness builds and builds, higher and tighter. As he pounds into me, sensation there blends with the tingle from my clit, twisting together up to a peak of almost unbearable beauty. I come apart, shuddering, wailing, my arms and legs quivering.

And Hunter comes too, pressing deep inside me, holding my hips and shouting.

I rest my head on my arms, trying to breathe, my heart slamming against my ribs. Hunter pulses inside me, my pussy still spasming. I'm going to collapse onto the couch, and as if he knows that, Hunter slowly pulls out, holding the condom.

He lifts me and sits me on the couch. My arms are lax as I sprawl back.

"Beautiful." He touches my mouth with a fingertip. "Be right back."

He walks into my bathroom and I'm not too far gone to watch his back view because holy hell it is delicious. He's got a hockey ass and it is exceptional. Also his thighs...they're like redwoods.

I look down at my own thighs. They're strong, but not as muscular as they used to be, even though I still work out and skate. At one time in my life, I bemoaned their thickness, but hockey was more important than thin thighs, so I got over that.

I reach for the soft throw folded over one corner of the couch and pull it over me.

Hunter returns wearing nothing but a smile. His cock has softened but is still hefty. He sits next to me, pulling me close, adjusting the blanket to cover us both. We snuggle there for a while. I drift off, not really sleeping, but I lose track of time until Hunter moves.

"Hey," he says softly. "You want to go to bed?"

"Sorry."

"No, no. I'm just asking."

"Will you come with me?"

"If you want."

"Yes."

He wraps the blanket around me and guides me to my bedroom. I pause as he pulls the covers back, then drop the throw and slip between them. He follows me, spooning me, my ass pressed to his groin, his hand on one breast.

"Naked cuddles are the best cuddles," I murmur.

He gives a low laugh. "Definitely."

"You're hard again."

"Yeah."

I smile. "It's all sweet and innocent until someone gets a boner."

He chokes on a laugh. "Guilty."

"I'm not sleepy anymore."

"Okay, then." He sounds amused.

"Do you have another condom? Because I have some if you don't."

"I do."

"Yay."

16

HUNTER

When Kate invited me to come to Chicago with her, I was surprised but glad. We've been spending so much time together and I was going to miss her. Meeting her father and her brother…is a step. But we've taken a lot of steps together lately, so it's just one more.

Also, not that she'd admit it, but she's freaking out about meeting her dad's girlfriend. I think she wants me there for the support. And I'm happy to support Kate. She's always the one looking out for everyone else. If she wants to lean on me a bit, or even a lot, I'm there for her.

We arrive at the Bridges' home in Bucktown late Friday afternoon. Kate lets us in, but the house is empty and quiet. She rolls her eyes. "I guess Dad's still at work."

The place is huge, a new build in an old neighborhood, all light and airy with high ceilings, cream walls and pale hardwood floors throughout. I bring both our carry-on suitcases in and set them at the foot of the staircase as I gaze around. "Your dad lives here all alone?"

"Yeah. It's way too much house for him but he doesn't want to move." She, too, looks around.

"You grew up here."

"Yeah." She frowns. "The décor could use some updating. Dad's not into that, though."

"Maybe Jenelle is."

"Eeek." She turns and heads into the kitchen. I follow. "Would you like a drink?"

"I guess it's five o'clock somewhere."

She laughs. "Let's see what Dad has. Maybe we need to make a booze run."

She pulls open the fridge. "Ah! Beer. Thank you, Dad."

As we open beers and lean against the kitchen island, we hear the front door open again. Kate pops up straight and hurries back to the front of the house. "Dad?" Then, "Oh. It's you."

I hear a low laugh. "Nice greeting, Katerade."

I grin. It must be her brother. I wait as they greet each other, and she brings him back to the kitchen. "Ryan, this is Hunter Morrissette. Hunter, my little bro."

I shake Ryan's hand. His grip is firm as he studies me. He's about my height, leaner but fit, and very tanned. "Good to meet you, Ryan."

"Yeah, you too."

"Where'd you fly in from?"

"Toronto. On to San Diego next. Hey, beer."

"Help yourself," Kate says. "It's Dad's."

She opens cupboards and finds a couple of boxes of crackers, which she sets on the island. We all pull up stools and sit to munch and drink and talk, Kate and Ryan catching up. I see the family resemblance, especially the eyes.

"So we're here to meet the girlfriend," Ryan says.

"And for business," Kate adds. "I'm meeting with a potential client tomorrow."

"Huge potential client," I clarify.

She sends me a quick smile. "Yeah."

"Good for you," Ryan says. "How is business?"

"It's going okay. It's free agent frenzy right now so I've been busy." She waves a hand at me. "Hunter's a free agent, and a few of my other clients. And next weekend is the draft, so I'm going to go to that and talk to a few up-and-coming players."

"At least you don't have to travel far," Hunter says. "It's close to home."

"Yes! Newark. That's great."

"Who's having a good off season?" Ryan asks, picking up a cracker. "I mean, which teams?"

"Hmm." Kate tilts her head and lists off a few moves that have happened and how they'll impact the different teams.

Ryan nods. Apparently, he follows hockey, even though he's a pro golfer. I guess with a dad and sister so involved in the business, he would.

"You didn't want to play pro hockey, Ryan?" I ask.

"Nah. I like golf."

"Good thing you're better at golf than you were at hockey," Kate says.

Ryan just laughs. "I was a great hockey player."

"Actually, you were pretty good," she admits grudgingly.

Another beer later, the door opens again and we all turn.

"*That* must be Dad," Kate says. "We're in the kitchen, Dad!"

A moment later her father strolls in. I've seen Joe Bridges many times, but haven't actually met him. Kate introduces us and I'm treated to a bone-crushing handshake and another inspection. "Hunter. Nice to meet you. Enjoying my daughter?"

I blink.

"Dad!" Kate's mouth falls open.

Ryan's shoulders shake with laughter, his head bowed.

"I mean, enjoying Chicago," Joe says quickly. "Shit." His face reddens.

I bite back my grin. "Haven't seen much so far. You have a great house."

"Yeah. Thanks." He clears his throat. "I'll have one of those beers."

Kate fetches him one from the fridge. Joe sits on a stool. He's casually dressed in a pair of khaki pants and a golf shirt. His mostly-gray hair is combed back from his forehead, a gray moustache and beard grizzle his face, and he too has the same blue eyes as Ryan and Kate behind a pair of black-framed glasses.

"Where's Jenelle?" Kate asks casually, picking up another cracker.

"She's busy tonight. Her sons have taekwondo testing tonight. We'll all go out for dinner tomorrow."

Kate blinks. "How old are her sons?"

"They're ten. Twins."

She looks at me, then back at her dad. "How old is Jenelle?"

"She's thirty-nine."

Kate swallows. "Oh."

I think Kate said her dad was the same age as Vern, which is sixty. That's a bit of an age difference, but hey, they're mature adults, who cares?

Kate, apparently. "Oh my God, Dad."

"What?"

"She's twenty years younger than you."

He rolls his eyes. "Yes, she is."

Ryan has his lips sucked in to keep from laughing. "You dirty old man, Dad."

Joe laughs at that, luckily. The air has thickened with tension, but most of it is coming from Kate.

"We're going to need more booze," Kate says. "We drank all your beer."

"I'll go to the store." Ryan stands.

"I brought something. It's in my suitcase." I stride out of the kitchen to where I left our bags. After quickly zipping it open, I retrieve the bottle of Macallan Sherry Oak that Kate told me her dad likes and return to the kitchen. "This is for you, sir. Thanks for having me this weekend."

Joe takes the bottle with an approving nod. "The good stuff."

"That shit tastes like my golf socks," Ryan says. "What do you want to drink, Hunter? Beer? Hey, come with me."

I glance at Kate. She lifts a shoulder, so I agree.

Ryan and I head out. Kate and I rented a car at the airport, and so did Ryan. He offers to drive, so we jump in and cruise to a nearby liquor store.

"Thirty-nine," Ryan says as he drives. "Wow."

"Ten-year-old twins. That must be…uh, fun for your dad."

Ryan chuckles. "Yeah, it's been a while since he had a ten-year-old. Jesus."

We buy some beer and I grab a couple of bottles of wine in case Kate doesn't want to drink beer.

As we walk down the street to where he parked his car, Ryan says, "Hey! The Royal Tuba!" He points at a neon sign above a door. "Let's go in and have a drink! For old time's sake."

"Uh, sure." Old times for him, I guess.

I follow him inside the tiny, dark bar. Like, honest to God dark. I've never been in such a dark place. What the fuck is happening in here?

My eyes adjust as we head to the bar and order beers. There are some pinball machines at the back, which Ryan checks out once we have a beer in hand.

"I haven't played pinball in years," I say.

"I was a pinball wizard."

I laugh, but he's serious, eyeing the machine with focused intensity.

"Hold my beer."

Uh-oh. Ryan gets into a determined game of pinball. When it's done, he raises a fist. "Yeah! Beat that, Morrissette."

Yikes. I hand him the beers and he drinks while I play, coming nowhere near his score. We go back and forth for a while.

"I'm hungry," Ryan says. "I wonder what we're having for dinner. Oh hey, let's grab some popcorn. And more beer."

We fill a basket from the popcorn machine and he orders more beer. I'm bemused by all this. Kate's probably wondering where the hell we are.

I pull out my phone and send a quick text message.

"Hunter Morrissette!"

I turn to see two old guys smiling at me. I smile back. "Yeah. Hi."

"What the hell are you doing here?" They each reach out to shake my hand.

"I'm visiting friends." I gesture at Ryan who's gripping a pinball machine in another game.

"You gonna sign with the Storm again?" one man asks.

"I don't know." I scrunch up my face ruefully.

"They'd be stupid to let you go," the other guy says.

"Well thanks. I'd be happy to stay. But I know it's a business."

"Fucking money," the first man snarls. "That's all those owners are in it for."

Well, yeah. That's generally why you run a business. But I get what he's saying.

"That fight with Younger was great," Man Two says. "You really cleaned his clock."

I grin. There's an expression I haven't heard for a while.

Ryan beckons me over to play again.

"Excuse me. I have to beat my friend at pinball, or we may never leave here."

"Isn't that Ryan Bridges?" Man One asks.

"Yeah."

There are a few guys gathered to watch Ryan. "Holy shit, you're good, man," one says. "That is some stellar flipper work."

Ryan grins.

Jesus. What have I gotten myself into?

Now Ryan has an audience, there's no stopping him. I let out a sigh and order another beer.

I do a double take when Joe walks in.

"What the hell are you two doing?" he demands, standing behind Ryan.

"Oh, hey Dad." Ryan talks over his shoulder. "Just playing some pinball."

I'm ready for Joe to drag us out of there. Instead, Joe says, "I want in."

"Go grab a beer." Ryan doesn't look up.

I stare as Joe heads to the bar and returns with a cold one.

When we finally make it back to Joe's place, I've been texting with Kate, who ordered pizza and has sent more than one message asking when we'd be there.

We walk into the house, laughing uproariously. "I think my retinas are scarred!" I shout. "All I can see is flashing lights! I'm blinded!"

Joe slaps me on the back. "You'll be fine."

Kate sighs. "I cannot believe this."

"We're home, honey!" I teeter over to her and sling an arm around her shoulders.

"I see that."

I don't even know how long we were gone. It feels like a few days. "Um, is there any pizza left?"

She rolls her eyes. "Yes. I'll heat it up."

"Nah, don't bother," Ryan says. "Cold is fine." He reaches for one of the boxes on the counter.

"Speak for yourself," Joe says. "I hate cold pizza."

"You can heat your own up then." Ryan lifts a piece out of the box. It slips out of his hand and it lands on the floor.

We all stare.

"Hell," he mutters, then bends and retrieves it. He eyeballs it, shrugs, and takes a bite.

"Ryan!" Kate closes her eyes.

"I'm hungry," he mumbles. "We had popcorn though."

I help myself to a piece from the box too. "It was good popcorn."

Joe is busy turning on the oven and finding a pan. He inspects the choices.

"Pepperoni and mushroom," Kate offers. "And a veggie special."

Joe turns up his nose at the veggie pizza, which I am eating. I shrug.

"I'm glad you all had fun," Kate says dryly.

Joe turns to her, pointing at me. "He's a great guy. Don't fuck things up."

Kate's eyes nearly fall out of her head. "Dad!"

I laugh. More likely it'll be me who fucks things up, but I don't want to say that because right now her dad likes me. I meet Kate's eyes and see the amusement twinkling there.

"You sleep in the guest room," Joe says to me. "I put a cot in there."

I run my tongue over my teeth, glancing at Kate. She shakes her head, eyes closed, then meets my eyes and shrugs.

"Okay," I say.

I feel a little less tanked after a few pieces of pizza. Then Joe opens his bottle of scotch. "Come on, Hunter, try this."

Oh sweet merciful Christ, no. "I...need to get to bed."

"Hell, no." Joe waves at me as he grabs glasses and the bottle and heads to the big family room attached to the kitchen. "Come on. Just one."

I look helplessly at Kate.

She makes a "yikes" face. "You don't have to," she whispers.

"Just one." I smooch her as I pass by, following Joe.

She heaves another sigh and follows too.

I'm pretty shellacked by the time we all head upstairs. But we're having fun! Joe and Ryan are hilarious, and so is Kate, even though she's not as drunk. She's kindly patient with our hilarity and bad jokes.

She shows me the spare room and the bathroom. I drop my suitcase on the floor and squint at the small bed. "I'm not sure I'm gonna fit on there."

She bites her lip. "This is ridiculous. Come sleep in my room."

"Nu-uh. Your dad said to sleep in here."

"I can sleep in here. You can have my bed."

"No. I'll be fine." I kiss her. "See you in the morning."

"Okay. Good night. My room is next door, if you need anything."

"Okay."

Once she's left, I hit the bathroom to take a leak, then strip off my clothes and lay down on the cot. It's small and hard, but I don't even care because I immediately pass out.

I'm jolted out of sleep in the morning when Kate creeps into my bedroom.

"Hunter!" she yells.

"Jesus! Shhh."

"Sorry. I was whispering but you didn't hear me. I want to get into bed with you."

My first reaction is hell yeah, but then I realize I probably smell gross. "Uh…"

She lifts the covers and slips in next to me. I wrap an arm around her and then WHAM. With a loud crash the cot collapses and we both hit the floor. Kate lets out a shriek and I grunt.

"What the fuck?"

We both lie there unmoving for a few seconds. What just happened?

The bedroom door flies open and bangs the wall. "What's going on in here?"

Joe stands in the doorway. He flicks the light on and glares at us.

Oh fuck me.

"Dad! The cot collapsed."

"I see that."

"She just came in here," I yell. "Nothing happened."

Kate fights her way out from the covers and crawls onto the rug. She sits and shakes her head. "This is ridiculous. We're adults."

Luckily she's wearing flannel pajamas that cover her up. And socks. I rub my aching forehead. "I need some Advil."

"Can't hold your liquor, Morrissette?" Joe says.

I risk a glance his way, which hurts, and see him trying not to smile. "That scotch is fucking rot gut."

"You gave it to me."

"And you can drink it."

Joe laughs. "I'm heading to work for a while, but I'll be back later this afternoon. We're meeting Jenelle at the restaurant at seven."

He leaves.

Kate falls to her back and starts laughing. "This is nuts."

"Advil," I remind her grumpily.

"Right, right." She rolls onto her hands and feet. "Do you want to go back to sleep? You can get in my bed. Dad's gone to work."

"I guess he didn't think we'd want to bang in the daylight." I drag myself out of the broken cot. "And he's right, because my mouth tastes like I licked the bottom of a litter box."

"Eew. I *was* feeling a little frisky, but that does not sound appealing." She stands. "I'll get you Advil and water."

Damn. Maybe later.

KATE

"Your dad likes me."

I pucker my lips and look at Hunter. "Until this morning."

Hunter grimaces. "Oh yeah. He'll forgive me though. But I may have to buy him a new cot."

"That one was probably fifty years old."

"Still."

"I don't know why he doesn't have a bed in the guest room. It's not like he can't afford it." I shake my head.

"Sorry about last night." Hunter sets his coffee mug on the counter. "We shouldn't have abandoned you like that."

"It was kind of weird." I shrug. "But I'm glad you and Dad and Ryan all got along." They more than got along. They all got drunk, ate popcorn, played pinball, and bonded like bros. Jeez.

"Thanks for understanding."

"I hope you feel better by tonight." He looks a little pale, with shadows under his eyes. I didn't get a good look at Dad before he left, since I was lying on the floor, and Ryan's still asleep, but I suspect they feel much the same.

"I will."

"Okay. Let's get out of here. I'm meeting Van at one o'clock."

We're meeting at Navy Pier, which is Van's suggestion, so Hunter's driving me there and he'll roam around and be a tourist while Van and I have lunch. Then I can join him and we can both be tourists for the rest of the day.

I give Hunter directions from Dad's place in Bucktown and we park on a street off Lake Shore and walk to Navy Pier. The lake is blindingly blue in the afternoon sun, stretching out to the horizon. "I love Lake Michigan," I tell Hunter, my arm tucked into his as we walk.

"Yeah, it's great."

"Have you been to Navy Pier?"

"Once, a couple of years ago. We had a bit of time off on a road trip so a few of us came here."

We find the restaurant where I'm meeting Van and stop outside. "I'll text you when we're done, okay?"

"Great. Good luck." He kisses my forehead and smiles into my eyes in a way that makes me feel like I can do anything.

I can do this.

I head inside and look around for Van. Not seeing him, I tell the hostess about our reservation and she seats me at a table for two. I face the entrance so I can see Van when he arrives and pull out my phone to catch up on emails while I wait.

Van grew up here in Chicago and he's staying with his family for the summer after a year at Princeton. He's been a huge Chicago Aces fan all his life, and when he was about fourteen, he won a chance to skate with the Aces. He met my dad and a bunch of the players. Marc Dupuis was the captain at the time, and he and my dad became mentors to Van, recognizing his talent and helping him figure out his path to the NHL. Dad got to be friends with Van's parents. I'm extremely grateful for the "in" I have because of Dad and the team, but I also know I have to earn this client.

Van is fifteen minutes late by the time he shows up. I'm not his agent yet, so I don't lecture him about punctuality. He's not even an NHL star yet. Some players operate on their own schedule, knowing that everyone will wait for them and let them get away with it, but I try to make sure my guys have respect for people.

I stand up to greet him with a handshake and a big smile. "Hi! Good to see you, Van."

"You too." He's wearing jeans, a sweatshirt and a ballcap, which he takes off and sets on the table, then pushes his hair back from his face. He sits across from me.

God, he's young. He's a baby.

Okay, I'm not that old. It wasn't that long ago I was eighteen. But imagining this fresh-faced young man playing in the NHL—oh my God. He still has acne and I'm not sure if he even shaves.

But he's hella talented.

He's been considered the top prospect in this year's draft for a long time now. He was NHL Central Scouting's top-ranked North American Skater during the midterm rankings and finished in the top spot for the final rankings as well. Pretty much every NHL draft publication or website has put Van at the top. He has high-end puck skills and the vision to create plays. He competes every time he's on the ice, and pressure situations actually elevate his game.

I'd fucking love to sign this dude as a client.

"So what are you doing this summer?" I ask once we've ordered.

"Mostly working out. I'm training with Greg Stewart."

"Good, good. He's one of the best. You'll be in amazing shape for training camp."

"Gotta get drafted first."

I smile. I like this hint of humility. It's not a done deal, even though he's considered the top prospect. "Yes. First things first. You're ready for the combine?"

He nods.

"You know what's involved?" I ask. The annual NHL Entry Draft combine assessment involves four days of interviews, medical screenings, and fitness tests.

"Yeah. I've talked to some of the guys I'm training with."

"The combine can be the most physically and mentally exhausting thing in your whole season. And it's your last chance to make an impression on scouts and executives from every team. Both in the physical testing and in the interviews."

"It's the interviews I'm worried about," he admits.

"We can do some coaching on that ahead of it."

"You mean, if I sign with you."

I smile. "Yeah. We've already talked about my background. I've given you my list of current clients, although I recently signed a new client—Hunter Morrissette."

"I heard that."

"I hope you'll contact them."

"Have you ever had a client leave you?" he asks.

"No. I have not."

Van asks me questions about my fee structure, how and when I get paid, the duration of our agreement and how to terminate. I suspect he's been coached on these questions to ask, but I respect that he's here on his own and not with Mom and Dad.

"What services do you offer other than contract negotiations?" he asks next.

I talk about tax advice and financial planning, and the financial planner I have a relationship with if he wants more advice about that. I also talk about endorsements and partnerships with other businesses.

We talk our way through lunch, both business discussion and some personal talk.

"I'm impressed with your maturity," I tell him. "Becoming a professional hockey player comes with a lot of pressure."

He nods. "Yeah. I get that. But I think I'm pretty down-to-earth and realistic. My parents keep me grounded. And having your dad's advice has helped too."

"That's great."

"Well," he says. "I'd basically decided before we met today, but Mom and Dad said meet one more time to make sure."

I'm holding my breath.

"I want to sign with you."

I slowly let the air out of my lungs and try to keep my smile professional. "Wonderful. I'm so glad. I think we can do great things together. You're going to be a superstar and I'm excited to be part of that."

"Thanks." He grins.

We talk about the paperwork we'll need to take care of. I pay the lunch bill and we stroll back out into the bright sunshine. We shake hands standing on the pier in front of the restaurant. "We'll talk soon," I tell him.

With his ball cap pulled down over his eyes, he walks away.

I resist the urge to jump up and down and scream.

I fumble to pull my phone out of my purse and text Hunter with shaky hands. *We're done. Where are you?*

I pace as I wait for him to answer. *On the Ferris wheel.*

I stare at my phone. *Seriously?*

Yeah. Cool view up here.

I laugh. *You couldn't wait for me? I love Ferris wheels!*

Sorry! We can go again.

I'll meet you there.

There's no missing the giant wheel. I climb the stairs to the upper level where the Ferris wheel is, looking up at the cars as they go around and around.

I did it!

I'm nearly dancing when Hunter finally climbs out of a gondola and jogs toward me. He breaks into a smile when he sees me. "Good news?"

"Yes!" I leap into his arms. "He's going to sign with me!"

"Holy shit! That's fucking awesome, Kate!" He picks me up and spins me around.

I love it that he's so happy for me. He knows what a big deal this is. Or will be.

I'm laughing and breathless when he sets me down.

"Congratulations." And he plants a big kiss on me.

"Thank you." I beam at him. "He seems like a good kid."

"Fantastic. Come on. Let's ride this baby again." He takes my hand and leads me to the ticket booth and then we wait in a short line to get on.

The view *is* spectacular from up here...the gleaming skyscrapers, the curve of the lakeshore, the colorful canopy of the merry go round beneath us. And when we're at the top, Hunter kisses me. The world is spread out beneath us and I literally feel on top of it. On top of the world.

Dinner's not what I expect. We meet Jenelle and her twin boys at Howard's Hot Dogs on North Damen. It's not the kind of place I would have chosen for a get-to-know-you dinner since it's noisy and crowded, but they have great food and it's a good place for kids.

My stomach hurts and I can't stay still, shifting in my seat all the way to the restaurant. I don't know why this matters. It's fine for Dad to have a girlfriend. I just want her to be...good enough for him.

Is this how he feels about me and Hunter?

Probably.

Sitting next to me in the back seat, Hunter sets his hand on my thigh and squeezes. I turn to him.

"Okay?" he asks in a low voice.

"Sure!"

His lips twitch. "You're as jumpy as a one-eyed cat watching two rat-holes."

I laugh so hard I snort. He laughs too, and I lean into him. "Oh my God."

"What?" Dad calls from the drivers' seat.

"Nothing," I answer, trying not to giggle.

"You better not be playing finger puppets back there!" Ryan hollers. "Save it for later."

"Jesus," Dad mutters.

"What!" I collapse into laughter again.

"Feel better?" Hunter asks, leaning near my ear.

"Yes." I shake my head, still smiling. And I know he made me laugh so I'd get over my nerves. This man.

We have to wait a few minutes for a couple of tables to empty so we can push them together and have room for all of us. So Dad introduces us to Jenelle, Ethan and Lucas while standing in the entrance of the tiny place. Despite the age difference, Jenelle doesn't look like she's way too young for Dad. She's about my height, her blonde hair cut in a wavy chin length bob, stylish glasses on her narrow nose, and she's dressed in slim black pants and a hot pink top. We exchange greetings, smiles and handshakes. Ethan and Lucas are in awe of Hunter, staring up at him.

"I hope you don't mind," Jenelle says. "The kids brought Storm pennants for you to sign."

They eagerly display their pennants.

"Don't mind at all," Hunter says cheerfully. "Are you guys Storm fans?"

"Sometimes," Lucas says. "I usually cheer for the Aces."

"Me too," Ethan chimes in.

We don't tell them that Hunter probably won't be playing for the Storm next season. He uses his ever-present Sharpie to sign his name, holding the pennants against the wall. This attracts the attention of others in the restaurant, but I don't think anyone else recognizes Hunter.

"I guess golfing's not cool," Ryan says, ignored by the boys.

I smirk. The boys give him a blank look.

"They do think it's cool," Jenelle assures Ryan. "They've been excited to meet you."

Ryan looks unconvinced as Lucas and Ethan continue to worship Hunter. When we finally move into the small dining room to sit, they're quick to take a seat on either side of Hunter.

I smile at Hunter as I sit opposite him. He grins.

We have to order at the counter, so Jenelle and Dad go up while we wait.

"Do you guys play hockey?" Hunter asks Lucas and Ethan.

They both nod vigorously. "Mom makes us do other stuff, too. Taekwondo. Baseball."

"Golf?" Ryan asks dryly.

"No." Lucas wrinkles his freckled nose.

"Maybe one day," I say. "Hunter likes to golf."

"You do?" They stare at him.

"Oh yeah. I'm not as good as Ryan, but I've been golfing a lot this summer."

Ryan shakes his head, smiling crookedly. "Thanks, man."

Soon we're eating excellent Chicago hot dogs—poppyseed buns and fresh toppings including a tangy pickle. Ryan and Dad have chili dogs.

"How was your meeting?" Dad asks me.

I've been dying for someone to ask! "It was great!" I smile proudly. "I signed him!"

"Wow! That's fantastic!" Ryan says. "Good for you, Kate."

I catch Hunter's proud smile.

"Wow," Dad says with less enthusiasm. "That's amazing. That kid's going to be a star."

"I know!"

"Congratulations!" Jenelle says.

"Thank you, I'm excited about it."

I'm doing it. People thought I couldn't, but I am. I really am.

I eye Dad. His muted reaction is a bit of a bummer. But it's okay. Because I'M DOING IT!

We tell the others about our Ferris wheel ride (which makes Lucas and Ethan envious) and our afternoon at Navy Pier, including a walk along the beach path.

Conversation jumps around, with the kids pelting Hunter with questions and me interrogating Jenelle. Just kidding. I'm trying to get to know her. I learn that she's been a widow for four years, she manages a bookstore, and she loves hockey. She also seems devoted to her kids and keeps them in line when they start getting carried away catapulting French fries at each other with their forks. So overall, I don't find anything about her to dislike. And the boys are honestly adorable.

When we get back to Dad's place later, I follow him into the family room where he turns on the TV. Ryan's gone out somewhere else with friends and Hunter's gone up to bed early. He's still a little under the weather from last night. I told him to go sleep in my room since the cot is broken and I'll deal with Dad if I have to.

"It must be different for you having two young kids around," I say, curling into a corner of the couch.

"Yeah, it is." Dad smiles ruefully. "It makes things a little harder, but luckily Jenelle has a good babysitter in her neighborhood she uses, if we want to go out alone. And her boys are great kids."

"They seem like it. And Jenelle seems nice."

"You sound surprised."

"Do I?" I purse my lips. "I'm sorry. I wanted Jenelle to be nice, because…I wanted her to be good enough for you."

"Aw. Baby girl." Dad coughs. "And your verdict?"

"Well, I've only met her this one time, but I like her."

"Good. And I like Hunter."

"Thanks. I like him too." I smile at him.

"I have to confess I was a bit concerned that you're dating a client."

My stomach tightens. "Oh." I swallow.

"I know how much you care about your clients. I worry about your boundaries."

"Oh," I say again. I don't have to think hard to know what he's talking about—performing a marriage ceremony for one player, bailing another out of jail, dressing in a bear costume. Falling in love. Eeep. "I know it doesn't look great, but…Hunter and I have a history. We knew each other in college."

He sighs. "There are a lot of things stacked against a woman in this business. Sleeping with a client doesn't help."

Ah. That's what the issue is.

"It's more than that," I protest, although with a knot in my gut I know he's right. "I care a lot about Hunter." I swallow again. "I've worked hard to build my reputation and my business, after a rocky start. And...it's hard enough to do this job as a woman, without feeling I don't have the support of my own father."

"Ah, hell. You do have my support, Katy. You know I put in a good word with Van."

"More than one good word," I mutter. "I figured that. But was it because you thought I couldn't seal the deal on my own?"

"No!" His frown is fierce. "That's not it at all! It's because I know you'll be a great agent for him."

I study his face. "Really?"

"Really. I can tell his family how great you are until I'm blue in the face, but in the end you're the one who has to convince them you're the right agent for him. And you did."

"Thanks, Dad."

"It's a hard business. Being an agent can be...tough. It's always been a man's business."

"Dad." I give him a reproving look. "You did *not* just say that."

"I know you're not the only woman agent, but men are assholes and they can make it difficult for you."

"They did make it difficult for me. At Pinnacle. When I left, they weren't happy that I took some clients with me, and they didn't have great things to say about me because of that. I didn't do anything wrong, but they were pissed. But I survived and I'm doing okay."

"Sometimes I worry about you getting hurt."

"Why would I get hurt?"

"Sometimes when we give a lot of ourselves, we expect the same in return. But we don't always get that. Not everyone is as honest and trustworthy as you are."

I narrow my eyes. "Are you talking about Hunter?"

He holds up a hand. "No. I told you, I like him."

"I know what you're saying, Dad. I saw that at Pinnacle. The things they did weren't always…ethical. Which was part of the reason I left. I wanted to represent my clients differently."

"I worried that the way you conduct your business might not be…respected."

"Again, are you talking about Hunter?"

"Again no. But having him as a client and a…boyfriend…could be complicated."

It already has been. But I don't say that to Dad. I don't want him to worry more than he already is. "We know that. And I know you always thought I was too player focused. But I think I *am* respected in the business."

He smiles. "You are. I hear that from people all the time."

"Oh." All the air leaves my lungs. "Really?"

"Yeah. I'm proud of you, Katy."

I didn't know how much I wanted to hear that. My throat squeezes. "Thanks, Dad."

Dad clears his throat. "Okay. How's Vern doing?"

"Last I heard, he was getting better. We don't know if he'll work again."

Dad shakes his head. "That would be tough."

"Do you think you'll ever retire?"

"Whoa. Why do you ask that? I'm still young."

"I know. But hockey and the team are your life. Or maybe not…now you have Jenelle and her kids. I just wondered if you thought about life after hockey."

"I haven't," he says slowly. "But I guess having a plan B is always a good idea."

"Yeah."

Dad shoots me a wry smile. "You're still looking after us."

I smile black. "Of course. I love you."

"Love you, too, Katy. And I am so, so proud of you."

My heart expands and I pull in a shaky breath. "Thanks, Dad."

I go up to bed and join Hunter. I close the door of the spare room, hoping Dad won't look in there and find it empty.

"This is much better," I murmur, sliding under the covers next to Hunter's body which produces heat like a blast furnace. I love this, since I'm always cold. My feet are aching, so I push them between Hunter's calves.

He jerks away. "What the fuck…"

"Sorry. My feet are cold and you don't like it when I wear socks to bed."

He sighs. "Go ahead."

I wiggle my feet between his legs. "I'm absorbing your bountiful heat. You have so much to spare."

"Maybe socks aren't so bad," he mumbles.

I smile against his back, my arms around him. "Okay then."

18

KATE

It's time for the draft. It's an exciting time for anyone involved in hockey. I've been following the scouting reports and the discussions (and rumors) about who each team might pick. Van and I have signed paperwork, talked on the phone, and met up a couple of times ahead of the draft to discuss the possibilities. Everyone expects him to go to Philadelphia, who have the first pick this year. He's okay with that. We've also done some mock interviews to get him ready to meet with the folks from Philly as well as other teams.

"Make eye contact," I coach him. "Shake hands firmly. Act confident."

"Okay."

"Sometimes they ask some wild questions in these interviews. So we prepare as much as we can, but who knows if they'll ask you about a hungry bear in the hallway."

"What?" His forehead creases.

I shrug and relate the question I heard about there being a hungry grizzly bear in the hallway and of the five people in the room, who should go out there?

Van gives me a deer-in-headlights look. Then he says, "I guess it's a metaphor for teamwork. Like, there's five of us on the ice and we're facing someone...hungry."

I nod approvingly. "Yes, yes. What do you do?"

"Um...communicate? Take the lead? Sacrifice myself? Get eaten by a grizz?"

I laugh. "Yeah, that's good. Not the getting eaten by a bear part. The other."

We talk about other potential questions. "Are you a virgin?"

"Whaaat!"

"Don't answer that." I hold up my hand. "I don't need to know. But they could ask you, just to throw you off. Also be prepared for questions about drugs. Or who your worst teammate was." We go over some strategies. "And if they comment about your game, engage with them and see what you can learn about what they think about you."

I've also arranged meetings with a bunch of other prospects, giving them my sales pitch on what I can do for them. Usually their parents are with them, which is fine. These are kids, after all, and big decisions are being made. The fact that I just signed Van, and I'm young and interested in them as people seems to kindle their interest.

I'm ecstatic when another prospect expected go in the first round signs with me. Jack Karey is a big, solid defenseman that teams like Santa Monica and Dallas will likely be interested in. I dance into my apartment later that night, excited to call Hunter and tell him about my day.

"That's great, Kate!"

"Thanks. I'm thrilled." I smile up at my ceiling, stretched out on my couch. "And tomorrow I'm meeting with the Théo Wynn and Claude Faucher to talk more about your contract while they're in town. Things are heating up now. There could be trades right up until the last minute, which could change things, but after the draft I expect we'll get offers."

"Fucking finally."

"I know it's been a long wait."

"Yeah."

"We've talked about all the moving parts."

"Right."

"I'll be able to tell you more after tomorrow."

"Okay, that's great."

"Are you going to pick me up at the Hargrave Center tomorrow? We can go for dinner. Friday night I'll want to be at the arena to cheer on Van and Jack."

We arrange a time and place to meet and end the call. I set my phone on my chest.

After our trip to Chicago, I feel even closer to Hunter. I love how he fit in with my family, and how he was there for me when I was nervous about signing Van and meeting with Jenelle. I loved how good he was with her kids and how they worshipped him. Despite my happiness, I feel a little ache in my chest. I miss him, after being together all the time for a few days. But I have work to do, and I'll see him Thursday.

I'm not here to do any serious negotiations. That'll happen later, and these teams are focused on the draft right now. But it's important to show my face in person. I have several contracts to negotiate, and I want them to remember me.

My first discussion is with Théo Wynn. It's short and sweet. Then I talk to the GM from Toronto, Claude Faucher.

Let's just say he's not my favorite person to deal with. But that doesn't matter. This is about Hunter.

I don't trust Claude. I have this weird feeling he's stringing me along. I have the feeling that he can't close a deal without team ownership approval and that makes me uneasy. I also feel he doesn't respect me. It's nothing specific he says, more how he says it, and the condescending smile he gives me when he mansplains entry level contracts to me. Ugh.

But I am my most professional, charming self.

I say hi to Dean Marlow, GM in Philly, who has the first pick. They've already heard Van signed with me and I get a friendly greeting. I'm sure they're going to select him.

I also talk to a few sports reporters who are eager to ask questions about Van, as well as some with questions about Hunter. I know these guys (and women). I tell them my standard lines that Van will be thrilled to play for whatever team drafts him. I'm not going to tell them anything on the record about Hunter, but I do mention that Hunter's disappointed about not yet getting a qualifying offer from the Storm. Fans aren't going to feel sorry for a guy going after a multi-million-dollar contract, but they will feel sorry for a guy who's basically being given the boot, especially a fan favorite like Hunter. It never hurts to have the fans on your side, and I've gotten better at working the media.

When it's time to meet Hunter, I head to where we agreed to meet. The buzz has died down here in the arena. Tomorrow will be the big day, and Saturday for the other draft rounds. I spot Hunter talking to a man I recognize as the coach of the Storm. They're laughing about something, Hunter's smile like a light beaming toward me and guiding me to him. I can't help but smile too as I walk toward them.

I'm stopped in my tracks by someone else. I stare into the face of Tarek Bennani, who I worked for at Pinnacle.

"Kate." He gives me an icky smile. "What are you doing here?"

What am I doing here? What the fuck kind of stupid question is that?

I hold back my first reaction and say, "Wow, Tarek! What are *you* doing here?"

He frowns.

"You still have clients, I guess," I say cheerfully. "Good for you!"

How's that for condescending? I give myself a mental high five.

He laughs. "I do. And you?"

"You know I do." I flash a toothy smile, holding back the word "asshole."

He shrugs. "I heard a rumor that you signed Van Halston." He eyes me coolly. "Good move."

Hunter appears behind Tarek's shoulder with an "are you okay?" look on his face.

"Hi, Hunter," I say calmly. "Hunter, this is Tarek Bennani. We used to work together at Pinnacle Sports Management. Tarek, Hunter Morrissette."

Tarek turns to Hunter, who towers over him and glowers down at him. "Hunter. Good to meet you. I hear you're a UFA."

"Almost." Hunter's smile is grim. Technically he can't sign a contract until July first.

"Haha, yeah." Tarek's phony smile feels like a spider crawling up my spine.

"Hunter's another of my clients," I tell Tarek, although I'm sure he already knows that too.

He nods. "Good luck. Rumor has it the Bears are interested in you."

Hunter's face tightens even more.

"I heard that rumor!" I say breezily. "Well, nice to see you, Tarek, but we have meetings to get to."

I move away and Hunter follows with a last narrow-eyed look at Tarek. We march out of the arena.

"Fuck him," I mutter.

"Er…I got the impression you weren't happy to see him."

"Hell no." I stare straight ahead while Hunter leads me to where he parked his car. "I fucking hate him."

"Whoa. I don't think I've ever heard you say that." He shoots me a sideways glance I can feel. "You okay?"

"I will be."

"Where do you want to go for dinner? Or do you want to just head back to my place?"

"Your place sounds good."

I hate that I'm this upset from seeing Tarek again. Goddammit. As Hunter drives, I take some deep breaths and try to tamp down my annoyance. Hunter doesn't say much, but I'm aware of the looks he's giving me. He knows I'm perturbed.

I think about how familiar this drive must be to Hunter after three seasons with the Storm. It's not a done deal, but I don't think it's going to happen. I wish I could make it otherwise, but I can't fight the dollars and the salary cap.

In Hunter's bright apartment, I kick off my shoes, drop my bag on the floor and stretch out on his couch. "Bleh."

"Okay, what's up with that dude? He's got you all riled up." Hunter sits next to me and pulls my feet onto his lap. He starts massaging them, and sweet Jesus, that feels good.

I let out a small moan. "Thank you." I wore flats because I knew I'd be on my feet a lot, but they still hurt.

He digs his thumb into one arch. "So? You worked with him?"

"Yeah." I sigh. "He was my boss at Pinnacle. And he's a sexist, racist jerk."

"Oh."

I haven't told Hunter about all the reasons I left Pinnacle. I've always felt like it was a failure on my part. Like I ran away. Like I couldn't handle being part of the boys' club.

"Tell me about it," he says softly, rubbing my foot.

"He was…inappropriate."

Hunter's hands still. I feel the tension in his arms. "What does that mean?"

He knows what it means.

"Did he touch you?" he demands. "If he did, I'm going back to the arena to fucking punch him in the face."

"No. Don't do that."

"He did."

"No." I sigh. "It was all talk or texts. When they hired me, he told me I was pretty, but I needed bigger boobs."

"Jesus Christ!"

"Yeah. He made personal comments all the time. He called one of the other new agents a racist slur. One time, he got mad in a meeting and threw a chair at me."

"WHAT?"

"He missed." I bite my lip. "It was fine, but it scared me. I managed not to cry in front of him, but I sure did when I got home. He was supposed to be my mentor, but instead he made belittling comments about me to other people. And that was *before* I left the company."

Hunter growls. Literally growls. Tension radiates off him.

"He didn't think I had it in me to be an agent. He kept telling me women are too soft, don't know enough about sports and contracts and what makes athletes tick."

"He told *you* that?"

I snort laugh. "Yeah. Idiot. He thought I was too "motherly." I swallow, the pain of that accusation still like a knife in my gut. "He said players would take advantage of me."

Hunter makes another rough noise.

"Anyway, I talked to a few other people at the agency and everyone agreed he's a dick, but people had complained to senior management about him before and nothing ever happened. I had to make a decision. I didn't know what to do. Report him and take a chance on losing my job. Also, pissing him off. Ignore him and try to get along with him. Or leave."

"And...?"

"I left." I close my eyes. "I felt like a coward, but I knew I wasn't going to change him and it looked doubtful I'd advance very far in the company with him there. And reporting him likely wasn't going to do anything except make things worse. I felt guilty. I felt like a loser."

"No. Oh, fuck no, Kate." Hunter moves my feet off his lap and reaches for me, pulling me up to hug me. "You did the right thing for you."

"Yeah." My mouth is muffled in his shirt. "But I didn't do anything to help the other women at the agency. Or anyone who came after me and had to put up with that shit."

"Ah. I get that. But sometimes you can't help everyone. I know you want to. You're a strong, amazing woman."

My heart squeezes. I grip his shirt tightly and hold on. He doesn't look down on me for what happened. How many times did I ask myself if I was responsible for Tarek's behavior? How many times did I wonder what I could have done differently? How many times did I beat myself up for being weak? And then question myself, wondering if he was right. "Thank you." I sniffle. "When I left the agency, some of my clients came with me. No one big, but still, it annoyed management there, and they didn't hold back from telling people in the business that I wasn't good at my job."

"Fuckers."

"Yeah." I lift my chin. "But I work hard. I'm showing people who I really am."

"You've done great."

"Thank you. And thanks for coming up to us at the arena. I was freaked out by seeing him."

"I could tell." His hand rubs up and down my back in a warm, comforting gesture. "I know you can handle anyone and anything, but I was right there and…I like helping you, sometimes."

The pressure behind my eyes is intense. I don't want to cry. I never cry. But having someone look out for me when I'm always looking out for everyone else… it's amazing. Touching. Glorious.

I snuggle in closer to Hunter, to whom I just confessed things I've only ever talked about to Dad and Soledad. It feels safe talking to him, telling him my secrets. My heart is doing weird things in my chest, flipping and expanding and contracting, making me breathless. What is this feeling?

It feels like love.

I wasn't supposed to fall in love with Hunter. I'm about to negotiate a contract for him that will send him across the country or possibly to Canada. I have to get him that contract, for my career and for him. I know how important it is to him.

I don't know how he feels about me. I think he feels something…

but is it love? Is it happily ever after, forever kind of love? Is that what *I* really feel?

Falling in love with a client probably isn't going to do my reputation good. It basically proves everything Tarek said about me. Oh God.

And yet…this feeling…it makes me feel hopeful…and safe…and strong.

I don't know what to do!

"Want to order in food?" Hunter murmurs.

I'm thinking about how much I love him, and he's thinking about dinner. Okay.

I inhale a slow breath.

That's good. That helps me. Dinner. "Sure," I mumble. "Sounds good."

He passes a gentle hand over my hair. "What would you like?"

"It doesn't matter."

"How about Indian?"

"Mmm. Butter chicken."

He eases away from me and I lift my head, pretending everything's okay.

"There's a little place a couple of blocks from here. They deliver."

"Great. I'm going to use your bathroom."

While he calls in the order, I shut myself in the bathroom and try to get control of my wildly messy emotions. I run cold water and wet my hands, then press them to my cheeks, staring at myself in the mirror.

"I love Hunter," I whisper to my mirror image.

It doesn't feel wrong to say that. The truth is, I've probably loved him forever.

Oh God, that makes it even worse!

Next week is the week. After the draft, we can officially talk to other teams. I'm confident that Hunter will have offers. Which means he'll be leaving. The ache in my chest nearly takes my knees out, but it's what I have to do. And I have to be strong doing it. For Hunter.

19

KATE

Monday morning the offers start coming.

I'm up early and ready. I'm dressed in an Alexander McQueen pants suit, ivory, with narrow cropped pants and a fitted jacket. I have a gold statement necklace at my throat and I'm wearing a bold red lip.

Claude Faucher from Toronto is still in New York, so I hop in a cab to go to his midtown hotel. We meet in the empty bar, sitting at a round table.

"This is what we're offering," Claude says. "It's non-negotiable."

I keep my poker face firmly in place. "Non-negotiable?"

"Yes. We're five hundred grand a year apart. You have to take this offer."

"I don't have to take this offer." I smile. "What about my client and his input? Isn't that important?"

"No."

I sit there stunned.

"We're the ones paying the money," he continues. "So we determine what's fair."

Calmly, I pick up my bag and stand.

"Where are you going?"

"You're saying my client's not important in this process and you're not going to listen to us. You're saying you'll determine what's fair. Since we can't accept your offer, I'm leaving."

In a miracle of perfect timing, my phone buzzes. It's in my hand and I hold it up to look at it. It's Théo Wynn from Santa Monica. I smile at my phone, then say to Claude, "Have a good day, Mr. Faucher."

Walking out is hard, but he's full of shit.

Now, I don't know why Théo is calling, but I'm optimistic.

I take the call as I walk into the lobby of the hotel. "Kate Bridges speaking."

Indeed, he wants to get together. At another hotel. We agree to meet in an hour. I could be there in five minutes walking from here, but an hour's fine.

Santa Monica offers the same money as Toronto but a shorter term. I know Hunter wanted a longer term. He's tired of the one year deals he's been getting. I tell Théo that money won't be enough for that kind of term. They eventually increase the offer to what I want. Yay! Except for the term.

"We feel we're taking a bit of a risk on Morrissette," Théo says. "He was slow to break into the league and slow to prove he's an NHL level player. The term is a trade-off for the money."

Trade-offs. Yes. There are trade-offs and Hunter will have to decide if he's willing to trade off the length of the deal for the money.

They want to meet with Hunter, so I know they're serious. I leave the hotel and head to a diner a block away. When I'm seated alone in a booth, I order coffee and a club sandwich, then pull out my phone.

It buzzes with another incoming call.

Brad Julian from the Bears.

My heart bumps. I'm excited but...shit. They're going to make this difficult for me. I answer the call.

Brad wants to meet. I hesitate.

Should I take the meeting? Hunter's made it clear he's not going to sign with them. I don't want to waste their time, or mine for that matter. But I feel I need to hear them out. And I can't hesitate too long. So we arrange a time.

I set down my phone on the table. Fuck. My stomach tightens.

The waitress brings my coffee and I curl my hands around the warm mug and lift it to my lips. I can meet with them. I don't ever have to tell Hunter about it.

That's completely unethical. I can't do that.

I've got two offers on the table. I can use this to sweeten whatever deal the others are offering.

Or maybe the Bears are offering such a crappy deal it won't be an issue.

My mind is racing, turning over options and possibilities. Should I call Hunter now? Or after I meet with them? Maybe I should meet with him later and lay out everything and see what he thinks. Yeah. That's what I'll do.

My stomach is in knots, but I make myself eat half the sandwich, then use the ladies' room to freshen up for my meeting.

I'm only a few blocks away from Brad's office at the Apex Center so I walk there.

It feels like I was just here a day ago, but it also feels like so much has happened since then.

I'm surprised that the owners of the Bears join us in the meeting, along with Brad and the assistant GM, Dale Townsend. I shake hands all around, keeping my smile pleasant but reserved. I hope my hands aren't sweaty.

I've got this. I know my stuff. Hunter's a desirable player.

"Has there been other interest in Morrissette?" Brad asks.

"Well, I'll be honest with you. Yes, we have offers."

He nods. "We expected that." When he presents their offer, it's a struggle to keep my features composed and businesslike. I listen, ask a few questions, and nod.

"This isn't far off what we're looking for," I tell them. "Hunter's interested in a longer-term deal, and I think he'd find this attractive. The money, on the other hand…"

And we negotiate. They push. I push back. They increase the money. And when we're done, I'm ready to float out of the room and all the way back to the Village, as if I have a thousand helium balloons tied to me.

As I sit on the subway train, my phone buzzes with another call. It's Claude. Upping their offer.

I can't hold back my triumphant smile but keep my voice calm. "I should tell you we have other offers on the table. I'm about to meet with Hunter shortly. We'll get back to you."

I could cry. I almost have to hold back the tears This is so fantastic for Hunter...but what's he going to do? Is he going to freak out on me again? I don't want this to be a trigger for him. But it's such a great deal.

I'm both excited and afraid to tell him, but once I'm home I call.

"Okay," I begin. "Can you come over? Or do you want me to come there? We have lots to talk about."

"I'll come there. See you soon."

I lay papers out in front of me on my desk and look everything over. There are lots of details that need to be ironed out in all the offers, but I have no worries about any of those things. I'm just worried about Hunter.

If I wasn't in love with him, this would be so much easier. If I was just his agent, I'd present the offers to him and he'd say yay or nay and I wouldn't be worried about how he's going to react. I messed things up by falling in love. I need to be able to do my job.

But the fact is, I do care. I can't stop caring. I want him to be happy. I want him to get the contract he wants and deserves, the validation he needs. I know he had a late start as a pro hockey player, playing college hockey for four years instead of entering the draft, and I know why. And I know how hard he's worked to prove himself since then.

Hunter arrives soon and walks in with an anticipatory smile. He kisses me then says, "I almost picked up a bottle of champagne on my way here, but I was worried that would jinx things."

I smile. Of course he'd think that. Hockey players and their super-stitions "Lots of time for champagne."

"Is it good news or good news?" he asks, walking farther into my apartment.

"Well." I get stuck here. Jesus.

"What?" He turns, frowning.

"It's good, it's good!" I wave my hands in the air. "But will you promise me something?"

His frown intensifies. "What?"

"Promise me you'll hear me out. About everything. Okay?"

His eyes narrow. "Okay."

I nod and walk over to my desk. "Okay. We have three offers."

I tell him about my day, how I walked out and then heard back from the Leafs. The offer from Santa Monica. And…deep breath…the meeting with the Bears.

"Kate!" He stares at me. "I told you I'm not playing for them."

"I know. But you said you'd hear me out."

"You said you wouldn't talk to them anymore!"

"And I haven't! Until today. I had to meet with them."

"No, you didn't! You could have said no."

"We don't have to take the offer. But it's a good offer. If you don't want to play there, I can try to use it as a negotiating tool."

He inhales sharply and lets out a long breath. "Okay."

Now he's tense. I can see the tightness in his mouth and eyes, the set of his shoulders. Shit.

We go over everything.

There's no way the other two teams are going to come up to the level of the Bears. I can negotiate more, but I know it won't happen.

"This has everything you want," I tell Hunter quietly, referring to the Bears' deal. "The term, the money. It gives you security. I think you'd fit into their long-term plans for the team, and there's a great spot for you on their second line. There's also the fact that you could stay in your apartment in Hoboken and not have to move. That's something."

He stands up and walks away from me. At the window, he shoves his hands into his pockets and looks out onto the street. For a long time, neither of us speak. Then he says, "You know why I won't take that offer."

"Yes." I pause, gathering my thoughts. "But Hunter…are you absolutely sure about that?"

His shoulders tense. "You don't understand."

Oh God. "I know, I can never know what you went through. But…" I stop. I shouldn't have said but. I *know* I shouldn't have said it. I try to regroup. "And I know the idea of seeing those guys and playing with them makes you uncomfortable." I almost say "but" again. "Maybe instead of running away from it or trying to ignore it, you could…face it."

He whips around. "Are you telling me to face my fears? Seriously? You?"

I jerk back. "No, that's not…I mean, maybe…"

"For Chrissake, Kate. You know me. You know I faced my fears. You know what I've overcome."

"I do! And I respect that and admire you so, so much for that. I…" I pull in air. "I think maybe there's still some stuff you need to overcome."

"Oh, fuck that!"

I flinch again. This isn't going well. I flail around mentally for a way to get things back on track. But Hunter's pissed, his eyes flashing, his hands curled into fists.

"You don't get to tell me to 'face my fear' and overcome shit."

I feel like he just shoved the butt end of a hockey stick into my gut. The air whooshes out of my lungs, leaving me without air and the ability to speak.

"I told you I don't want to play for that team, and you disregarded what I want. What kind of agent does that?"

I stare at him, blinking wildly. "I'm sorry," I manage to say. "I told you, we don't have to take the offer."

"Oh sure, I'll settle for what Santa Monica is offering. Two years." He makes a face. "That's all I'm worth, I guess."

I straighten. "Oh, no. No, no, no. You don't get to do that."

"Do what?"

"Feel sorry for yourself. Nope. Uh-uh." I stand and walk over to him. I feel terrible and I'm afraid I've messed up and I've hurt him, but dammit, he hurt me, and now he's disparaging himself. He has his flaws, but I'm not standing for that. "You got a fantastic offer. You don't want to play for that team. That's *your* choice." I point my finger at him, resisting the urge to stab it into his chest. "*That* offer is what you're worth. If you don't see that…if you don't want to accept that because you're afraid…that's on *you*."

He stares back at me. I watch his face as his eyes flicker, his lips press together. I don't know what he's thinking. But then he turns and walks to the door.

"Hunter! Where are you going?"

"I'm going home. I need to think."

My shoulders slump. But that's a reasonable request, I guess. Maybe it will do him good to think things through. "Okay." My throat constricts and I clear it. "Call me if you want to talk or if you have questions."

He glances at me, then looks away. "You can't fix everything, Kate. I know you want to. I know you want to look after everyone and fix things, but…you can't fix me."

He doesn't answer, just leaves, closing the door sharply behind him.

This is what I was afraid of.

I sink down onto my couch.

The last time this happened, we both agreed we had to communicate better. I go over everything I said. Was I too aggressive? Not clear enough about my strategy? My reasons for talking to Bears' management? Maybe? I don't know.

I shouldn't have said that he should try to face his fear. That's not my place.

He's right. I can't fix everything.

Except, I feel like *he* thinks he's...unfixable. And that's not true.

Obviously, Hunter is pissed. And I get why, I really do. This is a sensitive issue for him.

But...thinking more about it...what happens if he takes the deal from Toronto, and in a month Easton Millar is traded there? Hunter's not going to have a choice about playing with him at that point. I mean, it's a long shot, but it could happen. All three of these guys are young and have long careers ahead of them.

But maybe I shouldn't try to convince Hunter using that argument.

My throat burns and my chest aches. My stomach has a stone lodged in it.

I care about him so much. I hate it that he's hurting. I don't know how to fix this. Maybe there is no way to fix this. All I can do is let him decide what he wants to do and then make it happen. That's my role as an agent.

But goddammit, that's so hard! My job as an agent is to get the best deal possible. And here I have a client making a unilateral decision that doesn't match up with his stated goals!

I don't hear from Hunter the rest of the evening. Or the next day. Late afternoon, I send him a text. *Hey. Hope you're doing okay. Just want to remind you that Santa Monica and Toronto want to meet with you.*

I don't bother mentioning the Bears. That's a done deal, I assume.

An hour later, I hear back from him. *Tell them it'll have to wait. I'm in Calgary.*

I stare at my phone. What the fuck? *Now* he goes home to Calgary?

If he screws up any of these deals, his career is fucked. That's the *last* thing I want for him. I curl my fingers into my palms, my nails digging in. Heat burns through my chest at the thought. I remember how I felt when I heard he'd given up entering the draft, the huge opportunity he'd missed out on through no fault of his own. I'd felt sick and sad with sympathy for him. Now after working so hard all these years, after defying the odds and signing his first pro contract when he was twenty-two years old, I feel those same emotions. And I'm worried.

I'm also worried about our relationship. I love him. He's my guy. The only guy I've ever met who cares about me just as I am. The only guy I've ever met who I've been so attracted to—physically, but also in so many other ways. I love being with him. Talking with him. Laughing with him. We just found each other again. And I've fucked that up by not listening to him and his concerns about playing for the Bears.

This is the ultimate test, I guess. I can't fix everything. I can't control my clients. And that sticky issue of boundaries has come back to bite me in the ass.

How am I going to make this right if he won't even talk to me?

20

HUNTER

I got here late last night after a couple of flights. Very expensive, last minute flights. I surprised my family, showing up at home in a cab. We yakked a bit, then everyone crashed.

I'm a free agent.

That thought gives me a twist of panic in my gut.

And yet…I have offers.

I know they're not going to pull the offers after one day, but how fucking stupid am I to pick up and leave town? I deserve every fucked-up thing that happens to me. Like the last time, when I couldn't get my shit together enough to enter the draft. Even a year later, I couldn't do it. Now I'm screwing up again.

I had to get away. I paced around my apartment the night Kate told me about the offers, simmering and seething, unable to shut my mind off, unable to sit still. It must be the adrenaline giving me some kind of primal fight or flight instinct. And I chose to flee.

Now I'm here, I almost regret it. It was impulsive and childish.

On the other hand, I'm a mess. I can tell myself a million times to get it together, but it just doesn't work like that. I still feel like running.

So I literally go for a run, lacing up my shoes and cruising through the neighborhood where I grew up. That's healthier than a beer at ten in the morning.

When I get home, Mom's making waffles and Dad's sitting at the island with coffee and his iPad.

"Breakfast's almost ready," Mom says.

"I'll just jump in the shower." I wipe my face on the hem of my T-shirt. "It's already hot out there."

"Going up to thirty today," Dad comments. "Scorcher."

I've gotten so used to Fahrenheit it takes me a minute to make the conversion from Celsius. "Yeah. That's hot."

After a fast shower, I join them in the kitchen again. Arianna's up now too, also on a stool at the island wearing pajamas, her hair in a messy bun.

"Okay," she says. "Tell us now. What's going on? There are all kinds of rumors about which team you're going to sign with."

Ugh. Just what I don't want to talk about. I pour myself a mug of coffee from the pot on the counter. "What are the rumors?"

"Santa Monica, Toronto, New York. Bears, I mean. Also Pittsburgh and Boston."

I choke. "Definitely not Pittsburgh or Boston."

She grins. "I vote for Santa Monica. I want to come visit you in California."

"Oh, that helps make my decision."

She laughs. "Tell us!"

I wish I was as excited as she is.

With no emotion, I tell them what's been happening. But when it comes to the offer from the Bears, and everyone's screaming, I don't know how to explain that I'm not going to take that offer. After Kate telling me to "face my fears" I can only imagine what my family will say.

Nobody gets it. Nobody's been through it. Nobody knows what it's like to have those feelings.

Except...maybe Easton Millar and Josh Heller.

They went through the same thing. Except, they didn't. Obviously, they're both fine now. Josh has recovered from his injuries. Easton had nothing wrong with him at all. Even they don't know what I've been through.

"I haven't decided yet," I hedge.

Dad frowns at me over his reading glasses. "What's to decide?"

I shrug. "I want to consider every angle."

He squints. "Like what?"

"Like, everything." I sound like an idiot. "Don't worry, my agent is very smart. She knows what she's doing."

Fuck. I *am* an idiot.

"Why aren't you happier, Hunt?" Mom asks slowly. "This is exactly what you wanted."

"I'm happy."

They all give me a what-the-fuck look.

"I am. I just need some time to think. That's why I'm here."

"Well. We're glad you're here," Mom sets a big platter of waffles on the island. "Eat up."

I shoot her a look of gratitude, but I know it's a reprieve. This isn't done.

Maybe I should go to Tofino.

I could be totally alone. Stare at the ocean. Walk on the beach. Surf. It'd be perfect.

Another expensive flight to Vancouver and a ferry ride to the island later, I'm in Tofino. This time, I'm staying at a five-star resort that combines rustic with luxury. Nestled among ancient pine trees, my suite overlooks Chesterman Beach.

I love this place, even though I spent some of the worst days of my life here. It's quiet and peaceful. I love the scent of pines mingled with the salt of the ocean. I love the waves crashing onto rocks and sand. I spend hours hiking and walking along the beach, sometimes finding a warm, dry rock to sit on and look out at the ocean, sometimes exploring small caves. Vast and wild and mysterious, the never-ending rhythm of the water calms something inside me. It helps me think.

I do a lot of thinking.

What the fuck am I going to do?

I want that Bears contract. Kate is right. It's everything I wanted. The money's not top dollar but I'm not a top dollar player. I want them to commit to me for three years. I want to feel like I'm valued. I know I had an unusual path to professional hockey and I'm grateful every day to the Storm for taking a chance on me, and now the Bears want to do it for three years. I should be ecstatic.

But I keep thinking about Easton and Josh. I keep thinking about how seeing them every day is going to affect me. I'm terrified I can't handle that. What if I sign a contract for three years and in the first month I fall apart?

Fuck. I have to have more confidence in myself than that.

This whole thing has sent me spiraling back in time, to right after the bus crash, when I couldn't sort out what I was thinking or feeling. I can't feel like that again.

Walking on the beach, I pick up a piece of driftwood. I like the shape of it, the smoothness and soft curves. I carry it with me as I amble barefoot through the sand.

What if I've screwed up not only the Bears' deal but the other two offers as well? What if I've fucked up my whole career? *Again?*

The thought has me dropping to my ass on the sand to stare out at the water. I can't do that again. I can't let that happen again.

I've only been gone a few days. Surely Kate won't let that happen?

I was an asshole to her, though. It would serve me right.

It's easy to blame her for what's happening, but deep inside I know this is not her fault. I was pissed that she was pushing me, pissed that she thought she could fix me when I'm so broken I can never be fixed. I've known that all along.

I drop my head forward, closing my eyes.

That's the other issue. I love Kate. I don't want to be broken. I want to be whole, for her. I want her to love me back. And now I've pretty much made sure that'll never happen.

My throat closes up. In a way, this thought has me ganked up even more than losing my hockey career.

Kate.

My mind is full of images of her, going all the way back to college. Her red cheeks as I handed over her pink lace panties in the dorm. Her confidence and hockey knowledge that destroyed idiots who thought women didn't know anything about hockey. Her tears that day she was so overwhelmed with life, when she was always so disciplined and fearless.

The day I saw her kissing Henry in the kitchen at Bingo's. The crushing disappointment I felt, when I'd finally gotten up the nerve to ask her out.

And that night in Cancun. When she was finally all mine.

And then I had to leave.

Now, I've left her again. Fucking running away from my feelings, because I'm scared. Because I don't believe I can ever really have her. She'll never love me.

What the hell can I do about all this?

Maybe I should go see Roberta again. The counselor I saw after the accident. I wonder if she has time?

I pull out my phone, but service is weak here.

I start walking, my steps lengthening. I have to call her. I have to talk to her. She'll help me figure things out.

When I'm close to the resort, I sit on a bench on a bluff and unlock my phone again. I don't have her number anymore, but a quick Google search brings it up. Taking a deep breath, I set my thumb on the "call" button.

I have to leave a voice mail, which sucks, because this is *urgent*, goddammit. My heart is zooming and I feel like I'm going to burst out of my skin.

Okay, okay. Calm down. You can wait.

I enter the hotel and head to the restaurant. It's lunch time, so I should eat. I'm seated at a pine table at the window and I order a grilled ham and cheese sandwich and a Coke.

I'm taking a drink of the Coke when my phone beeps with a call.

Holy shit, it's Roberta already.

I answer the call. "Hi. Roberta?"

"Yes! Hi, Hunter. I'm so surprised to hear from you."

"I'm in town." I pause, staring out the window with hot eyes. "I'm, uh, having a hard time. I was wondering if I could see you."

There's a brief pause, then I hear the clicking of a mouse. "I am so booked up," she says, and my heart dips. "But you know what? I could see you tonight. Six o'clock?"

I lick my lips. "Are you sure?"

"Of course."

"Okay. Great. Same place, right?"

"Yes, that's right. See you then."

I end the call and blow out a long stream of air. Okay. Okay, that's done, that's good.

Now I'm really wired up. I walked all morning, now what am I going to do? Maybe it's a good day to rent a surfboard and hit the waves.

That's how I spend the afternoon, floating, catching waves, trying to keep my balance. It takes my focus away from my screwed-up thoughts until it's time to drive to Roberta's office a couple of blocks off Main Street.

I wait in the private entrance, which I learned is separate from the exit so people don't run into each other. I always appreciated the protection of privacy, and even more so now.

Roberta's door opens and she steps into the opening. "Hello, Hunter."

"Hi." I stand. "How are you?"

"I'm very well, thank you."

I feel a rush of almost affection. We spent so much time together and she helped me so much, but her demeanor is always professional and polite. We don't even shake hands.

I follow her and she closes the door. The room is the same, but she has new furniture, a nice blue couch and several armchairs. I sit in a chair. Through the window I can see the coffee shop across the street.

"Are you here on vacation?" Roberta asks me, also taking a seat. Her short silver hair frames a kind face with big red glasses, her lips also red.

"Sort of. It's the off season." One thing I learned about Roberta is that she knows nothing about hockey. I explain to her briefly how I came to be here.

She listens attentively as always and asks a few questions that get me talking. I tell her about my career and needing a new contract and a new agent at the same time, and what's transpired.

"So up until this happened, you feel you were doing well?" she asks.

"Yeah. I was. There are still things that bother me, but I handle them. I've put the accident in the past."

"Hmmm."

What does that mean?

"You've done very well with your life," Roberta says. "I'm happy to see it. You've overcome so much. You have the career you always wanted. You had the courage to go after it and do it."

I swallow. "Unless I've messed things up now. Again."

"You're worried that you've repeated what happened in the past?"

I nod. "Yeah." My chest is tight, my gut churning.

"It's human nature to hold on to what we know. Change is threatening. But the thing about trauma is that's it's part of your life forever. You say you've put the accident in the past, and that's where it is. But it still has power over you."

I slowly lift my chin in acknowledgement.

"If you try to deny that...if you try to bury it or ignore it...it can have even *more* power over you."

I gaze at her, trying to absorb her words and their meaning. "Are you saying that because I don't want to play with those guys, it's having even more of an effect on me?"

She gives a half-smile. "What do you think?"

I think…oh Christ. I think she's right. I close my eyes and relive my conversations with Kate, my protests that seeing them would affect my mental health. Meanwhile, I'm a fucking mess.

"Okay," I say hoarsely. "Yeah."

"Past trauma has a way of inserting itself into your future, whether you want that or not. But if you're willing to face it, you may find yourself open to the possibility of growth that brings."

Face it. Goddammit.

She continues. "The more comfortable you are bringing your past into your present, the less control it has over your life. I believe you have to honor and respect what brought you to this point of your life. At the same time, you have to create space to grow into where you are going. Staying where you are isn't growing."

I nod again, turning her words over in my head.

"If you sit with the discomfort instead of ignoring it, you can tap into a deep wisdom inside you that will help deal with uncertainty. There's a quote I often tell people, from an English author and spiritualist, Jeff Foster: 'True healing is not the fixing of the broken, but the rediscovery of the unbroken.' You feel you're broken…and that trauma will always be a part of you. But there is much of you that is unbroken. Those are the things you need to rediscover. To embrace. What you've done to get you to this point in your life is admirable. But it might not be enough to get you to where you want to go now. You might need to dig a little deeper."

I clear my throat. "There's also…one more, er, problem."

She tilts her head slightly. "What is that?"

"I've fallen in love with my agent. And I think I screwed that up too."

KATE

This is a shitastrophe.

My client has disappeared. I'm trying to hold off three different teams who want to meet him and want an answer. I told them Hunter had a family emergency in Calgary and would be back soon, but I don't know if that's going to happen. I've texted him a couple of times and haven't had a reply, so I have no idea what's going on.

I have other clients who need my attention. It doesn't take Philadelphia long to want to sign Van, who they indeed drafted as the number one pick. We've now inked a three-year entry-level contract, standard salary but with the potential for up to two million dollars in bonuses each season. He's thrilled and so am I.

I'm working on a couple of other negotiations as well, as well as a partnership with Nike for Van and a little issue Callum got himself into in Las Vegas. But...I didn't get on a plane and fly there to get him off the hook. I calmly gave him advice on how to handle it.

But I keep thinking about Hunter.

I swing wildly between furious and heartbroken. Also worried and frustrated. Damn him.

After a workout, Soledad and I head out for drinks.

"What the hell is with you?" she asks as we settle in at a table. "I thought you were going to have a heart attack you were pushing it so hard."

"Ha ha. That'd be just my luck right now." I sigh, then smile at the waitress. I need more than a beer tonight. "What's a good strong cocktail?"

"Do you like martinis?"

I wrinkle my nose.

"Okay, then I'd suggest an Angel Face," she says. "Calvados, which is an apple liqueur, apricot brandy, and gin."

"That sounds perfect."

The waitress looks to Soledad.

"Uh...I'll try that too."

"Of course."

"I'm a little scared of that drink," Soledad says when she's gone. "So, what is up?"

I fill her in on some of what's happened, as usual careful about personal details about Hunter.

"Your job is stressful," she comments. "But I've never seen you this stressed."

I look down at the drink the waitress served while I was talking, a martini glass with a little twist of lemon rind on the rim. "That's because I've never fallen for a client before."

Soledad nods and sips her drink. "This is delicious."

"I thought that would get more of a reaction from you."

She grins. "I'm not surprised, hon. The way you talk about him... the way you look at him. It was obvious to me."

I pout. "Not to me. I guess it should have been."

"So what's the problem? You two have been spending a lot of time together the last couple of months."

"He's pissed at me for trying to do my job." When I put it that way, his behavior seems ridiculous. "Because there's a team he doesn't want to play for, and I talked to them."

"Oh."

"I shouldn't have talked to them."

"Why did you?"

"I wanted to get the best deal for him. It's everything he wanted. But I should have respected his wishes. Now I've ruined everything." I sigh and take a big gulp of my cocktail. It warms a path all the way down to my belly.

"Why doesn't he want to play for that team?" Her forehead furrows.

"He has his reasons. Something in his past." Again, I don't feel comfortable sharing Hunter's story.

She purses her lips. "Huh. You'd think a few million bucks might help."

I give a dry laugh. "It doesn't work that way."

"What are you going to do?"

"I don't know. He left town. Went home to Calgary. And he's not answering my texts."

"Yikes."

"I know." I press the heel of my hand to my forehead. "Damn."

"If it's something in his past...well, you can't change the past."

"No. That's true."

"Is there anything you could do to help him deal with it?"

I tilt my head, letting that sink in. "I don't know...maybe..." Ideas play out in my head. "But if I do, Hunter will never speak to me again."

"Seems like he's not speaking to you now."

I blow out a sharp breath. "True."

"You're thinking about this."

I make a face. "I shouldn't."

"Yeah, you're probably right. Better to do nothing and let him screw things up."

Doing nothing has never been the way I operate. I take on challenges and get shit done. It's not like me to sit around waiting for something or someone.

Later that night, lying in bed, I think about it more. Hunter's already mad at me. If I wasn't so convinced that facing this problem would be a good thing for him, I'd drop it. But Soledad's prodding has

194

generated an idea. It could be a disaster...or it could be the best thing that could happen. Is that a risk I'm willing to take?

HUNTER

I spend the evening on the deck of the hotel bar, looking out at the ocean as the sun sets. The warm day becomes cool. I'm right under a patio heater and I brought a hoodie down with me, so I pull it on and continue to sit out here as dusk falls and the ocean and sky turn midnight blue. The trees are silhouetted black against the sky and stars appear, tiny sequins twinkling above.

All the things Roberta said earlier run through my head and I try to make sense of them.

If you try to deny that...if you try to bury it or ignore it...it can have even more power over you.

Is that what I'm doing? Burying it? Avoiding it, more likely. Avoiding seeing Josh and Easton. Is that giving my trauma more power over me?

The answer is certainly yes. I'm refusing to sign a dream deal because of it. How fucked up is that?

If you're willing to face it, you may find yourself open to the possibility of growth that brings.

I don't want to grow. I just want my life to go on the way it was.

But that can't happen. Life isn't going to go back the way it was. I'm done with the Storm. I have to move on. I've worked so hard to be the best hockey player I can be. Now...maybe I have to work at being the best person I can be.

I want to be the best man I can be for myself...but also for Kate. She believes in me. I want to deserve that faith.

I slump lower into the wicker chair on the deck. Right now, I don't deserve that.

But there is much of you that is unbroken. Those are the things you need to rediscover.

Okay. Hold up. Maybe there *are* parts of me that deserve that.

Like what?

It's easy to identify my flaws. It's not so easy to be kind to myself.

I'm a good hockey player. I'm gritty. I'm loyal to my team. I sacrifice my body to block shots. In the dressing room, the other guys like me. I've made friends. Especially Hakim.

I went through a traumatic experience and ended up still achieving my goal. I brush away thoughts about how long it took. I did it. That's what matters. That takes strength. Determination.

Deep down inside, I want more. This contract was all about esteem and recognition for what I've done. Being validated as a hockey player. But to be validated as a good person...that takes love.

I want Kate's love. I think that's what I've always wanted. Love. Acceptance. Belonging. She showed me those things and what did I do? Threw them in her face.

Pain slices through me like a knife. I almost groan aloud, which would attract attention from the other patrons out here, some who are talking and laughing boisterously, others sitting close together and quietly whispering.

I remember a coach saying to me once, if you can't take a hit, get off the ice.

I used to buy into that. But now I wonder if getting off the ice is quitting. We all take hits. We all need deal with them. It's *how* you deal with them that makes you who you are.

That's what I have to do.

I have to go back to New York. I have to talk to Kate. I have to take that deal from the Bears. And I have to talk to Josh and Easton.

In the morning, I shower and pack up the few things I brought. I go down to the restaurant for coffee and breakfast before I check out and head back to Victoria. While I'm sitting with my coffee at a table at the low stone wall separating the restaurant from the lobby, I pull out my phone to look for flights from Vancouver to New York, trying to coordinate with ferry times. I'm getting frustrated because it's not working out unless I want to drive like a maniac back to Victoria.

I drop my phone to the table and make an aggravated noise.

"Hunter."

I look up.

Holy shit. What is happening?

Am I dreaming this? Because I've been thinking about these two guys so much?

I stare at Easton and Josh, standing next to my table in the hotel restaurant. My mouth hangs open wide enough to drive a Hummer in.

They give me crooked smiles.

"What...?" I shake my head, closing my eyes briefly, but when I open them, they're still there. "What are you doing here?"

"Looking for you. Mind if we join you?"

Without waiting for my answer, Josh pulls out a chair opposite me and sits. Easton sits next to him. A waitress approaches with a coffee pot and a big smile. "Hi guys. Coffee for you?"

"That would be great." Easton pushes the cup on the table closer to her.

"Could I get a Coke?" Josh asks.

"You bet. Do you want to order breakfast as well?" she asks, after filling the cup. "I can get you menus."

"Nah, just coffee's good," Easton replies.

"What the hell is going on?" I ask.

"We heard a rumor that the Bears have offered you a contract," Josh says.

I blink. "You did?"

"It's just a rumor," Easton adds. "Who knows if it's true." He shrugs.

I stare again.

"But...if it was true...and it was a great contract...that would be fucking awesome," Easton continues.

I focus on breathing, because my heart is slamming so hard against my sternum my lungs are having a hard time expanding. "It would be."

"So you've signed the contract?" Easton hoists a challenging eyebrow.

"You fucking know I haven't." I glare at him. Then my lips twitch. I can't help it. I grin. "But I'm going to."

Now it's their turn to stare. "You are?"

"Yeah. Assuming I haven't fucked things up beyond repair. Assuming my agent is still representing me."

"Yeah, about your agent..." Easton pauses.

"What?" I frown.

"She's hot."

Josh gives Easton an elbow. "Hey. You're practically a married man. Shut up."

He shrugs. "Just an observation. Obviously she's not as hot as Lilly."

"Lilly's your girlfriend?" I ask.

"Yeah." His face goes soft and kind of lovey-dovey.

"That's great." I smile. "And yeah...Kate's hot. And smart. And..." I sigh. "Hopefully forgiving."

"I hope so too, for your sake," Josh says.

Easton rubs his mouth. "I have a good feeling about it."

"Wait. How do you know Kate?"

Their eyes go shifty. "We don't," Josh says.

"We may have talked to her," Easton adds.

"What?"

"She's worried about you." Easton gives me a ballsack-shriveling look.

Shit. Of course she is. "She called you?"

"Yeah."

My jaw drops. "Holy shit. Why?"

"Like I said, she's worried about you."

"That's why you're here?" I cannot believe this.

"Well, we heard that rumor. So we tracked you down to convince you to accept it. But...seems like you already made up your mind."

"After breakfast I'm checking out." I hold up my phone. "I was just trying to book a flight to New York."

"Well, fuck me." Easton regards me with disappointment. "We came all this way for nothing? Also, you're supposed to be in Calgary, asshole."

"I was. Then I wanted to come here." I pause. "You went to Calgary?"

"Yeah. Your mom told us you were here."

I shake my head. "Jesus Christ."

I'm so goddamn confused.

My breakfast arrives. I look between Josh and Easton. "Uh..."

Easton waves a hand. "Go ahead and eat. We grabbed something on the way here."

I pick up a fork to dig into my eggs. "I still don't understand what's going on."

"We need to talk," Josh says.

"We do?" I take a bite of sourdough toast. This makes me nervous. "About what?"

But weirdly...I'm not panicking.

"About why you disappeared off the face of the earth nine years ago."

22

HUNTER

I chew some eggs slowly. I guess this is it. I have to tell these guys. They're going to know how screwed up I am. When they went through the exact same thing and bounced back fine. I sigh. "Okay."

"Finish your breakfast. We can go somewhere else."

"The beach," I say. "We can walk on the beach."

"Okay. Sure."

"I've never been to Vancouver Island," Easton says.

"Me either." Josh looks out the big windows. "It's pretty awesome."

My stomach isn't as receptive to food as it was when I sat down here, but I shove in the rest of my bacon and eggs. I can't waste bacon.

I sign the check charging the meal to my room and we head outside. Today, the pale gray clouds hang low in the sky, obscuring the blue and the sun. The air feels damp against my skin, but it's not cold. I lead the way down the path to the beach where the ocean is calm, shifting in shades of silver and smoke, topped with whitecaps.

"Nicer when the sun is out," I comment.

"Still great, though," Josh says, staring out at the vast expanse of water.

We start walking along the firm, damp sand near the edge of the ocean.

"So." Easton speaks first. "Where do we start?"

"I don't know." I'm honest.

"I'll start," Josh says, surprising me.

I glance sideways at him. "Okay."

"When I got traded to the Bears, I thought it was the worst thing that could happen to me."

Relatable. I stay silent, waiting for him to go on.

"I was nice and settled in Dallas. I've had a hard time coping with change since the accident."

He doesn't have to say more about the accident. We all know what he's referring to.

"Getting traded was a nightmare. New city, new team, new coach. And Millsy was there. We tried to ignore each other, and it started impacting our play."

"Shit," I mutter, kicking a small, smooth rock. Sounds like they haven't been close, either.

"Yeah. Our coach had to get involved. He's a good guy, if you're wondering. Fair. Smart."

"Good to know."

"We still couldn't get our shit together," Easton says. "It was my fault, too. I wasn't thrilled when Hellsy showed up on the team. It reminded me of how pissed off I was that my two best friends disappeared out of my life just when I needed them most."

Guilt and astonishment slam a fist into my gut, nearly knocking the wind out of me.

"My dad and my brother died in the accident," he continues in a low voice. "I held my brother as he died. I kept telling him Dad would find us."

Easton's dad was our coach and his older brother played for the Warriors too.

Memories flash before my eyes, now. The darkness. The cold. The crunch and scream of metal, followed by utter stillness. Then the cries of my teammates. I saw Easton sitting in the snow in the ditch, holding his brother.

I saw guys thrown from the bus, lying in the snow. I saw our bus driver slumped over the steering wheel. I saw Cole walking in circles, crying.

I wait for the dizziness to come, the racing heart and shallow breaths. That's what happens when I have these flashbacks.

My heart is beating faster, but...I'm okay. I pull in a slow, deep breath.

"I had a concussion," Josh says, taking over again. "And a bunch of broken bones. I don't remember much about what happened that night. They took me to one hospital, then another, then I ended up in Winnipeg where my family is."

"I had funerals to arrange," Easton says. "My mom couldn't do anything. She collapsed and...she's never been the same since. I had to look after her and take care of everything."

Christ. "I didn't know that," I say, my voice scratchy.

"Neither did I," Josh says. "None of us were very good at communicating back then."

"Or now," Easton says wryly. "Getting better at it though. So, I was pissed that you were missing, and that Josh hadn't even called."

"And I was pissed that nobody called me," Josh adds. "I was in the hospital and then rehab for months. I didn't know if I'd be able to play hockey again."

A sharp ache stabs through my chest, thinking about Josh lying in a hospital bed dealing with that.

"I got drafted in June that year," Easton says. "I just focused on hockey. It was all I had. I had to get drafted. I had to make the team. It was selfish, but I was trying to survive."

I nod. "I get it."

"I felt like I'd been deserted," Josh says quietly. "I didn't think about what Millsy was going through."

"And I never knew Hellsy felt that way," Easton says. "I kind of felt like *I'd* been abandoned. We, uh, sat down one day and talked things out. I apologized. I did desert him."

"You were working on your own shit," Josh says. "Which I didn't know about. And I'm sorry about that, too."

I'm trying to take this all in. My mind is swimming, all these things flying around, and feelings coursing through me, and I'm confused and overwhelmed. The urge to turn around and run and keep running is real. I force myself to take deep breaths.

"Easton felt like hockey was all he had. For me, it's been a way to forget the real world. To forget my pain and my problems."

Yeah. I feel that right to my core.

"I was jealous when Millsy got drafted," Josh says. He clears his throat, and I can tell this is still hard for him to talk about. "I didn't know if I'd be able to play again. It made me bitter."

"And I felt guilty," Easton replies. "I felt guilty that I *could* play when others couldn't. The guys who were killed in the crash." He swallows. "Josh. And Mac." He mentions one of our teammates who had a spinal cord injury. "When I got drafted, I told myself I was playing for them too."

"I've felt guilty too." The words fall from my lips.

They shoot me sidelong glances as we walk.

"I didn't even have a scratch on me," I say in a low voice. "I was so lucky that way."

They say nothing. So many people have told me I was lucky. But these guys don't.

So I keep going. "But I couldn't play. I couldn't cope. With anything."

I gesture to a bunch of big rocks and head that way to sit. I face the ocean, and they sit too, all of us gazing out at the silvery brine. A seagull soars above us.

"I have PTSD," I finally say.

They both nod.

No judgment. No scoffing because I "wasn't really hurt."

"I met a kid," Josh says, then pauses.

I'm not sure where this is going.

"His name was Carter. We really connected. He was dying of

cancer. But he was so positive and strong. I wanted to control every-thing in my life. He couldn't. And he showed me how to be strong despite that."

My throat squeezes.

"We can't control everything in our lives," Josh adds.

For a moment, the only sounds are the swish of waves onto the sand and the cry of a seagull. Pressure pushes behind my eyes, my cheekbones. I'm afraid I'm going to cry. I cover my eyes with one hand.

As if they know, the other guys keep talking.

"Since the accident, I've had a hard time controlling my temper at times," Easton says. "That got me traded from Vancouver to New York, which I thought was a good thing, until I met my new coach."

"Asshole," Josh mutters.

"He was abusive and racist. He knew how to push my buttons and I was so afraid of losing hockey, because I thought that was all I had, I couldn't stand up to him. And I hated myself for it."

"But you did stand up to him," Josh says.

"Yeah. Lilly helped me see that I needed to do the right thing."

"Then *I* showed up," Josh says dryly.

"Yeah." Easton smiles.

"I think we both wanted to set things right between us," Josh says. "I was terrified, though. Talking about this shit isn't easy." I feel his eyes on me. "It's hard to be vulnerable. I felt like I wasn't worth caring about because my friends didn't care enough to be there for me after the accident, but—"

"I'm sorry," I interrupt. "I'm sorry I wasn't there. For both of you."

My chest feels hot and tight, my throat clogged.

"Thanks," Josh says.

"Yeah," Easton adds, his voice muted. "Thanks."

"Anyway, I wasn't there for you guys either," Josh adds. "I'm ashamed of that."

"Me too," Easton says.

Yeah. That's the word. Shame. This thickness in my throat, the ache in my gut, the heat and prickling in my face. I'm ashamed. I swallow.

"Hellsy and I both had reasons for not being able to help each other," Easton says. "We were both going through our own shit. But we could have made more of an effort." He pauses and looks at me. "Now, you want to tell us what shit *you* were going through?"

"Not even a little bit." I attempt to crack a smile, then I sigh. "I guess since you came all the way here…"

They both snort.

"I don't know what happened to your mom," I tell Easton. "Or what her diagnosis is. I fell apart, too. I had PTSD. I wasn't doing well." I remember how scared I was. "I kept reliving the accident and it freaked me out. My heart would go crazy and I'd feel dizzy. I got angry. I didn't want anyone to know, and I was afraid of how I might react in front of people. So I took off from Calgary and came here. I wanted to be alone. I especially didn't want to be around anyone who reminded me of the accident."

I meet Easton's eyes, then Josh's. They both radiate warmth and sympathy, not anger or blame.

"I wasn't sleeping. I couldn't shut off my mind. And when I did fall asleep, I had nightmares. I drank a lot of booze and smoked a lot of weed so I could sleep, but that didn't help." I look down at my linked fingers which have tightened. I consciously relax them. "I kept telling myself to get over it. I felt like it was stupid that this was happening, and I just needed to get control of my emotions. But I couldn't."

"I relate to that," Easton says.

"I was jumpy. On edge all the time. I didn't care about anything. I didn't care about getting up in the morning. I didn't care about hockey. I was supposed to enter the draft that spring, and I didn't." My voice breaks and I bow my head. "I beat myself up over that later. In fact, I still do, sometimes."

A hand lands on the back of my shoulder and squeezes.

"See?" Josh says quietly. "We didn't know that."

I keep my head down. "The best thing that happened was my

parents coming to see me. They were so worried about me and they convinced me to see a doctor and a counselor. I didn't want to, but by that point, even I knew I wasn't going to get out of that by myself, no matter how much I told myself to get my shit together."

"Did that help?"

"Yeah. The doctor gave me meds to help with sleep and depression. I didn't want to take drugs, but…it did help. The counseling was painful. Lots of days I didn't want to go. I'll never be really over it." I lift my head and glance at Josh, then Easton. "But I went back to see her yesterday and we had a good talk. Parts of me will always be broken, but I need to focus on the parts of me that *aren't* broken."

They're both silent, then Easton says, "Good advice."

I tell them more about what Roberta said and how I've been thinking about it. "I really was on my way back to New York," I tell them. "I knew I had to face you guys. And I have to face Kate."

"So, uh…Kate…" Easton pauses.

"Yeah?"

"More than just an agent? She seems to care a lot about you."

I bite my lip. "She's more than just my agent. But…I fucked things up."

"Haven't we all," Josh mutters. "I fucked up with Sara, too."

"You have a girlfriend, too?" I ask.

"Yeah. She's amazing. Look…it just occurred to me that Kate tried to do what Sara did. Sara tried to get Millsy and me to talk and I got pissed at her for interfering. Don't be pissed at Kate. She cares about you."

I lift my chin. "She sent you here."

"Sort of. She asked if we'd be willing to come talk to you."

I blow out a long breath. "Shit. I already did get mad at her for interfering. I didn't want her to even talk to the Bears, and she did anyway."

"Why do you think she did that?" Easton asks.

I turn that over in my mind. The only answer is that it was because she cared about me and wanted to get me everything I wanted in a contract. "I get it." I pause. "You fixed things with Sara?"

"Yeah. It was terrifying too, making myself vulnerable. But I didn't want to lose her."

"Same with Lilly," Easton says. "She wanted me to do the right thing and I wanted to be a big wuss." He smiles wryly. "But I didn't want to be a wuss in her eyes. Or my own."

"I always told myself I had to be a warrior," Josh says. "To me, that meant being tough. In control. But hell, falling in love wasn't something I could control. And you know what? Being a warrior doesn't mean not having feelings. The bravest thing you can do is talk about your feelings."

"Men aren't supposed to," Easton adds. "It's how we're raised. And especially hockey players, right?"

"If you can't take a hit, get off the ice," I say, my head moving up and down.

"If you get hurt, walk it off," Josh says.

"Yeah."

"Men are socialized to not be empathetic. To not be good listeners. Never ask for help."

"Look where that got us," I mutter.

"Hey, we're doing okay." Easton bumps my shoulder with his. "We're young guys. This is heavy stuff. Hard stuff."

"You gonna be okay, Morry?" Josh asks.

His question could be about so many things. Is my PTSD going to be okay? Am I going to be okay playing with them? Am I going to be okay with Kate?

"I don't know," I finally answer. I could have nightmares tonight, flashbacks tomorrow, and Kate may never want to see me again in which case I…I don't know what the fuck I'll do. My goddamn heart will be busted up, but…I've survived bad things. I can survive again.

I just need to make sure she knows I'm sorry and that I love her and that she's okay. My busted-up heart isn't as important as she is.

23

KATE

I wait anxiously for word from Easton or Josh about how things went. Did Hunter kick them out? Did he talk to them? Was it ugly? And…is he mad at me?

He probably is. I already know how he felt about me interfering in his life by trying to tell him he should face Easton and Josh and deal with his feelings about that.

I'm not a psychologist and I probably shouldn't have gone there. I need to tell him I'm sorry about that.

Would I have done the same for any other client?

I don't know.

I exhale slowly. Knowing what I know about his past and these players…I think I would have. But I don't really know.

Probably I've overstepped. Again. This could totally backfire and cause even more problems.

Maybe I do get too involved in my clients' lives. Maybe I should pull back on that. No more bailing them out of jail. No more counseling them on how to apologize to their girlfriends or what to get them for Christmas. No more house hunting for them.

I'll be like that with Hunter. Even though I care so much about him.

I stand up from my desk and roam my tiny apartment. I'm not getting any work done. I've read through a contract sixty-seven times and still don't know what it says. I check my phone and scroll through Twitter. I'm kind of hungry. There's a salad in the fridge I could eat, but I don't feel like salad. I'd like a big bag of potato chips and French onion dip.

What the hell. I grab my purse and my keys and jog downstairs. Out on the street, it's a gorgeous summer afternoon. I love my neighborhood and I take in the people and the shops and restaurants as I stroll the sidewalk to the nearby store. There, I grab my chips and dip, along with a six pack of Miserable Bastard brown ale (the name fits my mood). I carry my bag home, pausing to listen to a busker on a corner who's fantastic. The love song makes me wistful, though, so I continue on and climb back up the stairs to my apartment.

I open the beer first and glug back half of it. Excellent.

I'm opening the bag of chips when my phone rings.

I peer at the screen and see it's Josh Heller calling. Ack! My heart leaps, then races as I try to answer it, my fingers shaking. "Hi!"

"Kate?"'

"Yes." I close my eyes. I don't usually answer so unprofessionally.

"It's Josh Heller. Listen, we managed to track down Hunter. We're back now and we're wondering if we could meet up with you and talk?"

I can't breathe. *"Is he okay?"*

After a short pause, Josh says, "Yeah, he's okay. Can we meet?"

"Um, sure. Where?"

"How about Central Park?"

I frown. "Really?" I guess that's close to them? But I can get there. "Okay."

We arrange to meet inside the entrance on Fifth and Fifty-ninth.

"There's a statue there," Josh says. "Meet us there."

"Now?"

"Can you come now?"

I pout at my chips and dip and unfinished beer. "Sure. It'll take me half an hour or so."

Should I change? I'm wearing ripped jeans and an old Bayard T-shirt. Nah. They don't care what I look like. But wait. I'm an agent. I'm not *their* agent, but I should look somewhat professional. This is sort of a business meeting to discuss a client.

I quickly change into a long flowy skirt, a white T-shirt and chunky white sneakers. I grab a denim jacket and my purse and once more leave my apartment, this time going to the nearby subway station. It's about a twenty-five-minute ride, during which time I keep anxiously checking my phone and wondering what the hell they need to talk about.

It took me a while to track those guys down. Josh was in Winnipeg visiting family, so he wasn't far from Calgary, but Easton was still here in New York. I guess they're both here now? I gnaw on my lips and twist my fingers together until the stop at Fifth Avenue. I cross the street and make my way to the statue of General Sherman. He's accompanied by Nike, the Greek goddess of speed, strength, and victory. Oddly enough, she's a symbol I held on to during my hockey career. They both gleam rich gold in the late afternoon sun, and I pause to admire them.

Turning, I spot the two men sitting on a stone bench and start toward them. They look up and jump to their feet. "Kate?" one of them asks.

"Josh?" I smile and extend a hand. "It's nice to meet you."

"You too. And you know Easton."

I shake his hand too, trying to stay composed. "So what's going on?"

"Well." Josh gives me a toothy grin as Easton peers at his phone. "It took us a little longer than we expected to find Hunter. He wasn't in Calgary, he was on Vancouver Island."

"Ohhhh." It only takes me a second. "Tofino. He loves it there."

"Yeah. I'd never been there," Easton says. "Cool place."

"You went there?"

"Yeah."

"Jeez, I'm sorry. I didn't mean for you to be flying all over the continent. I thought it would be easy."

"No worries." Josh says. "It was kind of a fun road trip. I hadn't been there either, and it's awesome. Ocean, surfing, laid back…"

I nod, losing my patience, but my smile fixed in place. "I haven't been there either."

At that moment, two women walk up to us with big smiles. One of them has a little black dog on a leash. Oh please God, no, this isn't the time for autograph seekers.

But Easton reaches for the woman with auburn glints in her hair and the dog and kisses her, while Josh wraps the other woman with long brown hair in a big hug.

"Hey! I missed you," Josh says, and plants a big kiss on her lips.

She smiles up at him. "I missed you too."

Easton and the other girl are exchanging similar greetings. The dog leaps enthusiastically on Easton, and he bends to rub the dog's head. I love that dog's face!

I shake my head. What is going on? I just want to know about Hunter!

They make introductions. "My girlfriend, Sara Carrington," Josh says. "And this is Easton's girlfriend, Lilly Evans. And this is Otis." He gestures at the dog who smiles up at me, tongue hanging out.

"Nice to meet you." I force another smile.

"We had to come!" Sara says, beaming back at me.

I catch Josh sliding her a "shut up" glance.

"Oookay." How can we talk with their girlfriends here? I feel a headache coming on. Crossing my arms, I give Easton a look.

"It's okay," he says hastily, reading my expression. He looks around at the people strolling by and sitting on benches. A big crowd of seniors parade by, two by two, following a man; I guess it's some kind of guided tour.

I spot a big bear mascot walking along the sidewalk from Fifth Avenue. Ha. Good thing Hunter isn't here.

I remember his phobia with a pang. I miss him so much. I'm so worried about him.

I look back to Easton, then do a double take at the mascot. Isn't that the Bears' jersey he's wearing? I wore that costume myself.

"Is that…is that…Orson?" I point.

Everyone turns and looks.

"It is!" Sara says.

"It's not even hockey season." I shake my head. "Weird."

Orson has a weird, misshapen appearance. There's a gap between the furry legs and the big feet, revealing bare human skin.

"That's no good," I say with disapproval. "That costume doesn't fit properly. Even *I* made a better Orson than that.'"

"You were Orson?" Sara turns big eyes on me. "That is so fucking awesome! I would love to do that."

"It was only one time." I wave a hand. "Long story." I'm still staring at Orson as he nears us.

"Orson!" Sara waves. "Hi!"

Orson lifts a hand in greeting.

Sara grabs Josh's arm. "Josh. Seriously. I need to be Orson. When the season starts."

He gives her an incredulous look. "What?"

Sara's…interesting.

Orson lumbers toward us. People are pointing and smiling. A couple of kids run up to him and he gives them high fives.

Under his other arm, he's carrying a stack of big poster board cards.

"Why is he here?" I ask. "Is there some kind of Bears event in the park?"

"There is," Easton says. "Right here."

"What?" I swing my gaze from Orson to Easton and back again. Orson's smile is actually kind of creepy. No wonder Hunter didn't like me. Him. Whatever.

Orson struts up to us. No, to me. He stops right in front of me.

"Uh, hi," I say.

He reaches for my hand, lifts it to his fake mouth as if kissing it, then releases it.

What the...?

A small crowd is forming. I glance around and see that Easton, Lilly, Josh and Sara have backed off, leaving me and Orson surrounded by people. My eyes flick all over the place as my brain tries to process things.

Orson holds up one of the big cards he's holding. It says in handwritten letters, A MASCOT IS A GOOD LUCK SYMBOL.

I blink.

He drops that one to the ground and holds up another. This is like freakin' *Love, Actually.*

This one says, I NEED ALL THE LUCK I CAN GET.

My forehead tightens and my confusion deepens.

YOU TOLD ME I WAS RUNNING AWAY. YOU WERE RIGHT.

My eyes pop open wide enough that I might lose my eyeballs. "*Hunter?*"

The big head nods.

"Oh my God. What are you doing?" I step closer, hands outstretched. "You're in that costume...are you..." I stop, aware of the people around us.

He holds up another card. I'M FINE.

A smile tugs at my lips.

The next one says, I'M FACING MY FEARS.

I cup my hands over my mouth. "Oh, Hunter." I glance toward Easton and Josh, who are grinning. Their girlfriends are practically bouncing up and down with glee. Otis is sniffing a bench.

THIS ISN'T MY BIGGEST FEAR.

I suck on my bottom lip. "It's not?"

The bear head shakes negative.

LOSING A GOOD CONTRACT ISN'T MY BIGGEST FEAR.

I stare at him. Another card drops to the ground.

MY BIGGEST FEAR IS LOSING YOU.

My legs go shaky and my hands over my mouth tremble. My heart bumps unevenly.

I LOVE YOU, KATE.

I hear Sara and Lilly let out squeals behind me.

He drops the last card and reaches up to pull off the bear head. He tugs at it. It doesn't move.

My eyes widen.

Hunter wrestles with the head and I hear a muffled *fuck* from inside.

I rush over to help. "Not again," I say. "Oh my God. They need a better costume." I dig my fingers into the neckline and together we both fight with it. Finally, I loosen it. "There!"

Hunter yanks it off. His face is red and sweaty, his hair damp. He's never looked so gorgeous. I'm laughing and crying as our eyes meet.

He drops the head to the pavement. "I'm sorry, Kate."

I'm right in front of him and I reach to cup his face in both hands. "Oh, Hunter."

"I'm sorry I was an idiot. I'm sorry I didn't listen to you. I'm sorry I hurt you. You're the best thing in my life."

More tears stream down my cheeks even though I'm smiling. "Are you okay?"

"Yeah." He leans in to try to kiss me. His costume bumps me but we manage to get our lips to meet. "I'm okay. I'll tell you more...when we don't have an audience."

We each glance around. People are taking video of this with their phones! Jesus!

"Okay."

"I want to take the Bears offer."

My lips tremble and I gaze into his eyes. "Are you sure? I don't want you to do it for me."

He shakes his head. "No, it's not for you. It's for me. Because you were right."

I turn toward Easton and Josh. "I didn't expect them to bring you back."

"They didn't." His smile lights up my insides like Times Square on New Year's Eve. "I was coming back before they got there. I figured things out and I knew what I had to do. But...one of the things I had to do was talk to them."

I nod mutely.

"So we talked. It was good."

Typical male understatement. I'll get more out of him later.

"Okay, I gotta get out of this thing."

I grin.

Easton, Josh, Sara and Lilly surround us. Otis barks with excitement.

"Get me out of here," Hunter says to his friends. And possibly new teammates.

"We got you," Easton says. "This way."

On Fifth Avenue, they hail a cab. When the driver sees headless Orson, he gives us a sour look. Easton tucks a thick wad of bills into the driver's hand as Hunter and I try to climb in the back seat. I give his big butt a shove to get him in.

"Oooph. Thanks."

"This costume doesn't even fit you."

"I know." He grimaces and adjusts the fur garment.

"Where to?" the driver asks.

We look at each other.

"My place," I say, then give the driver my address.

I wave to the others as we pull out from the curb, catching the huge smiles on their faces. Lilly is holding Otis, Easton's arm around her shoulders.

I study Hunter as we drive, my gaze moving over his face and taking in every detail, including his tousled damp waves and ruddy cheeks. He's still so handsome and dear and brave.

"Are you really okay?" I ask softly.

"Better than I even knew," he says, the corners of his mouth lifting. "Don't worry, Kate. I did a lot of thinking. I'm good."

I nod and swallow past the knot in my throat. "Good."

"You?" He lifts a big bear paw as if to touch my face, then drops it. "Are you okay?"

"I am now."

Our smiles shine across the car and join in a sunbeam of joy and delight. For wordless moments we just look at each other as our driver blares his horn, weaves in and out of traffic, narrowly misses a pedicab, and eventually arrives in front of my building.

He waves off payment when I pull out my credit card. "Your buddy paid me."

I slide out and wrestle Hunter out of the back seat, catching the attention of a few passers-by. He carries the big bear head and follows me inside and upstairs.

"Déjà vu," he murmurs as we tussle with the costume to get him out. It's too small and that makes it even harder, but finally he's standing in front of me in a pair of athletic shorts and T-shirt. He shoves a hand into his hair, pushing it off his face. "Whew. That was…interesting."

I bite my lip. "I'll say."

He casts a baleful look at the head sitting on my island. "The guys who wear these things and jump around in them for hours are heroes."

I laugh softly. "Yep."

He turns to me. "Okay. I probably smell bad and look even worse, but I want to repeat everything I wrote on those cards." He sets his hands on my hips.

I move closer and curve my hands over his shoulders. His skin is warm and damp through the cotton of his shirt, but I don't care. "Do it."

His lips twitch. "I'm sorry. I was an idiot. I love you."

My heart swells up huge in my chest. "I love you, too."

He hauls me up against him and our mouths crash together in a long, hot, heartfelt kiss. I press myself to him and twine my arms around his neck while he wraps his arms around me and squeezes me.

Relief and joy pour through me, like sunshine and starlight and moonbeams, heating me from the inside out, warming my heart.

Finally we both pull back, panting. His eyes shine, his mouth curved into a smile. We stare into each other's eyes for a moment, my fingertips playing with the curls at the nape of his neck.

"You're so beautiful," he says in a husky voice. "I was so afraid I fucked everything up—my career, you…"

I grimace. "It's good that you're back."

"I'm sorry. Christ, I'm sorry for taking off like that."

I suck my bottom lip between my teeth. "I get it, but…yeah. It caused some problems."

"Shit." He gazes at me with his eyebrows sloping down. "Did the Bears withdraw the offer?"

24

KATE

"Let's sit down." I lead Hunter to my couch.

"Fuck," he mutters.

"It's okay. I think I've saved your career."

He closes his eyes. "I don't deserve it."

"Hunter. Stop that."

His eyes pop open. "Right." He swallows. "What's happening?"

"I told all three teams you had a family emergency in Calgary and you'd be back to meet with them as soon as possible."

He nods slowly and exhales. "Okay. Good. So the offer's still on the table?"

"As far as I know. I'd suggest we call the Bears in the morning and set up a meeting right away."

"Okay."

"You're going to be alright with playing for them? With Josh and Easton?"

"I think so. I can't guarantee what strange things my mind will do, but...I'm going to do it. I never realized that they had issues too, playing with each other."

"Oh?"

"Not to share all their personal deets, but I think we all learned things about each other. We all went through the same accident, but each of us experienced it differently. It impacted all of us, but in different ways. It actually felt good to tell them about my PTSD...they got it."

I nod, emotions swirling in my chest, rising into my throat and clogging it so I can't speak.

He tells me about talking to his counselor and the things she made him think about. About rediscovering the unbroken parts of him to be able to heal.

"I like thinking of it that way," I say slowly. "And its true...there are so many parts of you that aren't broken, Hunter."

"Hockey," he says. "My passion for the game. Determination."

It feels so good to hear him talk positively about himself. "Yes." I touch his cheek. "You feel things so deeply, and yet you try to hide it. I think that must make it even harder for you."

"That's what I need to work on. When Millsy and Hellsy and I talked, it was...okay. To be able to share things with friends who've been through the same things...who understand. And...I've always felt that way with you." He gazes earnestly into my eyes. "I felt safe telling you. You never judged me or laughed at me or thought I was weak because of it."

I close my eyes, a wave of both gratitude and dismay washing through me. I hate that he felt he couldn't talk about things to anyone else, that people might have ridiculed him for it. But I'm glad he felt that way with me. "You never judged me either," I whisper. "Even when other guys thought I was too...aggressive. You never did."

"I love how strong you are."

"Thank you." I deliver another long kiss.

"But I didn't share enough with you," he continues. "I should have stayed and talked to you about how I was feeling instead of bolting."

"Yes. You should have." Dammit, I might cry again. I never cry. "I love you Hunter, but if we're going to be together you have to promise me that you'll stay and talk, no matter how hard it is."

Our eyes meet and hold. I feel his gaze looking deep inside me and

I let him see my feelings…and I read the love shining through in his. "I promise." He takes my hand and presses it to his chest above his heart. "Roberta told me that by avoiding or ignoring my past—which I was by refusing to play for the Bears—it was still giving my past power over me. I thought I could keep it in the past, but the truth is, I can't."

I nod.

"I have to accept that. I have to be comfortable with it, and then it won't have as much power over me." He hesitates. "Are you comfortable with that? That it will always be part of me?"

I have no hesitation. "Yes. I always have been. You should know that."

"Yeah." He smiles. "You're right. So, Roberta said this is a point of change, a turning point, and what worked for me before to get through things might not work this time. She made me realize I had to do something different, and the first thing was to meet with Josh and Easton. Only, they showed up out of the blue." He pauses. "Or not so much 'out of the blue.'"

"Are you mad about that?" Anxiety tightens my insides. "I was afraid you'd be angry at me for interfering again. But I had a feeling they were the two people you really needed to talk to."

"And you were right. I might have been annoyed, but I'd already figured that out. And Josh also told me not to be mad at you because the same thing happened with him and Sara and I guess it almost ended things between them. But it made him and Easton sit down and hash things out, so it was all good."

"Whew. Okay, great." I bury my face against his chest. "I was so worried about you."

He strokes my back. "Thanks. I was worried about you, too. I was afraid not only did I screw up my career, but yours too." He runs his fingers through my hair. "And I was worried that I hurt you and I hated that. I shouldn't have said that you can't fix everything. Apparently, you can."

I take a deep breath. "No. I can't. I overstepped big time with you.

I'm so sorry, Hunter. I need to stop doing that. I have to step back with my clients and not get so involved in their lives."

He shifts and cups my face in both hands, looking directly into my eyes. "The fact that you care about your clients makes you a great agent."

I swallow, my throat thickening at his praise. "I can still care about them. I just need to learn how far to go."

His smile is so warm and proud it lights up my insides like a goal light flashing red. And I feel kind of proud of myself for coming to this realization. "I love how much you care for your clients and how hard you work to get the best for them. I love how smart you are. I love how nerdy you are about hockey contracts and the CBA. I even love your spreadsheets."

I choke out a laugh.

"I'm not perfect. I'll do dumb things, piss you off, then take it all back...but you'll never find someone who loves you more than I do. I love how you seem all cool and professional on the outside, but inside you're soft and warm. You encouraged me to go after my dream and helped give me the confidence to do it."

My heart lodges in my throat and I try to blink away the sting in my eyes.

"You make me smile...from those first days at Bayard, you were the one who made me smile. You also make me horny, but that's a different issue."

"Making you smile and making you horny are my two favorite things."

He grins. "Good."

"Also, you make me horny, too."

"I hope we never get tired of making each other horny." His smile makes my lower belly flip flop. "I love how strong you are. But I also love that you need me...I want to hold your hand and kiss your forehead and stand behind you. I want to beat up anyone who makes you feel bad."

"No. No fist fights. But thank you. So many guys couldn't do that. They couldn't handle that I knew more than them, that I skated better than them."

"That was their problem. Not yours."

"I'm glad you understood me. Nobody else did. And Hunter...I love your strength. When I first met you, I thought you were a jerk, but then I saw how you guarded your heart and hid your feelings. I love how you care so much. And I love how you make me slow down and enjoy the moment. Little moments."

"That's what life is. A bunch of little moments, all strung together to make up bigger moments and...a life. We need to appreciate every one of those moments."

I nod, my throat blocked again, remembering him stopping me to appreciate the beauty of the snowfall. The energy of Forty-Second Street. How much he appreciates those moments because of what he went through, and how I'm learning to do that too. I swallow. "I think I need one of those hugs that turns into sex."

He laughs softly. "Okay." He nuzzles the side of my neck, making me shiver. "I wanna do bad things with you."

"Yes please."

He kisses my mouth, then stands, lifting me with him. My legs wobble and heat floods my entire body as he slides an arm around my waist, then bends and slips the other arm beneath my knees and lifts me into the air. I wrap my arms around his neck, and he carries me into the bedroom.

In the dim room, he lowers me to my feet beside the bed. He takes my face in both hands and kisses me again, a gentle kiss of such devotion, tears spring to my eyes. I lay my palms on his chest, feel his heartbeat thudding beneath one, and give myself up to his endless, sensual kiss.

"So beautiful," he murmurs, rubbing his rough cheek against mine. "So strong and beautiful."

"Oh, Hunter."

He tugs my T-shirt out from the waistband of my skirt, and I raise my arms so he can draw it over my head. I reach behind me for the zipper of the skirt and let it fall to the floor. As I stand before him in my pink lace bra and panties, his eyes darken with appreciation. I feel beautiful and feminine. But also strong.

His hands move over my body, touching me everywhere, leaving trails of heat and sparks in their wake. When they come to rest on my shoulders, he turns my body so I face away from him. I close my eyes as he draws my hair to one side and kisses the back of my neck, and when he opens his mouth and so gently grazes his teeth over my flesh, fire flashes through me. A soft whimper escapes my lips.

He flicks open the fastener of my bra and pushes the straps down my arms, then whisks my panties down and off. Crouching behind me, he pauses for a moment to kiss the small of my back. My knees tremble and my belly heats. Then he pats my butt and says, "Get on the bed."

I climb on and lie down, rolling to my side to watch him as he reaches behind him and yanks his T-shirt over his head. Our eyes meet and hold with a sizzling connection as he shoves his shorts down his hips along with his boxer briefs. He kicks them aside, and my gaze tracks down over his muscled chest and abs to his erection, so bold and beautiful. I swipe my tongue over my bottom lip.

"Christ, Kate." He groans, taking the two steps he needs to reach the bed where he joins me, sliding his big, hot body against mine. My skin tingles voluptuously at the sensation. He rolls me to my back and moves over me, kissing me again. I hold on to him, parting my legs so he fits between them, so perfectly, and kiss him back with everything I have.

"I love you," I whisper as he moves his mouth from mine.

"Love you too." He kisses his way down my neck, then my chest, then he closes his mouth over the nipple of one breast and tugs at it.

My eyes fall closed and I give myself over to his touch. With his hands and his mouth, he draws a veil of magic and warmth and devotion around us, shrouding us in heat and light and love.

My hips lift into his, aching with need for him. "Please." I slide my hands into his hair. "Please. I need you."

"Say it again." He lifts his head, and I open my eyes to see his gaze fixed on me with his singular intensity.

"I need you." It feels so good, so liberating and giving, so I say it again. "I need you, Hunter, so much."

His eyes warm and his lips curve into a sexy smile.

"And I need you inside me."

His smile deepens. "Yeah."

He moves up on me, his knees pushing my thighs wide, and I watch as he fists his cock.

He hesitates and meets my eyes again. "Okay with no condom?"

"I'm okay. You okay?"

He nods. "Yeah."

He doesn't need to say more. We understand each other, understand that this is about trust and intimacy and deepening our relationship, and I love him so much for asking.

My body closes around him, pulling him in, and I wrap my arms around his back and my legs around his waist as he moves against me. Our bodies push together, seeking more, finding a rhythm that matches the beating of our hearts. His breath rushes hot over the skin of my neck.

Sensation spirals inside me, a taut coil of pleasure and heat, everything inside me tightening, pulling hard, up and up.

"Yes," I urge him. "Yes, yes…oh *God*."

He rises up again onto his knees, spread wide between my thighs. Once more our eyes meet, his blazing at me, full of adoration. He's letting himself feel everything, I can see it, I can feel it, and I love it. I love this gift of trust he's giving me. I love him.

Emotion swells and rushes through me. He reaches for my hands and holds them, and I tighten my fingers around his, still holding his gaze. I never want to let him go, never want him to let me go, and I grip his hands as my climax bursts upon me, an explosion of sparks and heat, pleasure sliding outward from my core, lovely and warm and sweet.

"Love you," I gasp. "Oh God, I love you." With our clasped hands at my chest, his eyes fall closed, his body tenses and stills for long, pulsing moments, and then once again he stretches out over me.

"Love you, too," he groans against my neck. "I love you, too."

EPILOGUE

KATE

Swift Current Warriors survivors encourage men to be open about mental health issues.

I smile at the headline on the article I'm reading on my phone.

"Easton Millar, Josh Heller, and Hunter Morrissette all played for the Swift Current Warriors. They were all expected to be drafted into the NHL after outstanding careers in major junior hockey. They were all on the bus the night of the crash that killed nine of their teammates, along with their coach, assistant coach, the bus driver, their athletic therapist, and a local radio broadcaster.

"Now, nine years later, all three former Warriors are playing together again...with the New York Bears. It's their dream come true, but it's been a long, painful road. Now they're ready to share their stories as a part of the NHL's initiative to raise awareness about mental health."

I pause scrolling on my phone and lift my head, pride and love swelling in my heart, then resume reading.

"It's hard in the beginning," Hunter Morrissette said. "Opening up and

talking about it is the biggest, bravest step you can take. There's no shame in showing emotion."

Tonight's game at the Apex Center is dedicated to promoting local mental health resources and to dispelling myths about mental illness. Hunter, Josh, and Easton have been making appearances and doing interviews. With the three of them together, it's easier for them to speak up about their experiences. Hockey players are the toughest athletes on the planet, but even tough guys can struggle.

I'm so proud of Hunter and even more in love with him than ever.

And he loves me too.

Even though he's no longer my client.

Vern got the okay to return to work about a month ago. He contacted a few of his old clients. Hunter and I had a good honest talk about the future. We've only been together about nine months, but both of us feel like this is forever. I don't want to lose a client, but I think it'll be better for our relationship if we're not also agent and client. And I trust Vern.

So we parted ways...business ways, ha...and in January we're moving in together. At first, Hunter said he wanted me to move in with Hakim and him, so he didn't have to desert his buddy. I was... alarmed. Turned out he was just joking. They easily found another roommate for Hakim, a new guy on the Storm. Hunter's going to move in here and we'll start looking for a bigger place. With his big, beautiful new three-year deal with the Bears, he can afford it.

I smile and mentally pat myself on the back for that contract.

Hunter emerges from my bedroom, yawning and rubbing his bare chest.

"Hey. How was your nap?"

"Good." He stretches, showing off that incredible lean and muscled body, his abs and obliques enough to make me drool. "I need my snack now."

He strolls over to give me a long, scorching kiss before moving to the kitchen to make his sandwich.

I accommodate his game day routine. I know it's important to him. After his nap, he eats a peanut butter and banana sandwich (whole wheat bread only) and downs a bottle of water. Then he dresses in his sexy game day suit and takes the train to the arena.

Today I'm going with him. I'm meeting Lilly and Sara and we're going to grab an early dinner before going to the game. There's going to be a special ceremony that Hunter, Easton and Josh will be part of, and we want to see it in person.

The guys have become close friends again, and I pretty much love Easton and Josh, too. And their girlfriends. Lilly and Sara are both amazing women. Also, I love Otis.

"I'm reading an article about you," I tell him.

"There's enough of them."

I ignore his sour tone. He hates the attention, but he loves the cause they've been working for.

"Have I told you how proud I am of you?" I stand and move to the island. I want to steal a piece of banana, but that might wreck his groove. I respect the game day routine.

He ducks his head, but he's grinning. "Yeah."

"I'll keep telling you. Gonna score a goal tonight?"

"Don't say that!"

I smile. "Sorry."

He smiles too. He doesn't take his superstitions as seriously as he used to. But all hockey players are superstitious to some degree. Lilly and Sara and I shake our heads at them, but hey, we love our dudes.

One thing we've all learned is that you can't just hope for a happy ending. You have to believe in it. You have to do the work. You have to take the risks. Taking risks is scary, but love is worth it. And we've all done that.

· · ·

Want to read more about Josh and Sara? Check out You Had Me at Hockey.

And read on for an excerpt from Easton and Lilly's story, Must Love Dogs...and Hockey!

ACKNOWLEDGMENTS

For a while, I didn't know if this book would get written or published! But I knew I had to tell Hunter's story and wrap up the three former Warriors' stories. Mental health is becoming more and more an open topic in hockey, with teams initiating events and dialogue about it. While my three hockey Warriors are fictional, many real-life players struggle with mental health issues such as Post Traumatic Stress Disorder, alcohol and substance abuse, depression, and anxiety, and the old way of toughing it out doesn't work. It's so important for players (and men in general) to be able to acknowledge their feelings, talk about them, and work through them. I want to acknowledge every hockey player who's been brave enough to talk about their personal experiences. Because hockey is such a popular and influential game, there's huge potential for conversations about men's mental health and reaching a wider audience.

I have many people to thank for helping me get this book written and out in the world. As always, to my agent Emily Sylvan Kim—thanks for encouraging me. Thank you also to the team at Social Butterfly PR, you are awesome at making sure the world knows about my books! Thank you to Stacey Price, who keeps me afloat doing so many things! Thank you to reviewers and bloggers who read my books and also help get the word out—I appreciate you so much! And special, HUGE thanks to editor Kristi Yanta. This is the first project we've worked on together. I am in awe of your ability to dig deep into the story and characters and pull out all the things I wanted to say but didn't. This book is so much better because of you. Thanks to my author friends for letting me vent and procrastinate and for motivating me, and most of all thank you from the bottom of my heart to all my readers. I am so grateful to every one of you!

EXCERPT - MUST LOVE DOGS...AND HOCKEY

Must Love Dogs...and Hockey
© Kelly Jamieson 2020

I've given myself the weekend. I cleaned and organized my bedroom and the kitchen cupboards. I threw out a bunch of crap I don't need anymore. Now it's Sunday afternoon and I'm taking Lola for a walk in the park.

Lola is my neighbor Kent's Jack Russell terrier. While I was out of work, I started walking Lola pretty much every day. Kent works long hours, and Jack Russells need lots of exercise. He was already paying someone to walk her and thought it might as well be me, since I needed the money and had the time, and I love him for that. I also love Lola. I love dogs in general. I also volunteer at an animal shelter once a week.

A couple of neighbors saw me walking Lola and asked me to walk their dogs too, which I was happy to do and it makes me a few extra dollars.

There's a park at the end of my street and I head that way. It's a nice fall day—in fact it's gorgeous. The sky is a brilliant blue, the trees are turning, and the sun is illuminating the leaves into glowing gold, fiery red, and rust brown. A few leaves layer the path in the park and it's so pretty.

Lola and I are strolling along the path when out of nowhere a dog appears, bounding up to us and jumping Lola.

I let out a scream. "Lola!" I pull on the leash and dash toward them to rescue her from being demolished by the other dog. Okay, okay, it's a smallish dog, just a pup, but still, he's aggressive. And Lola's not happy either, growling and snarling. Oh my God, it's a dog fight! What do I do?

I hear a man yelling, "Otis! Come back! Jesus, Otis, stop."

Lola is snapping and barking, but the other dog doesn't get the message, still jumping her and pawing at her. His tail is wagging wildly, although it's not much of a tail, just a furry little quivery stub. His tongue lolls out of his jowly mouth. Lola is freaked out, and so am I.

But I have to save her.

I try to pick her up, prepared to feel the other dog's teeth sink into my arm. She's squirming and jumping so much I can't get hold of her and I'm grabbing air and stumbling around, and then I fall on my ass.

Then Lola jumps the other dog, trying to pin him. Now I'm worried she's going to kill him.

The yelling man sprints up and grabs the leash dragging behind the dog. "Shit, shit, shit," he growls. He seizes the dog's collar and pulls him away from Lola. He glares at Lola. "What the hell?"

"What the hell is right!" Anger flares inside me. "What is your dog doing off the leash?" I demand. I grab Lola's leash and tug her toward me, pulling her into my lap where I'm sitting on the grass.

"He's on a leash! He yanked it out of my hands when he saw your dog."

"She's not my dog."

He frowns. "Whatever."

"You should have better control of him!"

"He's not dangerous! He's just a puppy. Your dog attacked him!"

"He attacked her!" I run my hands over her and bend my head to hers. "Are you okay?"

I know she can't answer, but I talk to her like this all the time. *Please, please be okay.* Not only do I kind of love her, but Kent will kill me if I let something happen to his precious pup.

The man crouches down and lays his hands on his dog. "You okay, Otis?"

I scowl at him. "I'm sure he's fine. Lola's not an attack dog. She was defending herself."

I watch him check out his dog and I'm even more annoyed. He's very attractive. *Very* attractive. Dressed in worn jeans and an old hoodie, his dark hair falls over his forehead in a defiant tumble but is neatly trimmed around his ears and neck. Stubble darkens his square jaw, and his eyes make me think of the syrup I pour over my pancakes —warm, liquid brown but with a cheeky glint in them. He's also got amazing shoulders and long legs, and I'm fascinated by his hands, which are a bit rough but with neat nails. Everything about him screams danger. Hot, sexy danger.

Too bad he's a jerk.

I drag my attention away from him, which is definitely not easy, and push myself to stand. He rises too and holds out a hand to help me, but I ignore it. I take a few steps to a nearby bench and sit there. Lola jumps up onto my lap and licks my chin.

The man and his dog follow us. The dog looks more worried than the man, with his furrowed forehead. Goddammit, even the dog is cute.

"I'm Easton," the man says. "This is Otis."

"I don't care who you are," I snap. I'm shaking a bit now, the adrenaline rush in my veins dissipating. God, I was so scared there for a few minutes.

Otis plants his butt in front of me and Lola, staring at us with sad but hopeful eyes. Shit.

Easton sighs. "I'm sorry. He caught me off guard and pulled the leash out of my hand."

I purse my lips, looking at Otis, not Easton. "He does look apologetic."

"He always looks like that. But I'm sure he is. He gets in trouble a lot."

"Maybe you need to take him for some obedience training."

"I would, if he was my dog."

"He's not yours?"

"It's a long story." He sits on the bench too and rubs the back of his neck. "I don't know how I ended up with him and I can't get hold of his owner so I'm kind of stuck with him."

"Oh."

"And I have to go out of town tomorrow." He shakes his head. "He'll destroy my apartment while I'm gone."

"You can't leave him alone while you go out of town!" I turn alarmed eyes on Easton.

"I know, I know," he says hastily. "What am I gonna do, though?"

I don't know. Not my problem. I slump back onto the bench and rub my hip where I landed on the ground.

"Are you okay?" he asks.

"I might have a bruise. But that's okay." I sigh. "It'll just match my bruised spirit."

His lips twitch and his eyebrow lifts into a slightly wicked arch. "Uh-oh. That doesn't sound good."

"I haven't been having the best luck lately. You could say my life is like the love child of a train wreck and a dumpster fire."

Easton chokes on a laugh.

I focus on Otis again. He's gazing longingly at Lola. Clearly he just wants to be friends. I cautiously set Lola on the ground and watch as Otis sniffs around her.

"He *is* hard to resist," Easton says, watching them too. "He seems to like women. What else is going wrong in your life?"

I'm not about to share all my woes with a douche stranger. "Nothing."

He shrugs. "You're too pretty to have a dumpster fire of a life."

I roll my eyes, even though my heart quivers at the compliment. Because, yeah . . . he's gorgeous. "This isn't the time for flirting. Read the room, dude."

He laughs, and it's a fantastic laugh—low and deep and rumbly. "I'm not flirting. I'm just being extra friendly to someone who's extra attractive."

"Oh my God."

Lola is now checking out Otis, sniffing his butt. Otis responds by checking hers out, and they do the canine version of shaking hands and introducing themselves.

"I admire how you jumped in to save your dog—er, your friend's dog—when she was being attacked. That takes guts."

I study him with narrowed eyes. Is he for real?

He gives off an air of bold confidence and a reckless charm, but his smile is genuine and his expression sincere. That annoys me even more.

I reach out and rub Otis's head. I'm not mad at *him*. "He's not vicious. And it wasn't his fault. He's a baby. He just needs to be controlled better." I give Easton a pointed look.

"I get it." Easton holds up a hand. "I've learned my lesson."

"How old is he?"

"I don't know."

"What? You don't know how old he is?"

"Like I said, I got stuck with him." After a beat he adds, "Although I admit he's fun."

"Of course you are. Aren't you? You just need to grow up and learn how to behave." I lean forward and kiss Otis between his big brown eyes. "You're a good boy."

"I don't suppose you'd want a job dog sitting?"

I snort and flash Easton a sideways glance.

"Really. I don't want to just get rid of him to a shelter."

I give him a look with my chin down. "You don't even know me."

"Babe. You're gorgeous, smart, and gutsy. And you like dogs. You rescued a dog that's not even yours. You have to be a decent person."

Heat washes down through me at the compliments from this hunk of hotness, but I laugh. "Wow, you *do* know me."

He smiles too, a sexy bad boy smile that heats me up and makes my belly flutter.

"Seriously, you don't even know me."

He nods at Lola. "Someone else trusts you with their dog."

"True."

"I'd pay well."

This piques my interest. Little does he know, but I'm in debt up to my formerly well-groomed eyebrows. But still . . . "What if I took off with your dog and your money and you never saw me again?"

"I wouldn't be much worse off," he says dryly.

"Ha." I play with Otis's funny ears. "How much?"

"How much what? Pay?"

"Yes."

"Hell, I don't know. Would you come to my place and look after him? Or take him home with you?"

"Well, since you're obviously extremely trusting and naïve, I'll point out that letting a total stranger have access to your home is probably not wise."

He rolls his eyes at the "trusting and naïve" comment.

"So I would look after him at my place."

"Okay. Five hundred dollars?"

I gasp. "You're kidding me."

He lifts his hands.

"For one night?"

"Sure. Except I won't be back until late Wednesday, like really late, so it would be three nights. Five hundred a night."

Holy shit. That would be fifteen hundred dollars. Is this guy for real?

I study him through narrowed eyes. He's holding my gaze and seems honest. "Cash."

"Sure. I can drop him off tomorrow morning."

This is all weird. The guy can't keep his dog under control. Except it's not even his dog. And he's kind of a flirty, cocky ass.

But watching him with the dog . . . he's gentle, if a little awkward. And he's willing to pay big bucks to have the dog looked after.

I'm trying to see the downside to this. Looking after a pup isn't that much work. It's not like I have much else going on. If I get the money up front, the worst thing that would happen is Easton doesn't come back for the dog and I'd have to deal with it. "Okay. Deal."

He lifts his arms in the air. "Yes!"

I grin.

"It doesn't put me in a good bargaining position," he says. "But I was desperate."

So am I. "Well, worry no more. I'll take good care of Otis."

"Give me your address." He pulls out his phone.

I hesitate. Giving my address to a stranger doesn't seem very smart. Would it be wiser for me to go to his place? I gnaw briefly on my bottom lip. "Maybe I should pick him up."

"Okay."

I remove my phone from the pocket in my leggings and he gives me his address. His place is only a few blocks away, on Riverside Boulevard. Given the address, I'm pretty sure his apartment is a lot nicer than mine. Maybe he really does have fifteen hundred bucks to spare.

"And your name," he adds, waiting.

"Right." I shake my head. "It's Lilly. Lilly Evans."

I give him my phone number in case anything changes, which wouldn't surprise me, because the way my luck is going that could easily happen. Let's just say I won't be going out and buying new shoes before I have that cash in my broke little hands.

"Can you pick him up around eight-thirty?" Easton pockets his phone.

"Yes. That's fine. You can give me all the instructions."

"Ha. Like I have any instructions for you. I had to google how often to feed him."

I bite my lip on a smile. "Oh." I stand. "Okay, Lola, let's finish our walk."

"Okay." He stands too, still gripping the handle of Otis's leash. "See you in the morning, Lilly."

Otis strains at the leash, trying to follow us, apparently enamored of Lola, or maybe both of us, as we walk away from them. I guess that's good if I'm going to look after him. Easton's a bit of a jackass and Otis is not well behaved, but . . . fifteen hundred bucks. Okay!

Must Love Dogs...and Hockey is available at all major retailers.

OTHER BOOKS BY KELLY JAMIESON

Heller Brothers Hockey

Breakaway

Faceoff

One Man Advantage

Hat Trick

Offside

Power Series

Power Struggle

Taming Tara

Power Shift

Rule of Three Series

Rule of Three

Rhythm of Three

Reward of Three

San Amaro Singles

With Strings Attached

How to Love

Slammed

Windy City Kink

Sweet Obsession

All Messed Up

Playing Dirty

Brew Crew

Limited Time Offer

No Obligation Required

Aces Hockey

Major Misconduct

Off Limits

Icing

Top Shelf

Back Check

Slap Shot

Playing Hurt

Big Stick

Game On

Last Shot

Body Shot

Hot Shot

Long Shot

Bayard Hockey

Shut Out

Cross Check

Wynn Hockey

Play to Win

In It To Win It

Win Big

For the Win

Game Changer

Bears Hockey

Must Love Dogs…and Hockey

You Had Me at Hockey

Talk Hockey to Me

Stand Alone

Three of Hearts

Loving Maddie from A to Z

Dancing in the Rain

Love Me

Love Me More

Friends with Benefits

2 Hot 2 Handle

Lost and Found

One Wicked Night

Sweet Deal

Hot Ride

Crazy Ever After

All I Want for Christmas

Sexpresso Night

Irish Sex Fairy

Conference Call

Rigger

You Really Got Me

How Sweet It Is

Screwed

Firecracker

ABOUT THE AUTHOR

Kelly Jamieson is a best-selling author of over forty romance novels and novellas. Her writing has been described as "emotionally complex", "sweet and satisfying" and "blisteringly sexy." She likes coffee (black), wine (mostly white), shoes (high heels) and hockey!

Subscribe to her newsletter for updates about her new books and what's coming up.

Find out what's new...
www.kellyjamieson.com

Contact Kelly
info@kellyjamieson.com

Made in the USA
Middletown, DE
06 August 2021

45067096R00139